The Mermaid's Child

Born and raised in the village of Arkholme near Lancaster,
Jo Baker was educated at Oxford and now lives in Belfast.
She is also the author of *Offcomer*.

D1494669

Also by Jo Baker

Offcomer

For my mother, my father, and my son

He that would see marvels, it behoves him sometimes to wend out of his way.

— Sir John Mandeville, *Mandeville's Travels*

One

I don't remember ever having a mother. I must have noticed other kids had them, though, because I do remember asking my grandmother about mine. Gran was stirring rhubarb on the range: I stood thigh-high, looking up. 'She was a whore,' Gran said, which didn't really explain anything, but was enough to shut me up. I went away bemused and thoughtful, and even now I can't disentangle the word 'whore' from the smell of rhubarb and the view up Gran's sooty nostrils. A whore: sugared, smutty, not-to-be-mentioned-again.

My Da was more forthcoming, less reliable. One afternoon by the river, when Da was sitting on the shilloe bank with the sun on the bald patch on the back of his head, I sat down on the top ferrystep and kicked my heels and asked him about my mother. It must've been after I'd asked Gran, because it was bothering me more by then, like a brushed-away wasp. Da was mending a bit of rope, a cigarette squeezed flat between his lips.

'We met when I was at sea,' he said, watching his fingers. 'She was the loveliest thing I'd ever seen. Just lovely.'

The rope turned and coiled as he tweaked at the frayed ends.

'She asked me to stay out there, with her people. I couldn't, not and leave your Gran all by herself, so we came back here. I thought she'd settle down, but she couldn't stay.'

The straggling threads came together in his hands.

'She had to go back to her own people.'

He held up the rope, tidy, finished, and glanced round at me.

'She was a mermaid, you see. Gave up her tail for me.'

Even at that age, small enough to swing my sandalled feet over the ferrysteps – can't tell you what age I was, though: I was never told, and I've never had a birthday in my life – even at that age I caught a whiff of fantasy. My father the ferryman, determinedly repairing and rejoining, thought that he could make things ship-shape for me, but I wasn't sure I could believe him. It just seemed too tidy to be true.

I, however, will tell you the truth, in all its untidiness, to the best of my ability and recollection: I promise you that much. Unfortunately, I can make no promises about either my ability or recollection. My memory isn't perfect; I know myself to be a partial, limited and uncertain thing; and I can't help but see, cast over every event, the shadow of what happened next. Things look different in that shadow.

So I may well get things wrong, but I won't ever lie to you. How could I?

The day the circus came I was at school, at my usual seat on Miss Woodend's dresser, with my back arched away from her willow-pattern plates and my eyes fixed firmly on my slate. I was conscious of the Clay twins perched on a bench beneath my feet, and of the Metcalfe boys, all four of them, squeezed into the settle opposite. Only half an hour or so before they had shoved me up against the schoolhouse wall and tried to pull down my shorts.

'Are you a boy or a girl?'

'What kind of name is that, "Malin"?'

'I think she's a boy.'

'There's only one way to tell.'

I was small for my age, or rather small compared with the other children. I didn't stand a chance in a stand-up fight. So I kicked the oldest in the bollocks, bit the second one on the hand, ducked between the other two and was away. I went and stood at the schoolroom door, where they wouldn't dare tackle me again.

There was no point in telling Miss Woodend. It wasn't so much that the others could do no wrong, more that I could never, as far as she was concerned, be in the right. When she found me waiting at the door before the start of lessons, she didn't praise my punctuality or say that I seemed keen to learn, she just eyed me suspiciously and let me in. I was there under sufferance, I knew it. At best, I was tolerated.

I didn't have friends. Because I didn't have a mother, and my father was the ferryman (he was considered only one step up from the lad who scared the crows and docked puppies' tails with his teeth), the other children said that I was dirty, that if I touched them they'd get gibs. Not that I wanted to touch them. I didn't want to go anywhere near them: bunch of lard-headed inbred mouth-breathers.

Usually when they saw me, they'd just squeal and run away from me, even though I'd never even considered chasing them; but from time to time they'd round on me to inflict some form of pain or humiliation, though it was rare that they came up with anything as imaginative or enquiring as pulling down my shorts. I've had far more than my fair share of Chinese burns in my time.

Sometimes, as I was sitting on Miss Woodend's dresser, I would reach down the toe of my sandal and stroke it along one of the Clay twins' poker-partings. It was discreet, easily done and extremely satisfying. The girl would squirm in silent horror, unable to protest, because, as we both knew, the moment that she opened her mouth Miss Woodend would be on to her. Miss Woodend was a precise and powerful chalk-thrower: crimes such as speaking, smiling, sneezing, coughing, sniffing, looking-around, wriggling, and, on one occasion, breathing-too-loudly, were punished, almost before they could be committed, by a sudden blow from a scrap of chalk.

The school's regime had its benefits, though. Condemned to stare for hours at a time at the plodding letters on my slate, my peripheral vision became extremely well developed. Being able to look all round me without moving my head has come in handy now and then, though at the time it was of limited use. I had no interest in my classmates, or in the schoolroom, or in the muddy green outside the window. There was only one thing there that I wanted to look at. The schoolroom map, framed and glazed and nailed to the wall above the Metcalfes' settle. It seemed to me the most fascinating object in the world, and I never got the chance to stare at it straight. In the corner of my eye I could just make out the barest outlines: a squarish landmass circled by green seas, a scooped-out central lake. An island country, washed by waves. One day, I told myself, I would hop down from my seat, scramble up the Metcalfe boys and stand on their shoulders to get a good clear look. Peppered with chalk-fire, I'd find the dot that marked out home, I'd pick out the pathways, the roads and the trackways my mother would have taken. I'd trace the way away from here.

Miss Woodend, invisible against the window's glare, creaked. I kept my eyes down, my toes to myself. I copied, my chalk grating on the slate:

Jj Kk Ll Mm

because when Miss Woodend creaked, she was leaning right back in her rocking chair, perching on the tips of its runners, a bit of chalk in her hand, waiting for the next glancer-upper. Target sighted, she would fling the chair forward as she threw the chalk. Weighted with the full force of Miss Woodend's momentum, it would sting worse than ever, worse than a wasp sting on your cheek or your calf or the tip of your ear.

Which was why, when we first heard the music, no one moved a muscle.

To be fair, it wasn't really music at first, just the faint clatter of bells that could well have been the Robinsons' goats frisking on the green, shaking their stinky mad heads. So I sat, back arched, and continued

Nn Oo Pp

in my best copperplate. Which was, by then, very good indeed, because writing out the alphabet, our names, and the numbers one to ten were the only exercises Miss Woodend had ever given us. By the time I left, I could barely count, I could write my name, and I could read a little, if the words weren't too long or unfamiliar. That was about it.

But it couldn't really be the Robinsons' goats frisking. Tethered on over-cropped turf, they strained all day against their chains, hooves dug into the mud, yellow eyes bulging for a bite of hawthorn, cow-parsley or my coat. They couldn't frisk. They could barely move. Once when I'd been taunting the old billy with a bit of dock, he'd unexpectedly ripped up his stake. I'd scuttled off, swarmed up the wall, but when I looked back, he'd just keeled over on to his chest, chin stretched out on the mud, and was munching on the dockleaf that I'd dropped.

So it couldn't be the goats. It didn't even sound like it

any more. There was a fiddle in there, I could tell that now, and something else that sounded rich and sharp, like blackcurrants; like wine, I would've thought, if I'd ever tasted wine. It was nothing like the music we had in church, Gran's cold hand clamped around mine as we held the small black hymn book and droned on out-of-tune to the wheezing organ. This music brought water to your mouth; it tugged at you.

By now I could also hear other distinct sounds: creaks of strained rope, shouted warnings, a dog's excited bark. The slate now lay flat on my lap, my eyes had climbed towards the window. Dark against the glare, Miss Wood-end creaked, stood up. The Metcalfe boys clambered over each other to get out of the settle. The Clay twins bobbed up, knocking their heads against my feet.

The snort of heavy, burdened horses, the jingle of brasses, the smell of something I'd never smelt before, but know so well now that I can smell it again as I think of it, as if it's permeated the membranes, stuck on to the hairs inside my nose, so that time and nose-blowing and probing fingers can't dislodge it. The smell of cheap perfume and sweat on old sequins; the smell of camel dung, hair dye, sawdust, straw and sex. The smell of the circus.

We stood in Miss Woodend's porch, gaping. Tumblers rolled across the green. A leggy sand-coloured creature loped after them, two wobbling humps on its back, followed by painted caravans and wagons drawn by heavy horses, their tack alive with bells and brasses. I saw a white-haired man with a top hat at the reins of the first, at the second a hugely fat and smiling woman, and at the third a pair of identical red-headed men who at the same moment reached up to scratch an ear. Then came a huge grey beast with a nose that moved like a blind man's hand; above it white birds fluttered. I heard fiddle-music, pipes, and that dark sweet sound that I still could not identify. And, last, came a closed crate on wheels. There were words painted on the side panel of the crate, each line smaller and more faint than the one before. At the time I couldn't make much of them, just picked out a word here or there. Most of the letters just swam around in front of me and wouldn't settle into any familiar pattern. Of course I know it now, know it as well as I know the totemic pattern of my own name:

Aldobrandi's
Circus of Delights

Specialists in Freaks, Fantasms, Ypotams
and
Other Zoological Oddities

*

We'll make you laugh, we'll make you cry
We guarantee we'll Change your Life

*

Warts charmed, teeth pulled, futures told

*

(no refunds)

My sandal squelched. I was standing in something warm and wet. The youngest Metcalfe boy squirmed, shook his leg and tugged at a dark patch on his shorts.

The tumblers were now hoisting each other up into houses of cards that held, teetered, scattered, slid back into a pack and then dealt themselves out again. Unnoticed at first, fabric flowed through their hands, red unfurling out of nowhere, pooling out over the grass. Ropes snaked across, attached themselves to the silk as the tumblers backflipped, cartwheeled, catapulted and caught. Pegs were struck into the earth, ropes knotted, cords tightened. The fabric stretched and bellied. Before any of us had quite worked out what was going on, the structure had gathered itself, heaved up, and locked joints. A vast red circular tent. Right there in front of us. On our muddy old boring old green.

A tumbler drew back a fold of cloth, a doorway into dim red space, and the troupe cartwheeled in. The horses, caravans, camel, elephant, doves and the sealed crate all wheeled about, half-circle, and followed the tumblers inside. The flap dropped back.

Silence.

We crept out on to the green; Miss Woodend, the Clay twins, the Metcalfe boys, including the musty-smelling one with the damp shorts, and me. We held our breath. Old Aggie Newhouse, stick-supported, came shuffling over from her doorway. Uncle George from the Public, Mr Metcalfe from the stores. They clustered together, began to talk.

Wetfoot dryfoot, I circumnavigated the tent.

Not a peep. Not a whinny, not a coo or whistle or trumpet or harrumph.

I ran my fingers over the silky, thick material. I couldn't find the join.

No more school that day, that was clear. Miss Woodend was in no mood for it. Her hand had settled on Mr Metcalfe's arm; she was leaning up against his apron for support.

'Just like the last time,' she breathed.

'Always trouble.'

'Yes,' she murmured.

'Must be ten years.'

'Twelve.'

She looked round at me and saw that I was listening:

'You. You filthy little beast. Earwigging.' She reached into her pocket, fingers searching for a stump of chalk.

I turned tail and ran. A scrap of chalk sang past my ear.

'You can stick your chalk up your arse,' I shouted back at her.

I scrambled up a wall, hoisted myself over, dropped down on the other side. The Robinsons' goats turned their heads and stared. I crouched there, breathing, listening, smelling the piss on my foot. Something very strange was happening, I realized. Something utterly unheard of. She had never missed before.

I didn't go home that day. I couldn't go back to the green in case Miss Woodend saw me, but I couldn't quite let the circus out of my sight. I kept the red glow of the big top always in the corner of my eye, waiting for something to happen. Nothing happened.

Wading waist-deep in grass through nearby fields, I thought in vast distances, pictured muscled tracts of sand, thick ceaseless canopies of leaves, gentle shambling creatures. I hitched myself up on to an underhedge bank, chewed on hawthorn leaves and wood sorrel, found a few wild strawberries. The sun was warm and I began to feel tired. I closed my eyes for just a moment, and the red was the red of rippling silk, and the sweet breathy noise in my ear was my own companionable sand-coloured creature and not, of course, a couple of nosy heifers snuffing at me through the hedge.

When I woke, it was dark and I was cold, and there was something happening on the green.

For one thing, it wasn't dark down there any more. A reddish golden glow lit up the sky like on bonfire night. A trumpeting, barrelling, swaggering tune, quite unlike the sounds I'd heard earlier, was bowling out like pace eggs through the night. I didn't stop to notice this, of course: I was up and in an instant blundering through the long (and now wet) grass, socks slumped around my ankles, knees bare and arms goosepimpling. I felt a little unsteady on my feet, a little feverish, but it didn't seem important at the time. I clambered up the wall, hitched myself up on to the capstone.

On the green, the tent glowed; it throbbed. I scrambled down the wall and ran across the grass towards it. I breathed in perfumed air, placed my hands on the fabric. It was warm. I dug my fingers in to grab a handful, to hitch it up and slip under, but the stuff was thick, resistant. As I held it in my hands, it seemed to pulse. I let go, stepped back. I watched the creases from my grip melt away, as if it were skin I had pinched, not cloth. I watched the redness swell, retreat, swell, retreat.

I felt warmer now, almost hot. It seemed as if the tent's glow had wrapped itself around me. I reached out again and touched it. Fingertips brushing the warm softness, I drifted round the belly of the tent.

Into what seemed to be a riot. A jostling crowd, loud voices, coloured light cascading over faces. Mechanical music was jangling out from everywhere. Someone had looped back folds of the red fabric, and rosy light and sawdust spilled out through the entrance. I tried to push my way through the crowd towards it: rough clothing scraped against me, my stomach heaved with the reek of tobacco, dung and damp. Boots, thick and muddied, scuffed my shins and crushed my toes. I was pressed between corduroy and tweed, between an old arse and a young crotch. Dizzied and sick, I stumbled.

And was caught. And not just caught. Caught, lifted, held aloft. Blurred and nauseous, I saw that it was the Reverend Carr holding me up. His parboiled face went blue then green then yellow in the coloured lights. My stomach churned. I couldn't speak.

'Malin Reed,' he said. 'I might have known.'

He hoisted me higher, dumped me down beyond the margin of the crowd.

'When all good children have been in bed for hours.'

Scarlet-purple-blue-green. The music shook and slurred. His features shifted, seemed to melt.

'I don't know what your grandmother ever did to deserve you. You're nothing but a nuisance and a bother to her,' he said. 'Now go home.'

His hand was pressing on my shoulder, trying to steer me out of the coloured lights towards the darkness of the village street.

'Go on, get off home, before you get into worse trouble.'

I looked up at him, at his rainbowing skin, and he looked down at me for a moment as I stood sandal-deep in the mud, feverish, with sick now rising in my throat. A keen sense of injustice was rising with it. I wasn't going to be kept out of this so easily. I lifted his hand from off my shoulder, raised it to my mouth, and bit.

'Why you little –' he jerked his hand away, cradled it to his chest.

I turned and ran, pushing my way through the crowd, shoving past legs and skirts and backsides without looking up. Someone cuffed me round the head. My ear stung with the blow. I kept on running, shot out from the crowd and into the dark beyond. Crouched down on the grass, I tried to listen for footsteps, for someone coming after me, but all I could hear was my own breath, my heart pounding in my chest, and the music from the tent, distorting, stretching, reeling in my head. I leaned over, on all fours. I puked like a dog.

When I'd sicked up the last of the hawthorn, sorrel and

wild strawberries, wiped my mouth and straightened up, the music had stopped and the rainbow lights had gone. A shaft of golden light streamed through the entrance to the tent. Sick-streaked and blinking, I staggered towards it. The earth was trodden into mire and there was a shiver in the wind. The last villager, his shoulders bullish in a Sunday coat, was pushing through the opening. Looking past him, I glimpsed a golden circle, a haze of faces, and a man in a red jacket who stood with his arm raised, a top hat in his hand:

Ladies and Gentlemen!

And the cloth dropped back. I rushed forwards and tugged at it. It wouldn't budge. Alone, in the dark, on the trodden turf of the green, I opened my mouth again. I howled at the sky.

I didn't stay like that for long. I was pretty well used to not being wanted. And despite the fact that my skull now seemed to be squeezing my brain like a sponge, and my skin was rough as cows' tongues in the cold, and there was bile in my mouth, I wouldn't consider myself defeated. There was no way I was going home. I put my ear to the side of the tent. Voices came muted, words undifferentiated. All I could hear were inflections. I caught the polished rhythms of annunciation, soft rumblings of excitement, the bullet shots of command and confirmation. I was boiling with frustration. I was outraged. Because, let's face it, even first-cousin-marriages for four generations hadn't produced, in that place, something quite as unusual as me. Sure, there were six-toed feet, webbed fingers and tucked-away tails enough among the audience – it's a small village, you can't help knowing that kind of thing – but whatever the inherited distinction, none, I felt, matched me for sheer difference. Birthdayless, born to a fishwoman and a ferryman, I was, I always had been, different. That fact had been made abundantly clear to me every day of my short life. I was a freak. *I* was a zoological oddity. If I belonged anywhere at all, it was inside that tent. I had to find my way in.

In the darkness round the back, an untidy village had sprung up. Caravans and wagons described a street, courtyards, alleyways. Embers glowed inside circled rocks. A red pinprick picked out a cigarette: someone smoking on the steps of their caravan. If I wasn't careful I would be out on my ear before I'd even got in. I edged over to the nearest conveyance, ducked down underneath it, shuffled backwards into the dark. So this was their world. Pack-up-able, wheeled, off-in-a-minute. For them, home could be anywhere; home was, perhaps, in the space between places, in the journey itself.

A roar of applause and I jumped, hit my head on the underside of the caravan floor. A sudden corridor of light streamed past my nose and half-a-dozen pairs of silky legs flashed by, bringing with them warm scents of overworn footwear and perfume. Counter-current came a torrent of yellow longjohns. From the tent, another happy roar as the tumblers cartwheeled out across the ring. Close by, young female voices, a giggle, then feet on wooden steps and a door slammed. Overhead, the boards creaked and shifted. I caught my breath. They were just above me. Someone lit a lamp and light slipped through the gaps between the boards, blinked out here and there as they moved around. Peeling off stockings, loosening laces, smoothing out hair. I'd just turned my head and was looking for a gap or knothole that I could look through, when I heard the music. Not the swaggering come-and-get-it barrel-organ stuff, but the earlier sound, the dark sweet music that was not quite a tune, but which made me think of the way in springtime the rocks on the riverbed look golden through the peaty water. I turned, crawled towards it underneath the caravan. I scraped my toes on something sharp, dragged my leg over a thistle, put my palm in what could only be goat shit. On the far side, I peered out between the cartwheel's wooden spokes into stark moonlight and shadows. By now, my head was singing in sympathy, my jaw was clamped tight, my cheeks were burning hot.

Wordless or filled with unknown words, the song spun loops out into air like spiders' webs, like the travelling lines that sweep across your face in autumn, invisible till suncaught. Crouched underneath the caravan, I looked up, looked round.

I saw the wheeled crate standing in the moonlight. Its side panel had been taken down and left leaning against the wheels. Light caught on the gilding, and I was aware, in the corner of my eye, of the words:

make you laugh . . . make you cry
we'll change your life . . .
. . . no refunds . . .

But I wasn't looking at them.

It must have been moonlight that caught the curve of her arm, silvered her tail and stroked the fall of her hair, because oil-light makes everything warm and dirty, and she looked as clean and cold as frost. She was reclining on cushions in the opened crate. Someone had painted waterweeds, fishes and bubbles on the inside to make her feel at home. She was singing. And as she sang she dipped a tiny brush into a tiny pot beside her, studied her nails, then applied paint to each of them in turn. I crawled out from underneath the caravan and scrambled to my feet. Mouth open, eyes wide and bright with fever, I was vividly aware of my dirty knees and palms, my sick-stained clothes, the dried urine on one foot. My head was pounding, but I watched transfixed as she dropped the brush back into the pot, then screwed it neatly shut. She shifted her position, blowing on her fingernails. And as she moved, the scales on her tail rippled, catching the moonlight. Her tailfin was lacy, like frozen spiderswebs. I may have stumbled, staggered slightly with the centrifugal force of my dizziness, or made some noise, some whimper, I don't know, but certainly something drew her attention to me. She glanced up, looked over in my direction, squinted.

'Who's there?' she asked.

Speechless, I found myself stumbling forwards into the moonlight, wiping my hands down my shorts.

'Who is it? What do you want?'

I stared up at her. She was beautiful and fresh and clean and indisputably there. I tried to blink it away, but darkness was already gathering round my vision. I reached out to steady myself, but there was nothing to my touch. The mermaid shimmered in my fevered sight, seemed to slip away, grow distant, tiny. The darkness blinked. It swallowed her.

'Mother –' I said, and then I fainted.

Two

If you're wondering how I remember all this, word for word, smell for smell, taste for taste, I wouldn't blame you. After all, I did say that my recollection isn't perfect. The truth is that time is seared into my memory with a clarity I myself sometimes find astonishing. Something to do with the virgin quality of my senses then, I suppose – I had seen so little, smelt so little, felt so little back then that an event such as this could record itself precisely and in minute detail on my mind. Like pissing on new snow, it was bound to make an impression.

A lot has happened since.

There's another reason for the clarity of my memories: after these events there came a break in my consciousness as neat and round as a full stop. After that comes the scratchiness of a blanket and the stickiness of hot skin and a burning sensation in my eyes every time I blinked, then the scrape of a spoon on teeth and the taste of liquorice and metal and alcohol. Some kind of fever.

Caught while sleeping under that damp hedge, or contracted perhaps from the scarlet of the tent.

I don't know how long I was ill, but by the time I was able to elude my grandmother for long enough to shuffle up to the village green, the circus had gone, the sawdust had been swept away, and all that was left was a ghost of a circle, like a fairy-ring, where the grass caught the light at a different angle.

Three

The following year saw the worst weather I've ever known. Not bad in the sense of extreme, not ice and snow and hail the size of apples: not weather you'd write home about. The danger in this weather was that it was so dull that it could bore you to tears, or to death. It began with a wind, so light at first that you'd hardly feel it, though the women began to notice it was good drying weather and fired up the coppers for a titanic wash. Then, gradually, over the course of several days, the wind became infested with water, droplets so minute that at first you could barely tell that it was raining, until the women began to notice that the sheets and shirts and underskirts they'd boiled and scraped and pounded and pegged out on the line were not even beginning to dry. And over the space of days and weeks, the wind grew ever stronger and its water content ever greater, so that the sheets, which had at first gently stirred in the breeze, now snapped, soaking wet, on the line, like sailcloth.

There was no autumn that year. Leaves, debilitated
by the wind and wet, turned muddy brown without
bothering with the intermediate shades of red and
gold, then lost their grip and fell. They gathered in wet
drifts in the lee of drystone walls and hedges, and
would not, despite my efforts, rustle. Depressed, the
days retreated in upon themselves, so that come
October it was dark by four o'clock. Dark, but you
could never see the stars: dirty clouds tumbled almost
incessantly across the sky. I remember one afternoon
standing in the haymeadow, the cut grass rotting in
neatly combed rows, and squinting up at the sky
through the stinging rain. Briefly, the clouds had
broken and a weak golden light had penetrated, catching me there, making the droplets on my eyelashes and
on the tip of my nose glitter, glossing the silken threads
of the dying grass. And I thought, come and take me
now. Come flying down through that gap in the grey,
come pick me up and take me away to warmth and
sunshine and the blue.

I was not a holy child, and this was not a spiritual
experience. I'd developed a rather pragmatic notion of
religion, constructed out of bits and scraps I'd picked up
in the Reverend Carr's Sunday School, when I couldn't
otherwise distract myself from lessons. What with the
biting incident, and getting myself expelled from Miss
Woodend's school, I was lucky, I was told, that he'd let
me join the class at all. Christian forgiveness, he had told
my grandmother, palming the coin she offered him. He
would turn the other cheek.

'But remember, Malin, I only have one more cheek to turn.'

I resisted the temptation. I nodded solemnly.

His instruction was made up of much blather about duty, obedience, and meekness. He was particularly keen on meekness, and sometimes I'd glance up when he was delivering one of his disquisitions on this virtue, and notice he was looking right at me. I couldn't see myself hanging around indefinitely in the hopes that I'd inherit the earth, but in the meantime, the advantages of being good were not entirely lost on me either. If you were good, as I understood it, and asked very nicely, God might just do you a favour. So I had resolved to be very good and see what came of it, which was why I was there, standing in the haymeadow in the rain, when the clouds parted and a beam of sunlight illuminated, briefly, the grey wet world and me, and I thought for just a moment that all my efforts had paid off.

It was all part of my grandmother's scheme to combine convalescence with punishment. In practice, this meant my consumption of as much fresh air as possible, and my undertaking of endless, thankless tasks. Anything that kept me busy and out of her way. Every morning she sent me out with a receptacle (bucket, basket or bag, depending on the nature of the errand) and instructions to collect something. One day I would be easing apart bramble bushes to tease blackberries off their hulls and staining my fingers blue with juice, another I would be following the sheep-paths along hedgerows and across the fields and moors, to collect the scraps of fleece that had been tugged off by a thorn or nail. She had me pacing out the cowfields for mushrooms long past the mushroom season, when the only ones left were sodden and worm-raddled. Put roses in your cheeks, she said. Put hairs on your chest. I wasn't sure that I wanted either.

She made jelly with the blackberries, dyed the wool with onion skin, bottled the mushrooms in brine, and never once said thank you. The jelly tasted of rot, the wool took on a nasty shade of yellow, and the mushrooms, even the early, pearly white ones, grew mucousy and grey in their cloudy bottles. Perhaps it was this early experience of preservation that made of me the squanderer that I am today. The phrase waste-not-want-not, though commonly repeated, has always seemed wrong to me. To boil up perfect blackberries into nastiness, just so that the resultant jelly can be consumed at a later date, seems much less sensible to me than gorging on the fruit in season. Waste, want. That's the idea I have come to hold to. At least then, in times of dearth, you have the memory of pleasures to sustain you.

And even when all the summer's last fruits were exhausted, my Gran still had me out there gathering driftwood for kindling. And I, trying to be good and curry favour up above, still went uncomplainingly, and did not mitch or shirk or skive.

There was a great deal of driftwood that year, deposited in skeins across the watermeadows. With each flooding came a new tideline thatch of broken branches, fenceposts, upwashed roots and reeds, like the nests of giant waterbirds. I trod these high water marks, gathered the driftwood into damp bundles, and carried them home to stack in the shippon.

Thinking back, Gran's main motive in enforcing this regime might well have been to keep me out of my da's way. It was an anxious and a busy time for him. There's something about persistent bad weather which seems to make people all the more determined to travel. He must have had twice the usual volume of traffic that year. Shrouded in oilcloth and hessian, the village women would be clanging the ferry bell at all hours, demanding to be taken across the river to visit a sister or an aunt or a sick cow stranded on the opposite bank. The Reverend Carr and the rector of Melling had come upon an intricate and dusty difference-of-opinion on a point of theology, so our curate was forever shuttling back and forth to and from Melling rectory with heavy books bundled in canvas and his hatbrim dripping. And of course the doctor was called out more than usual, to sick children and the elderly who found the constant wet debilitating, and as his practice was based across the river, that meant my father was also called out for every illness and for every death in the village. Warming his hard red hands at the kitchen fire, his head would twitch up at the first clang of the bell on the far bank, and he would be halfway out of the house before he'd even pulled his oilskin on. He didn't like to keep people waiting in the rain, and hated to think, as he pulled out across the water, of the dark figure of the doctor standing underneath the dripping bell, and of the sweating feverish child, or the old woman burning with rheumatics, all of them waiting for him as he battled with the current. He was a good man, my father. He was kind.

It was an uneasy time for me too, though my discomfort was almost entirely selfishly motivated, if you consider the desire for forgiveness to be a selfish motivation (and I do). If I ever managed to be home at the same time as my father, and escape my Gran's notice, I would huddle at his feet, pull my yellow itchy jumper down over my knees, sit in sympathetic silence and hope for stories. I didn't ever ask, I didn't feel that I could ask, not after doubting his word so unjustly. My experiences at the circus had revealed to me that I could take his word as gospel truth, and my experiences at Sunday School had revealed to me that as he was my father I should have taken his word as gospel truth anyway, and not required corroborating evidence. It seemed I had a good deal of ground to make up with Him Upstairs.

Looking at the situation in daylight and good health, I wasn't really convinced that the mermaid at the circus had been my mother (that would have been too much of a coincidence, I reasoned) but she was nonetheless living speaking proof that not only did these creatures exist, but they were prepared, despite the obvious discomforts of the journey, to travel to this village at the arse-end of nowhere. It should have made no difference, but I couldn't help but find that this cast my father in an entirely different light. He had lived. He'd seen the world. He had attracted, however temporarily, the affections of an extraordinary being. He was more than good: he was great. So I sat and waited patiently for stories. And then I sat and waited impatiently, as, in exhausted silence, he passed down cigarette after cigarette for me to light for him at the fire.

It was rare that we got to stay like that for very long. Gran would stagger in with a bucketful of something-or-other and spot me; she'd bundle me back into my jacket and hat and push me out of the door. Or the ferry bell would sound far off on the distant bank, or nearby, fierce and sudden, making us both jump, sending him running out of the house, heaving his oilskin on to his broad shoulders.

It's hardly surprising, then, that before spring could even bring a break in the weather, he had caught a cold and died, though at the time it did surprise me. I found him lying cold on the kitchen table, where, it only occurred to me years later, Gran had laid him out. I concluded, as one tends to conclude something even when faced with irreconcilable impressions, that tiredness had overtaken him there and he was resting. I sat on the flags, my back against the dresser, and waited for him to wake. I ate a jar of Gran's raspberry preserve with a spoon. Still he didn't stir, so I went to fetch a blanket and covered him up, and tucked it in around his cold white toes. His feet were strong and broad: he could almost, I thought, have walked on water. When Gran came back into the room, and saw what I had done, she sank down on to a chair, put her face in her hands and began to cry. I thought at first it was because of the raspberries.

At my father's funeral, the Reverend Carr spoke of Heaven and God's goodness. He spoke of my father's willingness to shoulder a burden, and the honesty and dignity of hard work, and what a cross he had to bear, and what a worry I must have been to him.

My grandmother rowed his coffin across the river and, sweating and speechless, dragged it on to the jetty, then came back for the mourners. The men carried him across the floodplain, the pools and backwaters reflecting a silvery sky, and I followed, last, and no one spoke to me.

They buried him in the sodden earth of Melling graveyard, because ours isn't a proper church. It's only a chapel of ease.

As I stood at my father's graveside, I looked up at the tumbling clouds and felt the cool clear air on my skin, and heard the faint trickle of retreating waters, and I thought that's it, never again. He's dead, and now I won't hear the stories he might have told me, or know the things I should have known, and all because he was good, and I was trying to be good. Well, I thought, it won't happen twice. I won't get caught out like that again.

I wonder now, though I didn't think about it then, as my head was full of the ache in my throat, what happened to my father after death. I've read somewhere that you get what you believe in, but I've no idea what my father believed. I can imagine him, though, on the bank of the Styx, greeting Charon with professional courtesy, glancing appraisingly at his punt and pole while handing over the coin he has ready in his palm. He wouldn't want to keep anyone waiting, my father, wouldn't want to be any bother. On board, his strong hands folded as he sits quietly on his bench, he would gaze round politely at the plains and mountains of the underworld, but all the while be more intensely aware of the tug of the current against the hull, the dip and splash of the puntpole, the strain of the ferryman's back and shoulder muscles. He would know it, he would feel it all instinctively, he wouldn't have forgotten yet. And he would be itching to give a hand.

Following his death, things were, of course, immediately different. The weather changed, as if it enjoyed a joke. Spring came all in a rush and flushed the trees with leaves and blossoms, and the earth began to dry. My Gran, having developed a taste for it, took to the ferry trade like a duck to water. She spent all day, and often long into the night, down at the ferrysteps; caulking the hull, greasing the rowlocks, splicing rope, endlessly smoking a thin clay pipe which she filled with her son's old tobacco. I'd watch her, sometimes, from a favourite perch halfway up a sycamore tree, leaning back against the trunk, stretching my legs out along a branch.

The cottage grew dark and cold as the sky's blue deepened into summer, and there was never anything cooking on the range, and there was never anything to eat, not even gluey blackberry jelly or slimy mushrooms, and I never spoke to my grandmother from one day's end to the next. When by accident we did bump into one another her eyes would drift past me, then she would just turn away: I'd catch the scent of his tobacco-smoke on the air, and for a moment my heart would quicken, expecting him.

I grew thin and ravenous that summer, fending for myself. I stole eggs from underneath the neighbours' hens and henfood from their feeders. I grazed the currants off the currant bushes, stripped pea-plants of their pods. I chewed carrots with the earth still clinging to them and got grit between my teeth. I was chased from outhouses and vegetable plots all over the village. From my perch up in the sycamore tree, I would watch the villagers gather at the ferrysteps to complain to my grandmother. Sometimes they would have to form a queue.

Then one evening when I brushed past her in the doorway, she held out a strong brown hand to stop me. I looked up from the stained creases of her palm. She stood there looking over my shoulder, the broken veins like elderberry stems patterning her cheeks, the white of her eyes almost blue against her skin. She told me, without once meeting my eye, that I was to be off up the road to work for Uncle George at the Public, and I found that I was not surprised at all.

'You're too much for me. He'll keep you in line, if anyone can. Bit of hard work for once, that'll straighten you out.'

Still she didn't look at me. I don't need straightening out, I wanted to say.

'I expect there's food there,' I said.

'I expect so.'

'When do I start?' I said.

'Tomorrow.'

I ducked under her hand and was off, down towards the riverbank.

I sat on the ferrysteps, the slate cool through worn cloth, my legs grown too long for me to swing my heels. Above, the sky was deep blue, the night full of river-sounds. The water caught the moon's reflection and teased it into ripples. I put a hand on the bulwark of the boat.

A grey hollowness filled my chest, my throat. My nose began to prickle; on the river, slivers of moonlight bleared and swam. There was no one, nothing left for me now. Not even this.

So I was to work at the Anchor. The public house. Forbidden to children, disapproved of by women, possessed of an irresistible attraction for the village men. It was unknown territory. A new, mysterious world. God only knew what went on in there. The Metcalfes and the Clay twins would be so jealous.

I wiped my eyes. The smear of moonlight resolved back into ripples. Somewhere in the night a sheep called, baritone; and another, younger one answered her.

I wasn't going to leave empty-handed. I took advantage of my grandmother's absence the next day and had a thorough hoke around. Da must have kept something, some keepsake or souvenir. If I could just find something that was important to him, it would give me a glimpse of the man he had been, of the stories I had lost when I lost him.

In his room, the light shafted in through the deep-set window, fell on the enamelled bedhead, the crocheted counterpane. She still hadn't stripped the bed. For a moment I considered pulling back the pillow to see if his nightshirt was still there, but I couldn't bear to look.

His old sea-chest stood at the foot of the bed. It had always been there; plain, slate-blue, and with his initials stencilled on it in black; but I couldn't remember him ever mentioning it, and had never seen it open.

I knelt down, ran my hands over its dusty surface. A keyhole but no key. Experimentally, I tugged at the lid. It flew up, unlocked and unexpectedly lightweight. There were dustmotes in the sunlight. I looked inside. I sank my hands into folds of soft pale stuff.

There was nothing there, not really. Just a lavender-bag made from the same fabric as the front room curtains, and a couple of old shirts, one white, one white with blue stripes, which must have fitted my father as a boy. These, and a pair of boys' clogs, black, nailed and laced, the wooden soles splintery with wear. But apart from that, nothing. I ran my hands over the grey inner surface of the trunk, not quite able to accept its emptiness. No letter, no note, not even a smudged address label: nothing. And for a moment I felt almost angry. How could they have left me with nothing, without even a clue? I turned back to the shirts, lifted one, examined it unsuccessfully for pockets. The fabric was soft, smelt of mustiness and lavender. I peeled off my scratchy jumper, by now so outgrown that a clear three inches of sunbrowned belly was visible beneath it anyway, and lifted the white shirt over my head. It fell around me in cool folds. I tucked it into my shorts, then bent to unhook my sandals. The clogs were too big, but I took a pair of my grandmother's yellow ribknit socks from the press. I tucked the striped shirt into one of her old wool-gathering bags. I slung it on my shoulder. I would, at least, be bringing something of him with me.

Bag on back, my feet somehow, despite the ache for change and proper food that was gnawing at my belly, would not take me straight to the Anchor. Instead, I found myself scuffing along the riverbank. I followed without thinking the bend in the river round to where Thrush Gill falls into the water, and turned to walk the shallows upstream.

Half a mile up over loose rocks, then pushing through hanging branches and slithering over water-filmed slabs of sandstone. Easier going in my new clogs; no knocks to vulnerable ankle bones, no stubbed toes. Half a mile under dripping mossy overhangs, dark loamy banks, then up over a rocky shelf and out into open evening sky: the buzz of a waterfall, and the pool, a single perfect cup of sandstone, worn by the constant stirring of a single skull-sized boulder in its bottom. Above, one twisted hawthorn tree and the brackened sweep of moorland up to the sky. A hawk sailed by, carrying something small and soft and dead. I stripped naked. I felt the deep moss beneath my feet, the air around my skin.

It was my place. It always had been. I shared it with a blackbird: she bathed in the shallows sometimes. No one else ever came there.

I swam in the cold hillside water, turning and diving like a fish, legs together, as my mother would have done. I washed off domestic dust and darkness, let the waterfall pound the breath out of me.

And clean, breathless and damp-skinned, I pulled on my clothes. It felt oddly like putting the skin back on a rabbit. As I clattered back down the stream, my feet, still unused to the warmth and support of the clogs, glowed comfortable and secure. The air tasted sweet. A new life, I thought, was opening out in front of me. I had prospects.

Four

'Right,' Uncle George said, 'let me make myself clear.'

He held my shirt bunched up at the neck, his fist pressing into my throat. I'd barely got in there: he was pushing me up against the doorjamb, he'd almost lifted me off my feet.

'I'm not your grandmother and don't you ever forget it. You can't get round me the way you did with her. I know what you're like, and I know how to deal with kids like you. There will be no nonsense. You won't get away with anything. Do you understand me?'

'I never got round –'

He lifted me still higher, growled.

'And I won't take any lip from you either. You're here to work. The moment you step out of line I will beat you straight back into it. If I have to, I will break you. It won't bother me one bit. Do you understand?'

'Yes.'

*

Uncle George wasn't really my uncle. He wasn't anybody's uncle. He was the principal tallyman and moneylender of the area. Maybe Gran gave me to him to service a bad debt: certainly what with the funeral and the weather it had been a difficult year for her, and I don't recall ever being paid. But like I said, my memory isn't what it ought to be. Maybe I got that wrong.

Uncle George assumed that I was ignorant of everything: mostly he was right to do so. He stood in the kitchen, armsfolded, and told me the best way to pluck a hen, to clean enamel, to prevent a loaf from spoiling. He pushed the larder door open and gestured me in. The cool slate shelves were laden with jars of pickled eggs, vegetables and nuts, a grey and cloudy canister of mushrooms looking unpleasantly familiar. These preserves, he told me, were to be served with his meals. He had, he said, a taste for vinegar.

Behind the bar, he showed me the appropriate angle at which to hold a pint mug while filling it with beer, how to wipe the lip-prints off its rim after use. He opened a cupboard door to reveal a broom, a scrubbing brush and pail, and explained the sweeping, and, following that, the scrubbing of the flagged floor. He tossed me a donkey-stone, informed me of its use in rubbing down front steps, and that this activity was to be performed once a week, on Thursdays. He mimed the action of rubbing. The enquiry as to how his last slave might have died was on the tip of my tongue, but I managed to swallow it back down. Such good behaviour on my part could not go on indefinitely, but for the time being my throat was still sore from where he'd held me.

He led me out of the back door, towards a long low building that half covered the burgage plot. As we passed, he pointed out where I was to collect the necessary water for my chores: a conduit brought a clean rill down from a nearby beck, and spilled it into a cool stone trough. He opened the brewhouse door: I caught the soft rich whiff of malt, and in the dim light saw heaped sacks, silken grain spilling out on to the floor. He pointed out the bags of hops, the pyramids of loaf sugar. He took down a broad-bladed knife from a hook on the wall, lifted a sugarloaf and peeled back the paper. He showed me how to scrape the sugar into flakes. He rolled up his sleeves and picked up a shovel to demonstrate the stoking of the fires for the mashing process. Leaning over the vast malty vats with a paddle, muscles standing proud on his arms, he showed me the best manner in which to stir the wort. And, at the end of the room, warmed to drowsiness by the mashing fires, he pointed out the yeasty, quietly bubbling fermentation casks.

In short, he showed me the instruments of torture, and there was nothing I could say, no confession I could make, which could get me out of the ordeal. He didn't want to hear a word from me.

But, I told myself, all was not lost. I could handle the work, I'd keep quiet, and I'd manage to stay on the right side of Uncle George. It would be worth it. I'd experience first-hand the after-dark masculine world of the bar room. I'd see what no other village kid had seen.

It took slightly less than two minutes, that first evening

at the Anchor, for me to realize that the pub's dim corners held nothing more exotic or unusual than the village men I'd always known, just a little worse the wear for drink. They sat hunched over their beer in pairs or threes while Uncle George leant armsfolded on the counter, talking loudly to whoever came up to buy a drink, or bending his head to hear an appeal for funds or for a period of grace. Throughout the evening, coins were passed back and forth, even to my untrained eye clearly much more than was necessary just to pay for the quantity of beer that had been drunk, and a tally was notched up in a copybook kept underneath the counter. Sometimes a basket of produce, a dead hen or rabbit, a jar of pickles, was passed across the bar and handed on wordlessly to me, with just a jerk of the head towards the kitchen. For a man so forthright with his opinions, Uncle George was unusually reticent when it came to the intricacies of usury.

And that's how things went on, day after day, with little differentiation. Mornings were spent in the brewhouse, afternoons preparing a meal from the previous night's offerings, then in the evenings I worked on the bar. My nights I passed up in the attic, lying awake on a thin mattress, listening to the rain on the roof, or the wind rattling a loose slate, or the call of a nightbird. I'd find myself thinking of my father, of his presence at my shoulder as I sat on the hearth and he passed down cigarette after cigarette for me to light at the fire. I'd remember my grandmother in the doorway, her arm stretched out to block my way, not looking me in the eye.

The grey hollow feeling would threaten to swallow me entirely.

I didn't have much sense of passing time. There were no landmarks. The boredom of my situation was so intense that if I had allowed myself to think about it, I would almost certainly have cried. So I refused even to consider thinking: I must have drifted into a kind of stupor, and completed my daily and weekly rounds of tasks in a daze, though I can't really give a clear account of it, having not paid very much attention at the time. Season must have shifted into season, must have shifted back. I grew to fit my father's clogs: I outgrew my shorts. Uncle George provided me with a pair of blue worktrousers. I barely registered these concrete changes. I barely registered anything at all.

This state must have gone on for some considerable time; it could have gone on for ever, if I hadn't been shaken out of it. It was a shock, or rather a series of shocks, that did it. Apparently as usual, I held out my jug to catch the water as it fell from the conduit's lip into the stone trough, and I found myself slowly waking, becoming aware of the continued lightness of the vessel in my hand. I can see myself slowly turning to look, slowly lifting the pitcher to my face, my eyes focusing on the concentric circles of the glazed brown base, a mere smear of water. That was the first shock. The second came when I turned back, ever so slightly quicker, still half expecting to see the fall of clear water, and saw instead soft stalactites of moss, a single gathering drip. Then the third shock – to find myself standing there, an empty jug in my hand, the sun beating down on my neck and shoulders and on the crown of my head, with no sense of how long I'd been there, or where I'd been before, or how I'd got into that state in the first place.

And as I stood there a cog in my brain began slowly to revolve. Its teeth locked with another, which turned a clogged-up axle, which gradually coiled a spring, which sprung, nudged a lever, and the penny dropped. My pool.

I should have already known what I would find, of course, and shouldn't really have needed to go and look. That slowly dripping stalactite of moss should have been evidence enough. But because my brain was still just crunching through its disused gears, its lubricants cold and thick with disuse, and a good proportion of my mental cogs and wheels had yet even to become engaged, I was halfway down to the riverbank before I even noticed that the jug was still dangling from my hand, and the strings of my apron were fluttering loose. I tugged the apron off, stuffed it into the pitcher, set them in the bottom of the hedge and marched on.

If I hadn't quite managed to accept the significance of the dry stone conduit, I should have realized when I saw the whitened rocks in the riverbed, the baked and cracked mud at the banks. But even the dusty scrape of my clogs on the beck's dry bed was insufficient to prepare me for what waited up above, underneath the twisted hawthorn and the sky.

It was the silence that hit me first. I had always thought of the pool as a peaceful place, but now I realized that it had never quite been quiet: there had always been the hum of falling water. Now, the unaccustomed hush brought my heart to my mouth. I stepped up towards the bank. The waterfall was just a damp stain on the rock. Beneath me, bare stone sloped down to a shallow pond of algaed water. Dimly visible in its base, the pestle-stone rested, motionless. The place was dead. And I would have sank down, I suspect, on the parched moss, and put my head in my hands, had I not heard footfalls on the stream bed behind me. Someone had followed me there. I turned round. It was Uncle George.

I wasn't thinking. I barely noticed the angry flush of his face, the sweat of rage and exertion dampening his shirt. All I knew was that I couldn't let him be there, couldn't let him see. It was the one thing left that was mine. I grabbed his arm, shoved him away.

'Get out of here,' I said. 'Get out.'

Which was, I soon discovered, just about the worst thing I could have done.

For a week afterwards it was agony. The following fortnight was painful, and I remained uncomfortable for the best part of the next month. I couldn't really blame him for the thrashing that he gave me. He had warned me, after all. I didn't even blame him for using, from time to time, the buckled end of his belt. My first night back in the bar, Mr Robinson, who always smelt of goats, made it his business to point out to me that I had had that flogging coming, that it was the only way to deal with the likes of me. That George would put me finally in my place. Around the bar, the other men's heads were nodding in agreement.

The beating did let me know, quite clearly, where I stood, though at the time I wasn't, strictly speaking, standing. And afterwards, the tack of the weals against my Da's old shirt, the sting and lingering smart when a scab cracked open, kept me awake. Which was good: I couldn't risk drifting again, couldn't let myself sleepwalk through my life.

Senses vividly alert, I began to experience my circumscribed existence with a clarity and intensity I hadn't known since I was a tiny child. The patterns of wear in the stone flagged floor became beautiful to me. In the garden, the failed fallen apples, hard as shot, seemed perfect in their minuteness. The scent of mown grass on cooling evening air could make my throat swell with longing for I didn't quite know what. In the evenings in the bar room, I observed the way the day's dust lingered in the men's hair, the slopes and shadows of their faces as they leaned lower and lower over their drinks, how their nails looked white against their sunscorched hands, the reek of their unwashed and hardworked bodies. No one spoke to me, but I overheard that the cows were now licking daylong at the damp places in the river bed, that someone's hen had laid an empty egg, that my grandmother now sat, head in hands, on the ferrysteps, and desiccated in the sun. And that somewhere, not so very far off, a wagon was coming pulled by steaming glossy horses, brasses jingling, courtesy of Lord Carus, barrelled up to the gunnels with water from the demesne wells. It would be here any day now, but:

'It'll be too little and it'll be too late.'

Each morning I joined the queue at the village pump, head pounding with the heat, and would become, in spite of the discomfort, utterly absorbed in the observation of the way the light caught the curls of hair escaping down the nape of the woman in front, or the workstained and cracking skin on her sunbrowned hands. Then the queue would step, as if ratcheted, one pace forwards, as someone came staggering back along the line, laden with the regulation two buckets, sweat standing out on her skin from the exertion of cranking the pump. With the passing days, the work grew ever harder as the flow of water gradually diminished. The regulation two buckets was first cut to one, then to a quart pitcher, then to a pint, then to half a pint per person per day, which decisions were made and enforced by the Reverend Carr, who stood by the pump, day after day, pink-faced and sweating in his clerical black, blinking lizard-like under his hatbrim. And, once each household's rations were supplied, he clunked the pump's padlock into place, slipped the key into his waistcoat pocket, and walked away. He went up, I have to say, in my estimation, for that. I wouldn't have wished that job on anyone.

All that time I was constantly aware of the dryness of my mouth, the way my tongue stuck to my palate, the dusty catch at the back of my throat. Against my instincts, I was forced to spin out my half pint of water throughout the day, depleting it in mouselike sips. The urge to drink it down in one quick swallow was fierce, but I kept the impulse at bay. It was necessary, this slight refreshment, even though it was never quite enough to dampen down my thirst. At night, sweltering beneath the hot tiles, no breath of air coming in through the opened window, I slept shallowly: I dreamt of rain.

The heat turned a whole tun of beer: it reeked of rot and no one, despite their constant thirst, could be persuaded to drink it. Uncle George had me empty it on to the vegetable patch, where the leeks had dried into straw and the feathered carrot-tops were parched as tinder. The plants were past revival: the only possible benefit of emptying the cask there was that the earth, dampened, would at least cease to blow away. Uncle George's other response to the loss was equally pragmatic: he trebled the price of a pint.

Waterless, I had taken to cleaning the glasses with vinegar. Each time Uncle George finished off a jar of pickles, he would leave me the vessel and remaining liquid. I would stand behind the counter, dipping a rag into the jar, polishing each fingerprinted glass back to clarity. The vinegar evaporated quickly in the heat, and left the glasses with just a faint acidic whiff, a taint of onion, cabbages or eggs. No one seemed to notice these slight contaminations: every mouth was already bitter and polluted (after a while Uncle George even began to regret the disposal of that rotten barrel) and, unable to perform even the most meagre of ablutions, let alone launder clothes and underclothes, each of us perspiring like cheese left out in the sun, there was not one single villager who did not reek to high heaven, whose skin was not filmed with oily filth.

My first thought, therefore, when I saw him, was how clean he was. He came into the bar room with a breath of mist and moss, and looking up, I saw a fold of crisp linen, the dip and curve of skin over collarbone, and was suddenly acutely aware of my dirt-embedded fingernails, the stickiness beneath my arms and between my legs. My second thought was that I hadn't met him before. And I'd never met anyone I hadn't met before.

His hat and suit were clerical, black and clean, and his shirt was white and obviously of fine quality, but he wore it open at the throat and collarless, like a working man. He wore boots, not clogs: he'd come in softly on the usually clattering stone floor; and that spoke of quality, but a glance revealed the boots to be worn and dusty, and the laces were frayed with use. He raised a hand to his hat, and the hand was brown and strong, but wasn't scuffed or callused with work. His nails were neat.

He said, 'Good afternoon,' and the vowel sounds were clipped and unfamiliar. I glanced round to see who he was speaking to. There was no one else there. I turned back to him, opened my mouth, and then remembered what happened the last time I stepped out of line. This would, I suspected, count as stepping out of line. And so I moved back from the bar (mouth still hanging open, no doubt) and turned to go into the kitchen, where Uncle George was finishing his dinner. As I came through the doorway he lifted his head to look at me, his jaw working as he chewed.

'There's a stranger –' I began to say. A line appeared between his eyebrows. 'In the bar room.'

He scraped his chair back, turned down his cuffs, wiped his mouth with the back of a hand.

'What does he want?' he said.

'I don't know.'

'What did he say?'

'He said, "Good afternoon."'

Uncle George shook his head. Still chewing, he pushed past me and through the doorway into the bar room.

I stood there in the kitchen, looking down at his plate of food: the bits and scraps of hen meat, the messed heap of pickled cabbage, the black crescent on the plate's rim where the enamel had been chipped. I felt my heartbeat slow back down to normal. I listened to Uncle George's loud and over-friendly greeting. I could spit on his food, right on to the heap of cabbage; maybe if I stirred it around he wouldn't notice. I heard the softer, deep murmur of the stranger's voice. I felt my skin prickle.

I moved back towards the doorway. From the threshold, I caught sight of the stranger's passing profile as Uncle George gestured him up the stairs. For a moment I watched as he climbed but then my view was blocked by the bigger man following him up. I listened to the light scrape of the stranger's boots as they syncopated with Uncle George's heavier footfalls, heard the distant creak of a door, the shift and strain of floorboards as the men moved around the room above. I came back to my station behind the bar, lifted a glass from the stack, picked up my vinegary rag. I watched the stairwell's empty shadow until Uncle George came back downstairs again alone.

'What are you looking at?'

I dropped my eyes back down to the glass and rubbed at the oily tracery of fingerprints, the lace of lipcreases patterning the rim. I watched in my peripheral sight as he turned his shirt cuffs again and went through to the kitchen and his unfinished dinner. I should have taken my chance and spat. Because upstairs, stretched out on the best white candlewick, eyes closed, shirt open; chest rising, falling, rising, falling, as the air cooled around him, was this stranger. And in the kitchen was Uncle George with elbows spread, stabbing at scraps of brown hen meat, shovelling heaps of pickled cabbage, the sweat soaking through his tide-marked shirt. He would keep me side-lined, silenced, out-of-sight. I knew it. And it made me want to spit.

There was nothing to be done that afternoon that couldn't have been done another day, another week, ten years later. But still he made me work.

He had me clean the brewhouse. No brewing going on of course, not without water: but as far as Uncle George was concerned, this was no reason for me to slack off. Quite the opposite in fact. It meant that I could give the task my full attention.

It would, in the best of circumstances, have been a Herculean task, but my work was rendered Sisyphean by the fact that I could not be spared one single drop of water with which to do it. A thick rime of dust, generated by years of hops and grain and fires, covered every surface: it misted windows, weighed down cobwebs, caught in my throat; it had caked hard wherever the mash or wort had been spilt. Even without the fires, it was still baking hot in there, hot enough to keep the latest and, for the foreseeable future, final batch of beer fermenting quietly in its tuns, hot enough to have me sweating like a horse. My efforts at cleaning served only to move the dust around, to heave it into fine clouds, which slowly settled back on to trestle tables, windows, the slabbed stone floor and me. As I shuffled around the room with my broom and shovel, coughing, wiping my eyes, spitting thick black spit on to the floor, I cursed him. Even now, he'd be leaning over the counter, a pint of table beer warming in his hand, listening to the stranger's stories. Or, more probably, I thought, not listening at all: probably talking long and loud and uninterruptably about the same old same old stuff. Delighted with himself and with his new audience.

What a waste, I thought. What a godawful waste.

The interior of the brewhouse was fading into blue, my sight becoming grainy in the dark, and there was still no sign of Uncle George come to tell me I could stop. It must have been seeping into my mind gradually for hours, the sound of gathering voices, but I only became conscious that something was happening when a shout of laughter stopped me dead in my tracks. I straightened up, caught a rising wave of talk. I listened, tried to catch a word or two, but couldn't. From the pitch and weave of the voices, it was clear that a crowd had gathered in the bar, that the bar was far fuller than I had ever seen it, and that the crowd included, unusually, the village women. Obviously, the news had spread like cattlecough. Everyone (it certainly sounded like everyone) had turned out to get a look at, exchange a word with, the stranger. Everyone, of course, except me.

Outside, the air was cooler. The pub's back door was open. From where I stood I could see into the dark and empty kitchen, see dirty yellow oil-light spilling into it through the half-open bar room door, illuminating a corner of stone sink, an arc of flagstones. I leaned my broom against the wall, stretched cautiously. The muscles in my back and shoulders were sore, and a scab had cracked open and was weeping, the lymph sticking to my shirt. My head ached; a vein was throbbing in my temple. I had been entirely forgotten, I knew. Or, rather, no one cared enough to notice that I wasn't there. And if no one noticed that I wasn't there, then presumably no one would check up on me, so it wouldn't matter if I stopped work. I left my broom leaning against the wall, made my way into the kitchen.

Uncle George's dirty dishes were still set out on the table. I moved into the shadows, outside the lamplight's glow, and peered through the half-open door into the bar. The counter was thick with glasses, full, half-full, and empty, and the villagers were thick with drink. I'd never heard so much noise from them. There was a look of blurred relief about their faces, as though something grand had been achieved, as after haymaking. But all that had apparently been accomplished on this occasion was the consumption of a large quantity of strong beer which no one, I would have thought, in the current circumstances could really afford to pay for.

In profile, I could see the bulge of Uncle George's thick forearm upon the bar, the greasy curl of his rolled-up sleeve. His jaw was working vigorously as he talked, his Adam's apple sliding up and down his bristling throat. And across from him, one arm leaning on the bar, shirt-sleeve turned back to reveal a curve of muscle, light soft hair and brown skin, was the stranger. His fingers were arched upon the counter beside a slightly-sipped pint. He was nodding, looking down at his arched hand, his head turned a little to listen to Uncle George. He gave every impression of being utterly absorbed in what was being said. Uncle George must have paused: the stranger shifted his balance, glanced up, and said something. I watched his lips, the changing lines of his face. I watched as, still speaking, his eyes turned towards the open kitchen door, and me. I didn't look away in time. His eyes caught mine and held them. He smiled.

It was an odd smile, brief: just a moment, then he looked away, glanced back down at his arched hand, his clean nails, then up again at Uncle George's glistening face. Nonetheless, I knew that it had been intended to communicate something, though that something remained frustratingly unpindownable. Just a faint twitch of the lips. *I can see you* sung out as in a child's game, but something else too, something like complicity. *I can see you, I can keep a secret, I won't say a word.* And maybe, less playfully, *I know as well as you do what this man is like,* and also, perhaps, *we both know I'm keeping other secrets too.* Or, I had to concede, as I climbed the stairs to bed, none of the above. Perhaps he'd just seen me standing there, alone and forgotten in the shadows, and had smiled.

I sat down on the mattress to loosen my laces, then lay down on top of the covers and eased each clog off in turn with a toe. They hit the boards with a thud. Voices still rose from the bar below, slurred with distance and drink. My cheeks were burning. The whole village, with very few exceptions, was gathered down there with him. A real celebration. Was there something I didn't know, something he had told them? What, after all, had that smile meant? That I was the only one who wasn't in on the big secret?

I must have dozed off: I'd been dreaming. Diving deep into the pool, the water clear and soft as air, and the pool deeper and deeper, diving down and down, and never coming to the bottom, just one smooth cup of water, filling the hillside and the valley, taking up the space where the village should have been. My mother, diving there beside me, said, 'The pestle-stone has worn it all away,' and that was when I woke, thirsty, sweating, on top of tangled sheets.

It was still dark. It was quiet. Everyone must have either passed out or gone home. My door stood at an angle, open: moonlight slipped in through the gap and fell across my face, illuminating a stretch of silvered floorboard. Standing on the floorboard was a pint glass, filled to brimming with clear water. It was beautiful, laugh-out-loud beautiful: it could not possibly be real. I found myself leaning up onto an elbow, stretching out a hand towards it. My fingertips touched cold glass, sensed the unmistakable press of water against it. The tightness of the scabs across my back made me wince. I took the glass's weight in my hand, lifted it to my lips, and drank.

The first mouthful covered my tongue like a clean sheet, so fresh that my mouth seemed all the fouler for it. The second I let roll around, pulling it between my teeth, letting it trickle gradually down my throat. My tongue slid around my mouth like an eel woken by rain. I drank some more. My headache seemed to soften. My eyes felt wet and heavy: I blinked a few times, just savouring the sensation. The glass was empty: just a beading of droplets traced the water's flow to the brim.

There was only one person who could have brought it.

When I woke the next morning the glass was still standing there quite casually with my fingerprints on its side and a tiny puddle of water, constrained by its meniscus, resting in the bottom. And behind it, my bedroom door still stood open at an angle, though it was now rinsed in plain morning light. But even if someone had come back to take the glass, and maybe stood and watched me sleeping for a moment before shutting the door, I would still have known that it hadn't been a dream. I felt saturated, soft and full.

I had woken early, I could tell; the air was still cool before the day's long heat. I lay and listened awhile, conscious of the increasing pressure on my bladder, the intermittent sounds of the sleeping house. I heard the scratch and twitter of vermin from within the lath-and-plaster walls, the phatic communion of doves on the roof, the scrape and flutter as one lost, momentarily, its footing. But other than that, silence. Beneath, in the house, no one was stirring. Uncle George would be lying, sheets peeled back, chest all tangled hair and oily sweat, mouth open, sour, stinking of old drink. And just across the landing from him was the stranger. That thought, even more than the ache of my bladder, made me shove back the sheets and scramble out of bed. Hunched under the roof's low pitch, I heaved on my shirt and hitched up my trousers. Belt buckled, I picked up my clogs and slid out through the still half-open door. I knew which of the stairs creaked: clogs in hand, I placed my bare feet on the corners of the treads.

That's what the smile had meant. He'd noticed me, and had thought of me, when no one else had thought of me at all. And he, crisp and clean and smelling sweet as a sheet just off the line, must have known something that no one else here knew, because he must have got that water somewhere. Something was swelling up inside me like a balloon, almost lifting me off my feet. Happiness, I realized.

I came to the landing, paused to look at the guestroom door, the pale boards of bare wood, the smooth metal lip of the latch, the wear-glossed thumbhole.

Last night: everyone drinking and laughing and not a care in the world.

They knew already. He'd brought me the glass of water, but he'd told them hours before.

He'd be stretched out on the bed, the morning light cool through pale curtains, the white candlewick counterpane, brown skin against linen. I could, ever so quietly, cross the landing floor; I could hunker down, press my eye to the thumbhole. I could observe, for some moments together, the rise and fall of his chest, the pulse in his throat, the movement of his eyes behind their lids. And then I could just rise and turn and continue down the stairs in silence, through the kitchen and out to the back yard jakes, for a long, luxurious piss. And no one need ever know, neither that I'd looked where I was not supposed to look, nor that I'd peed where I was not supposed to pee (things being the way they were, Uncle George had dictated that we micturate on the vegetable patch, take our leaks, as it were, on the leeks).

And Uncle George could get up at any moment, could come staggering out of his room, sticky-eyed and still half-asleep, heading downstairs in search of a hair of the dog.

It was with these conflicting possibilities in mind, caught between temptation and anxiety, that I was hovering there on the turn of the stair when I heard, from behind the guestroom door, the sudden and uncanny crash of water.

His back was turned to me: he stood on the far side of the bed, naked. The smooth slow slope from his shoulder down to his hip, the shift of shoulderblade beneath the skin as he lifted up the ewer. All over, the same soft honey-colour. As far as I knew, the sun only browned men's skin up to the elbow, reddened napes of necks and sharp vees of chest flesh. But this man was honey-coloured all over: he must have been born that way. He lifted the ewer higher, poured a flood over his head. Crashing down over him, the water flattened his curls, divided into veins and rivulets across his back and shoulders. He shook his hair, sending squalls of rain around the room, darkening the plaster and the parched boards. From the nightstand he took up a clean white cloth, ran it over his shoulders, chest and flanks. He turned.

I stumbled back from the door.

He had looked straight at me. Straight through the thumbhole.

I dropped my clogs. The noise seemed to resound through the sleeping house. I scooped them back up and ran down the stairs. I heard Uncle George stir and curse. But from the guestroom I heard nothing: the silence was so complete that it seemed conspicuous, felt almost conspiratorial.

As I slithered down the final few steps into the bar, I became aware of an unfamiliar and distracting pressure in the pit of my belly, quite different from the ache of an over-full bladder. But once I'd bolted myself into the jakes I didn't give it another thought, such was the pleasure of unburdening myself there, of that discreet rebellion against Uncle George. I recall, even now, with fondness, the impressively copious, hot, and pungent waterfall, the aching pleasure of release. There is, I will always maintain, nothing quite like a good and long-awaited piss.

I'd been right. They knew already. He'd told them something.

I was standing in the bar room, doing nothing. There were glasses everywhere, spilt drink on the tables, and the floor was filthy, but as there was no one there to see me cleaning, I wasn't going to do it. I leaned against the bar, chewed on a fingernail, and drifted.

He had a knack of observing me, I was thinking, just when I thought I was the one doing the watching. A slow blush spread across my face, and I glanced over a shoulder, but this time there was no one there.

I heard footsteps cross the landing, then Uncle George's feet heavy on the stair-treads. I picked up a glass smeared with last night's dregs, wiped it round the rim to take off the obvious marks, then held it underneath a tap and flicked the lever. As the beer began to flow I leaned over the glass and let a long slow streal of spit fall into the foam. I glanced up, wiped my lips. Uncle George was just coming to the foot of the stairs, a shaking hand resting on the newel post. He raised the other hand to his face, wiped it. His skin was almost as grey as his cuffs. I lifted up the glass, held it out towards him. He registered me, grunted and came over to take it. He gulped down half the beer. I smiled. I wasn't going to miss these chances any more.

'Lot of noise, this morning,' he said.

'Must've been the stranger,' I said. 'I expect he's packing.'

He narrowed his eyes at me.

'I don't think so.'

Which was my first indication that he was in on something. Then there was a knock on the door, which made me jump. It was the wrong time of day. No customers, no callers, nobody came to the Anchor before noon. It was unheard of. I glanced back at Uncle George. Even in his weakened state he hadn't flinched, and didn't seem surprised. He grasped the nearest chairback, drew the seat out from underneath the table and sat down.

'Fetch me the book,' he said, 'then let them in. And get this bloody place cleaned up.'

There was already a crowd outside, standing in the morning glare in their stained and stinking workclothes, their shawls and hats tugged down low against the sun. They filed in, one by one, across the darkened bar room to where Uncle George sat, stubby pencil in hand, copybook open on a fresh page.

'Is he about yet?'

'He'll be down soon.'

As each of them handed over their leather, felt or netting purses, Uncle George would tug at the strings, spill the coins out like grain across the table top. I watched as he steered the pence and halfpence with a fingertip, sorted them into piles, then pillars, counted them, noted names and payments in his copybook. He glanced up, saw me still leaning on the bar, and said:

'Do I pay you to do nothing?'

I looked at him a moment.

'No,' I said.

'Then get to work. This place is a kip.'

I pushed myself away from the bar, began collecting glasses, scrubbing at tables with a vinegary rag. The villagers kept on coming.

'How long will it take to get here? Did he say?'

'He said three days.'

'You know, once that's gone it's all gone,' someone said. 'We've nothing left. Not a bean –'

As the copybook page darkened with his scrabbled handwriting and the stacked coins grew to form a colonnade, Uncle George's hangover seemed to dissipate, and before long he seemed to be almost cheerful. I'd refilled his glass twice.

'Thank the Lord, George, thank the Lord.'

The Reverend Carr was reaching out, his purse cupped in his palm, and Uncle George had his hand stretched out to catch it when it fell.

'You'd do better thanking me, Reverend.'

The voice came from the stairwell. I looked round: every head turned the same way. The stranger. The vowels were clipped, the consonants thundering out like rolling barrels:

'Or him there for his organization. But not the Lord. This has got nothing to do with him.'

A shiver of delight raised the hair on my arms, goosepimpled me. The thrill of transgression. I looked back round at the clergyman.

The Reverend Carr had bridled. I watched his face grow pale beneath the flush of summer, then flood deeper red. His fingers, on the verge of letting his purse drop onto the table, tightened instead, regripping the leather pouch. Uncle George's hand fell to rest on the table. He looked up, but only as far as the Reverend's narrow leather belt, then he glanced round unfocusedly in the direction of the stranger. I waited, my teeth tugging at a scrap of skin near a fingernail. The Reverend Carr was thinking. I watched him weighing up what he would say. Eventually, he decided on:

'I had thought better of you, George.'

Uncle George said nothing, just returned his gaze to the cassock buttons, the narrow leather belt.

'I had thought better of you than to get embroiled with such a man, in such an unholy affair.' There was a tremor in his voice. The hand, gripping his purse, was shaking. The strip of skin came off my finger. I tasted blood.

The Reverend Carr stood there a moment more, vacillating, flushed, then he turned on his heel and stalked towards the door, his vestments rustling like a woman's dress. As he passed me I caught his smell: camphor, sweat, and boiled meat. I watched as the stranger came forward from the shadows. He came up behind Uncle George, put a hand on his shoulder.

'That's all right,' the stranger said. 'We'll do just fine without him.'

A pause.

He patted Uncle George's shoulder lightly. 'These men of God are all the same.'

'Aye, but,' said Uncle George, 'if he doesn't pay, and we all pay, it isn't fair. He'll be taking advantage.'

'Don't you worry yourself,' the stranger said, leaning

over to check the copybook. 'Don't give it another thought. He won't see a single drop fall on his land. That's the beauty,' he added, straightening, his eyes wandering across the room, catching mine, his face beginning to pucker with an expression that again I could not quite fathom, 'of a Rain Machine.'

Five

He would leave tomorrow, he'd be gone for three days, then he'd return with the Rain Machine. And then he would go away for ever. All day the idea of his coming and going and coming back again had stretched ahead of me like running stitch come adrift, like an unfinished seam.

The Rain Machine was to be hired as you would a threshing machine. I found myself imagining a vast conglomeration of whirring spinning cogs and wheels, taut drivebelts blurred with speed, and the villagers gathered on the green, gazing in wonder at these reassuringly unfathomable complexities. And, above, the clouds rolling in, massing, pale grey-brown and yellow, forming into the outline and expanse of the parish. With just a bite taken out from above the glebe, where the Reverend Carr would be standing alone, looking up desperately on clear blue sky, his purse still bulging through his fingers. Then a single clot would gather, fall, thwack down on to the earth, making someone jump, sending up a corona of droplets, a puff of dust. Then another, and a third. Hatbrims pushed back, a whistle, laughter. And then, uncountable, the rain would come in earnest, thick and heavy. Summer rain, drenching shirts, blouses, shawls. Saturating leaky clogs. Summer rain that would poach the fields, rot the dead grass where it lay, fill the dried-out river, swell it to bursting. My grandmother, afloat for the first time in months, would sit laughing in the ferryboat. My father, the earth growing damp around him, the water table rising, lapping at his flanks, would bloat up white and fishy, would crawl with worms. And Uncle George, whooping with delight, would push me back into the brewhouse and lock the door, leaving me there for ever to brew up vast vats of mouldy beer, and everyone else would drink themselves stupid in the rain. And locked into that dark swelter, sweat dripping and shoulders aching as I stirred the steaming wort, I would not even be able to watch as the stranger's figure diminished in the distance, as it grew indistinct through the thickening grey veils of rain.

I could get nothing done that day, nothing finished. Late into the night, after Uncle George and the stranger had scraped their way up the stairs to bed, I sat at the kitchen table, cleaning glasses. I'd never get the chance to speak to him before he left, I thought. Not now he was confederate with Uncle George. And I had to speak to him. Because beyond the bend in the valley road, over the cusp of the hill, there were places familiar to him, which seemed to him entirely unremarkable, but which would be strange and wonderful to me. As he walked out from underneath our tailored-to-requirements fully-guaranteed parish-shaped rain cloud, he would shake the water from his hat, begin to steam in the heat of the sun. He'd watch his scuffed boots as they swung out along the road, consider, perhaps, the urgency of their need for dubbin. In front of him, first would rise whalebacked slate-grey moors, then the smooth rolling slopes of the fatter land beyond. After that, perhaps, there would come an expanse of tree-pooled silvered grass that seemed to stretch forever, until at last you heard the sound of the waves, tasted salt, and realized that what had seemed to be just the continuing sweep of grassland was in fact wet sky-reflecting sand, and the sea. The sea, where my father had travelled, where my mother might still be found. Thick crashing waves, a bite in the air, and the ever-present dark enticement of the mermaids' song. My people. At last my people. The schoolroom map behind its dusty glass, observed peripherally and years ago, came again into my mind; the outline of this island country, green waves nibbling round its coastline, pale waters lying in its heart. I could almost see the dust trails rising from the paper, as together he and I paced out the pathways, the roads and the trackways my mother might have taken. As we traced the way away from here.

I was going with him, I realized. So I should probably let him know.

It was not a voice that woke me, not a jolt. I opened my eyes on a battlement of dirty glasses, my cheek pressed to the hardness of the kitchen table. From my curled fingers came the sharp stink of vinegar. I straightened up, raised a hand to my aching neck. Moonlight poured in from the deep-set window, silvering the tabletop, conferring on the glasses a temporary beauty. I swallowed dryly. Silence. No sign of what had woken me, no sound from the bar, no creak from overhead. My eyes came to rest on the back door, shut, slightly askew on its hinges. It could not, I knew, be closed without the boards scraping on the flagstones, without the door thumping against the frame.

I was on my feet and out in an instant, the door flung back and left gaping. Outside, the moon was full and high and cast only the most slender of shadows. I hesitated, looking round. The burgage plot was empty. And, beyond, the fields stretched out bare and silver, the hedges stark in the moonlight. No one to be seen. Out the front, then. Of course. Off along the valley road. I ducked into the ginnel, pounded along its darkness, clogs clattering on the cobbles loud enough, it seemed, to wake the dead, and in spite of my haste I found myself recalling for a moment my father's gentle presence, the hard skin of his hand, the smell of his tobacco. I swallowed again, gulping at the unexpected ache in my throat.

I came to a halt out on the road, skidding to a stop. The dust settled round my feet. I felt the hooded gaze of the sleeping pub on my back; the straggling cottages, village green and schoolhouse were monochrome in the moonlight. He was there. Ahead, a hundred yards down the valley road, he had heard me, and stopped. He stood, half-turned, his eyes shadowed by his hatbrim. A slight misty trail of footdust slowly settled back to earth around him.

A moment passed.

Standing on the crossroads, looking out down the valley road at the stranger. Body feeling light and hollow and disconnected. Fingers fluttering lightly at my sides. Not the faintest idea of what to do. And then, moonlight caught white: he had smiled, I realized. And on such slight gestures are whole futures founded. I grinned back, then clattered up to him, fingers still fluttering uselessly at my sides. I halted some feet away. Now that it came to speaking, I was once more at a loss. Again, that faint whiff of mist and moss off him. I opened my mouth. And for some unfathomable reason, my voice sounding creaky and uneven, I said:

'You know me, don't you.'

A slight turn of the head, as if in acknowledgement. I swallowed.

'When you come back,' I said, 'with the Rain Machine . . .'

The creases from nose to lip deepened. His eyebrows, in the shadow of his hat, seemed to rise a little, to tilt sideways. He looked down at me directly, his eyes bright and clear in the moonlight, and I realized that I had always known he was never coming back. My skin bristled again with that sweet and sudden thrill of transgression. He hefted his bagstrap up his shoulder, settled it there with the air of someone just about to go, and, once gone, be gone for good. I found myself stretching out a hand, placing it on his arm, noticing as I did so that my hand was shaking. The fabric of his sleeve was cool and soft, and beneath I felt the long smooth curve of muscle.

'Can I come with you?'

He looked down at me looking up. The lines on his face mapped out, I thought, a whole world of experience.

A long moment passed.

'What do they call you?' he asked.

My mouth was dry. The word felt strange on my lips: 'Malin,' I said. 'Malin Reed.'

'Malin.'

He seemed to consider this a moment, to weigh it up. Then he said:

'It's not what you think it is, you know. It's never what it seems to be.'

I nodded, alert only for a yes or no, happy to accept this, happy to accept anything. I told myself it would all make sense, when we knew each other, when we were travelling together, when I'd been to all the places he had been. I looked up at him, witless and tenterhooked.

'All right then, young Malin,' he said, and I felt a smile begin to broaden across my cheeks, 'if that's the way it is, you can come along.'

For a while I was so dizzy with excitement that just following him required me to be conscious of each step as it was made, to concentrate on the flexing of each knee, the lifting of each foot, the necessary swing of each hip in turn. His easy lope, half a pace ahead, made me all the more aware of my ungainly eagerness. I couldn't see his face. Above us, the stars were bright. A breeze, the first one that summer it seemed, caught at my hair. Clouds scudded, gathered above, tumbling across the stars. The breeze stiffened and grew sharp. The night darkened, the clouds thickening and curtaining the moon. At the road's bend I turned to take a last look at the sleeping village, and thought of my grandmother. She'd said I was too much for her. She'd said Uncle George would straighten me out. Well he hadn't.

And as I stood there, looking back, something passed swiftly before my face, hit the road in front of me with a thwack. I glanced round at the stranger: he too had stopped and turned to look. Something fell again, just over to my left. Then something else, further off, towards the village. I squinted into the dark, at the outlines of the public, the schoolhouse, the shambling cottages. Suddenly, a precise but painless blow to my collarbone, and an instantaneous cold, which rolled over the round of my shoulder, ran down my chest, lingered in the linen of my shirt.

'It's raining,' I said, unbelievingly.

A low growl of thunder, another whipcord lash of wind, and the heavens opened.

I don't know who laughed first. I remember seeing him push back his hat, his mouth open with a great shout of laughter, his eyes closed to let the rain run over his face, and I found myself thinking of his nakedness, his honey-coloured skin. I remember him turning to me, laughing, and me laughing too and being surprised that I was laughing so naturally, so comfortably, with him, and him putting an arm around my waist, and the cold wet linen of my father's shirt pressed against my skin. And him lifting me off my feet and spinning me round and the water falling all around us and the darkness blurring, and the breath squeezed out of me and still the laughter. That was the first time I had ever been kissed, and it is typical of me that I should spend that moment in which his body was first pressed against my own, just thin wet fabric between his limbs and mine, his hand on the small of my back and his lips wet with rain on my lips, thinking how badly I must have stank.

Six

I loped through the downpour at his heel, not hunched and collar-turned against the wet, but loose-jointed, shoulders low. After that kiss, the rain fell on me like a blessing. As I walked, I licked the water off my lips, tasted the bitterness and salt of unwashed skin. I blinked away the rain-smear from my eyes, pushed the hair back from my forehead, and lifted my face to the heavens. I felt cocksure, expansive, light-of-heart. I was glad to be alive.

Beneath the falling rain, the villagers slept on, unaware of the puttering of water on to slates, of the quiet gathering of puddles outside their back doors. In the morning, they would wake to find the world transformed; muddied, damp, and unfamiliar. They would step outside, lift their faces to the cool sky, tears gathering in the crooks of their eyes and rain running down their skin. And in their rapture, they would not forget to bless this extraordinary man, whose doing it must have, somehow, been.

And Uncle George, who would wake to a house empty of all but vermin, who would thump downstairs head-achy, parched and farting, to find the bar room untidied, the floor unswept, and a barricade of dirty glasses on the kitchen table. He would call for me, thinking me just out-of-sight, and be answered only by the scratch of mice behind the wainscot. Then he would shout, lifting his voice to the low ceiling, his anger growing as, in his drink-muddied mind, an image began to form of me still up stairs in bed among tangled sweaty sheets. But he would hear nothing back; not even the surprised clatter of distant feet coming to his call. So he would curse, snatch up a glass from the table, and throw it at the wall. And only as he turned away from the shards and sparks that skittered out across the floor, considering what he would do with me when he finally found me, would he notice that the back door was standing open, and feel the cool breath of weatherchange on his thick old skin, and see that it was raining.

'My mother was a mermaid,' I said, by way of intro-duction.

'Oh really.'

'She left us. She went back to her own people.'

The rummaging of branches overhead, the creak of limb on limb in wind. We walked into a deeper dark where the rain fell in fewer, fatter drops, leaf-gathered. Above, the canopy was cacophonous with birds.

'They always do.'

'Mermaids?' I stopped dead. He kept on walking. I ran

to catch up with him. 'You know about them? You'd know where to find her?'

The road was rising: I felt running water tug my feet. A stitch pinched at my side. I knew, though I couldn't see anything but him, and he was just a grainy flicker of movement to my left and a lightness where his collar curled above his jacket, that I was in a place that I had never seen: from the village, the track disappeared beneath these trees. The thought made the hairs stand on the nape of my neck. The air sang in my chest.

'I know a few places you could try,' he said.

I stopped again. The stranger walked on without a break in his stride, without turning his head. I stared after him a moment, or rather at the darkness where he'd been. I could hear him walking on though the murk, water sluicing round his legs, stones clattering out from underneath his feet. My mouth was opening on some still unformulated question, and I was just breaking into a run to catch up with him again when my foot snagged on something and I went flying.

He caught me. An arm across my chest, winding me.

'All right?' he asked, setting me back on my feet.

I nodded, hadn't got the breath to answer him.

'Not far now,' he said, 'Not far to the watershed.'

And he set off again into the dark. I followed him unevenly, gasping, looking forward to the watershed. We'd rest in there a while, I thought. Perhaps we'd stay the night.

We had come out from underneath the trees: it was a little lighter, and the rain fell more gently. Underfoot, the

angle of the climb grew shallow, the water's tug less
fierce. Soon, we were walking on flat ground.

And I realized that the rain had stopped.

I wiped my face. A fullish moon had risen out of
nowhere. Its pale light picked out the road in front of us,
twisting away into the distance, serpentine, declining,
dry. To left and right, the darkness of moorland heaved
up towards a cloudless, starry sky. Blonde grasses rustled
gently in the breeze. My clothes were sticking to my skin,
dripping: my skin bristled with goosepimples. A droplet
rolled down my nose, hung, then fell into the open throat
of my shirt.

But the rain had stopped.

He had stopped too. His face, shadowed by the
hatbrim, was unreadable. I glanced round over my
shoulder, back the way we'd come. I could still hear the
rain thwacking down on to foliage, splashing into
standing water, trickling away in rivulets downhill. I
stretched a hand back into the dark behind me, and three
drops landed there in quick succession, soft and heavy. I
took a step back, and the rain was falling thick and fast
and cold, drenching through the skin-warmed wetness of
my shirt. I lifted my face up to the sky, spiralled slowly
round, open-mouthed. I turned back to him, and stood
there a moment, just looking at him.

'How did you do it?' I asked.

He pushed up his hatbrim and stood looking at me for
a long moment, but even so I still couldn't quite read his
expression. A slight shake of the head perhaps. Perhaps
half a smile.

'C'mon,' he said, and turned to go. 'You'll catch your death.'

I stepped out of the rain, into the dry.

I stayed at his heel, always half a pace behind. As we walked I was vividly conscious of the sigh of his breath, the creak of his bootleather, the crunch of his footfalls. The moors reared up above us. The air was cool with mist. From high up and to the left came a distant reedy birdcall, a kind I'd never heard before, and I caught the sweet wild smell of honey.

'Where are we?' I asked.

'Nowhere,' he said.

'It's lovely.'

It must have been hours, miles, that we walked that night. We crossed becks, running fast and shallow across the track, cutting down through the turf, and when we crouched to cup water to our mouths it tasted like the smell of currant bushes. I drank, squatting there on the gravel beside him, conscious of his crouching presence, his lips open to his cupped hand. Once, straightening, I found my legs had stiffened, become weak and heavy, and as we walked on my feet seemed just to swing out ahead of me volitionless, like plumblines. Blisters began to burn my feet. And then came the cold; slyly incremental, relentless. No matter how often I reminded myself to keep my shoulders down, to keep my back straight, to step out, no matter how persuasive were my recollections of hot sun freckling my face, warm slate step on the back of my legs, or winter fires crackling on the sandstone hearth, there was no getting round it. I was frozen. I wrapped my arms around myself to hold back the shivers, but this pressed my wet shirt against my skin. I let go, but then the night air slipped in around my body. Jaw clamped tight, stumbling along, flapping my arms around me like some giant waterbird, I became absorbed in the kernel of warmth inside, focused on the slight ripples of comfort that followed each shiver.

I didn't notice the sun rise, or hear the dawn chorus. I wasn't going to complain, wasn't going to show any weakness. I wasn't going to make him regret, even for a moment, that he had brought me with him. So I just stumbled on, still half a pace behind the stranger, wondering if he would never stop, if we would keep on walking until I crumpled in on myself like a struck tent and lay where I fell, shivering, unnoticed, while he strode on ahead, believing, if indeed he gave it any thought at all, that I was still there, still half a pace behind him, following at his heels. I glanced up and caught him looking round at me. I tried to smile. He laughed.

'You look fit to drop,' he said.

He glanced up beyond me, up the empty moorside.

'Best get you sorted out.'

And he set off uphill through the heather. As far as I could see, there was nothing up there but a sheer rise, a patch of broken-stemmed bracken and a stand of gorse bushes, and after that the sky. But I sucked in a breath, gritted my teeth and set off after him, following like a balloon tugged along on a string.

It was a difficult climb, that hundred yards or so up the hillside, footsnared and stumbling in the heath. As I passed the gorse I was engulfed by its sudden thick cloud of scent. When, some years afterwards, I first encountered a coconut, I found myself transported by the perfume of its unexpected milk, its blue-white flesh, back to that shivering stumble through the moors. Coconuts, to me, will always smell of gorse.

Behind the gorse stand there was a dip in the moorland, where the hill gathered itself a moment before taking another leap towards the sky. And here he'd stopped and slid his knapsack from his shoulder, and I almost stumbled into him.

'This'll do,' he said.

I saw nothing but a dip in the ground, an overcrop of rock. I didn't like to ask about the watershed.

'Sit yourself down,' he said. 'Soon get you warm.'

I made to sit, but found that I couldn't. Everything seemed to have locked solid. I stood swaying, looking down the length of my uncooperative legs, past the black scuffed leather of my clogs, to gaze at the soft mossy turf. It looked so comfortable I could have cried. Then I felt his hands pressing against my ribcage, under my arms.

'Here,' he said. 'I'll help you.'

I glanced up at him, thinking he was laughing at me, but his face was all sympathy and seriousness. He took my weight and lowered me, stiff-legged, down on to the ground. I whimpered: I couldn't help myself. He straightened up and turned away. I just sat there, my legs stretched bolt out in front of me, looking down at my feet, and it was wonderful just to be still. Each specific pain, each throb and cramp and chafe, sang out through the fog of overall discomfort. I was conscious of his presence as he moved around, but only vaguely. I was preoccupied by the deep structural ache within my feet, by the burning tackiness where the skin had been worn away. It would be wonderful if I could just lean forward, reach down and untie the laces, ease off my clogs. But it wasn't worth the fight against the tightness of my muscles, it wasn't worth giving up being still just to do that. And it would be even more wonderful if I could be warm. If the shivers would just melt and the goose-pimples smooth themselves away. And then something dense dropped round my shoulders: his jacket, dry inside, and still warm from his body. I reached up a hand and held it closed around my throat, and dipping my nose down into the collar, smelt leather. I shivered, felt the shiver warm my flesh, the jacket catch the warmth and hold it to me. I heard the hiss of grass, of heather rustling as it grazed against his boots and trouserlegs, I heard the clean snap of dry wood, the tear of greensticks, the click of stone on stone. A pause, a breath held, the scrape and silence as he struck a light and held it to the kindling. And then the first cough of smoke. I looked up. A flame begin to curl itself around a parched gorse twig, to lick at the tip of a thorn. Crouched, intent and precise, his face half cold in the morning light, half aglow from the fire, he fed uprooted heather stems into the flame.

He looked up at me, that same intent look on his face.

'We'd best get you out of those wet things,' he said.

It was an agony even to consider peeling that jacket off

my shoulders, let alone standing up to ease down my trousers and pull my shirt up over my head. I could have cried at the thought of moving, of exposing my flesh to the cold dawn air. But as he crouched to tease out my laces and ease off my clogs, and paused for a moment to admire the raw and oozing blisters on my feet, he insisted that it had to be done, and done soon. And that once it was done, I would feel so much the better for it: 'Then,' he said, 'we'll have you wrapped up nice and warm.' I didn't doubt that he was right, and I wanted to do as he said, but it seemed utterly impossible, and not just because of the cold. Because after I'd shed my clothes, for however short a moment, I would have to just stand there, naked, as he unfurled a blanket and cast it round me. Skinny white flesh patched with rusty sunburn. All bones and joints and angles, pimpled as a plucked hen. And for some reason, for the first time in my life, it seemed to matter. Again I felt that pressure swelling low down in my belly.

He was still kneeling down there at my feet, his hands on his knees, his hat pushed back. There was a crease between his eyebrows, a slight shadow beneath his eyes, but I didn't really know if he looked annoyed or weary or just cold. I didn't know him well enough to tell.

'I don't think I can,' I said. 'I'll just stay like this. I'll be fine.'

'You won't,' he said. 'You'll be dead.'

This was delivered solemnly and with a deepened crease between his brows, and my eyes filled unexpectedly with tears. Pathetic, really, that I should be so

easily affected: it's hardly a dazzling compliment, someone preferring that you didn't die in their company, but
I was dazzled. I struggled to move myself. He leaned in
to help me and I felt his hands underneath my arms
again, supporting me, lifting. I was upright unexpectedly
quickly, my head light, balance not what it might have
been. The turf gave beneath my feet, stung at the raw
skin.

Pretend he isn't there, I told myself. Strip off as
quickly as possible, don't even think about what he
thinks. Because probably he doesn't think anything at all.

I fumbled at my cuff. My fingers shook. I couldn't feel
the buttons. 'Here,' he said. 'Let me help you.'

His head was bent to see what he was doing, so I
couldn't quite be sure, but I thought I caught a faint
smile as he moved in closer to me. Both of us watched in
silence as his fingers undid the buttons at my wrists.
Then his hands moved up to my throat, and his face was
close, and I couldn't turn away because his hands were
beneath my chin, teasing out the topmost button. Then
one by one he plucked open the shirt buttons, and our
eyes followed his hands down. My breath had caught
high up in my chest. As he unhooked the fastening of my
trousers, tugging each fly button loose, the back of his
hand grazed my skin.

'There you go,' he said, and moved away. I stood there,
my shirt hanging loose, my trousers sinking low around
my hips. He crouched to open his knapsack. I grabbed a
handful of my waistband and held my trousers up. I
watched him for a moment, crouching there, absorbed,

then I eased my shirt off one shoulder and let it peel itself away from my back. I shook it off the other arm then bundled it to my chest. I watched as he pulled a blanket from his knapsack, watched as he straightened and came over towards me. He moved behind me, his hands lifting to lay the blanket over my shoulders. I couldn't breathe.

'Who did that to you?' he said.

'What?' I twisted to look over my shoulder.

I felt a fingertip touch a trace of Uncle George's belt. 'Did he do it?'

'Oh,' I said. 'Yes.'

'Bastard,' he said.

His breath was warm. He bent closer. I felt the soft pressure of his lips, the warmth of his mouth on my flesh. A nerve prickled down my arm. He kissed a scar.

Seven

It was at once a strange and a familiar sight, that little village staggering out from the crossroads. Blue wood-smoke curling up from chimneypots, doves brooding on a slate roof, a dog sleeping on a hot stone doorstep. Even a pair of tethered goats wearing bald circles on to the green. A quiet, weekday place, which could so easily have been home, but wasn't. Uncanny. A shiver slid down my spine, shuffled my shoulderblades.

I had come so far, you see, and so much had changed, and I'd thought for a while that the journey would kill me. Rising at dusk that first time, my bones still sore, my feet already worn to shreds, just two things kept me going. One of them was a joyful sing-song in my head: I had got away from there, I had got away: I had left it all behind me and was going to see the world. The other was less clear, and I couldn't quite have put it into words. I found myself imagining the stranger stricken with illness in some deserted place, and me at his side looking after him; or I'd see him fallen down a cliff face or a grike, his face just a pale oval below, and I'd haul him back up hand-over-hand, though it would nearly kill me. But he didn't need looking after, he didn't need rescuing, and anyway I didn't have a rope. All he required of me was to follow and keep up, so I had to redirect my heroic impulses towards putting one foot in front of the other, towards not complaining.

We stopped at a moorland farm one evening. A thickbuilt house, a shippon, a few outbuildings round the side. A skinny girl answered his knock. The way she looked out at us it was quite clear that no one ever called there. He told her our needs, held out a palm on which rested a couple of coins, and she closed the door in our faces. We looked at each other. He curled an eyebrow. We waited. There was whispering inside, then the scrape of a chair on flagstones. Then a little later the girl returned, handing through the narrow gap a misshapen brack, a shook of dried meat, and a loosely bundled jacket. He took them, held out his hand in turn for her to take her payment, but she just looked down at the coins, then up at him, her face blank. He reached out and took her by the wrist, unfurled her fingers gently and placed the money in her palm. Then we turned and walked away, leaving her standing there, looking suspiciously down at the coins. After meeting her, it was hard to believe that there could be anything beyond, that there could be an end to this wilderness.

Striding down the darkening track, he tossed the bundled jacket to me, and I shook it out, shrugged it on to my shoulders. He tore the brack in two, stowed one half in his pack and then divided the remaining half again. He handed me a piece, and as I chewed on the densely doughy stuff, conscious of the slight weight of the jacket, the resistance of its sleeve as I raised and bent my arm, I couldn't help wondering whose elbows had worn the fleece thin, whose sweat had stained the collar.

'That was stupid,' he said.

'What?'

'Could have got all those things for nothing, if I'd given it some thought.'

Suddenly I saw Uncle George spilling coins across a table top, his blunt finger steering and sorting. The jacket's supple warmth seemed to settle more comfortably around me, its faint scent of sheep and someone else. I felt I'd earned it.

'Thanks,' I said. 'Thanks a lot.'

He glanced round at me.

'You're welcome,' he said. 'Easy come, easy go.'

The journey didn't kill me. It didn't even take me very long to get accustomed to it. I'd been bred strong, I suppose, and I'd never had the opportunity to get soft. Before long I was stepping out eagerly, westward, face to the setting sun. I was happy.

We would walk all night, sleep out the day. He never told me why and it didn't occur to me to ask. As the sky paled behind us and the first warm touch of sun caught us on the back of the neck, we would slip into the lee of a tumbled wall, an abandoned shepherd's cabin, or a sheltering dip in the moor. We'd spread our blankets on the ground.

Not that we just slept. Sleep would come afterwards, would seep into that dreamy, sated state that followed. In the warmth between the blankets, our flesh damp, his breath on the back of my neck, sleep would come for him, then eventually for me.

He never hurt me, even that first time, but the way my body ached for him was often painful. I've never wanted anyone so much. There have been others since, of course: too many. But no one, not one of them could make me feel like that. There's been lust, and there's been comfort, and there might even have been love, but there has never been desire like that. When I looked at him it brought water to my mouth. And when we lay down together, I wanted him so fiercely that it could almost make me cry.

I always knew that he never felt the same. He liked me. I knew he liked me.

By the time we had climbed the bald crown of the last fell, I considered myself quite changed, someone alto-gether new, and had expected to find the world beyond as different as I felt. So when I looked down at that village straggling out along a crossroads, smoke curling from chimneypots, doves, goats, a sleeping dog, I couldn't quite believe it.

'Don't worry,' he said, standing at my side, his rounded, dark-sleeved arm visible in the corner of my eye. I wanted to take him by this arm and steer him away, head off in another direction, anywhere.

'You can't step into the same river twice,' he said. And, a moment later, 'You take the bag.'

So we walked down there together, strides stretched by the steepness of the hill, the bag thumping against my back. His eyes were narrowing on the quiet settlement, one hand resting, ever so briefly, on the nape of my neck. 'Just remember,' he said, sliding his hand up the back of my head, his fingertips raking my scalp, making me shudder with pleasure, 'If anyone asks, you're my apprentice. You're my boy.'

'Is this it, then?'

The question had been bothering me some time. As had the faded pattern of the sheets, the chipped enamel ewer, the bleached-out wooden floorboards. A difference merely of design, colour, grain.

'Mnh?'

'Is this it? Same but different, again and again, the world over?'

A pause, a slow breath.

'Isn't it enough?'

I considered this for a moment, head pressed back into the pillow, a mattress coil pushing up into my back.

'Isn't it enough that you're lying in a warm dry bed, that downstairs someone is making you your supper, that within the hour we'll be sitting down to a dinner of roast mutton and parsnips? Isn't that better than skivvying for that old bastard?'

'Yes,' I said.

Another pause. I studied the knots and whorls in the

beam above us, listened to him breathe.

'What did you expect?'

Sweeping stretches of sand, forests alive with birds. A whispering, silver plane of sea, and the dark enticement of the mermaids' song. My mother.

'I dunno.'

'Well, then,' he said, and shifted, making the bed-springs jangle. I craned my head round to look at him. The lines as he smiled. The blue of his eyes. I smiled too, would have reached out to touch him, but didn't feel quite able to. He looked away.

'It's early days yet,' he said. 'First things first. We have a job to do here.'

I turned back, looked vaguely up at the bulging plaster of the ceiling. At least this was a decent room, I told myself. At least I could stand upright in it. I thought of the skinny kid I'd seen downstairs, hovering in a doorway. It was better than that.

'What do you mean?' I asked after a while. 'What job?'

I looked round at his profile. He was gazing up at the ceiling.

'I solve problems,' he said. 'It's what I do.' A moment, then he looked round at me again. His eyes were serious, intent.

'We're here to save the village,' he said.

'Really?' I said. 'What's wrong with it?'

He blinked.

'There's always something.'

'Oh.'

'It's just a case of finding out.'

I turned to look at the ceiling again.

'And if there isn't, then you can bet your life there's a game of cards to be had.'

What I remember best about that time is the sense of wonder. Wonder at what he did, and wonder that such an extraordinary person should want me as his companion. Everywhere he went, he seemed to generate a warm glow of gratitude and admiration, and as I went everywhere with him, I felt the glow fall on me too.

I never doubted him for a moment, but somehow I was still always amazed by him, by the successes he could pull out of what often appeared to be an entirely empty hat. He would look at me and seem a little puzzled, perhaps, by my admiration, but then he would shrug, and laugh, and say that it was nothing, that I should merely watch and learn. And though I did watch, and I watched intently, I was not a quick learner. I couldn't begin to understand the transformations that he wrought. He gave people what they wanted, I suppose, and that is so much more satisfying, and so much more appreciated, than giving people what they need.

Where the shitty stink of cholera hung about a town, he revealed that he was in fact one Dr Crawford, patent holder of Dr Crawford's Infallible Blue Pills, and sold tiny blue bottles, rattling with pastilles, from his knapsack in the market square. We departed from these places with all possible haste, avoiding handshakes, breakfasts, cups of tea. Because, he said, you shouldn't go tempting fate.

Where murrain, foot-rot or distemper was felling

livestock, leaving bloated bodies lying by the roadside, hoofs pointing at the sky, he offered up similar bottles, now filled with bovine, ovine and equine medicaments of unheard of efficacy and power. But we had to leave by moonlight, slipping through the darkened rooms of the public house and out along the dusty road like banished ghosts. Because, he said, all the attention he was getting was embarrassing.

With the wind in the right direction, you could smell the potato blight from a league away, the sweet foul smell of panic. In these blasted districts he offered the villagers their only prophylactic against starvation. Tiny blue bottles again, the contents to be ground in a mortar to produce a patent powder of limitless potential, which, sprinkled on the earth, would not only prevent the rot, but also restore affected tubers back to health. I was only disappointed that we never stayed around long enough to see this transformation, to watch the soily pockets of grey-blue slime resolve themselves into wholesome, earthcrumbed boilable potatoes. But there were other villages in similarly desperate situations. We were needed elsewhere.

And while I stood in his shadow holding his seemingly bottomless knapsack as he delivered a lecture on the contents of his little phials, or as he bantered with some thick-necked publican as a pint of small beer warmed in his hand, or as I carried his bag up the stairs to our night's lodging, everyone we encountered seemed to take for granted my relationship with him: they had me neatly trapped under the jamjar of the young apprentice. And I suppose, in some ways, they were right. In the space between places, in the underhedge shadows, or hayloft mustiness, or waking cold-nosed beside an ashy fire, I was learning. It all seemed to be wrapped up together, seemed equally magical to me.

The villages changed. Houses snaked along the valleys in long terraces. At night the manufactories were brilliant with light, making the dark seem even darker: you could see them from miles away. And from miles away too, faintly at first but then more insistently, until it filled your head entirely, you could hear the constant hum of spinning cotton.

In these towns the public houses were high-ceilinged, men wore waistcoats and aprons behind the counter, and the customers were slight, pale creatures who looked at us sidelong over their drink. He didn't try to save these places. He'd just settle down in a stall with a glass of beer and a pack of cards, and wait to see who'd play. I'd watch him, watch the spiderlike deft movements of his hands, the patterns of his game. On the table beside him, the coins would soon begin to accumulate. Dirty, tarnished discs of copper and silver. Afterwards, in our room, he'd show me how the play had gone, the counting of the cards, the decisions he had made, the ways in which he'd won. Before long, I began to recognize his tactics, understand his choices as he made them.

I don't think I ever knew his name. I called him Joe, though I don't quite remember why, and he called me Mal, or Kiddoe, or Malin.

Eight

Sailortown. A town built on, covered in, obsessed with mud. Mud on the wharves, on the streets, on the hems of ladies' dresses. Mud spattered up the walls. Mud caking the piers of the town's three bridges. In the river-bed, at low tide, silty chairlegs could be seen pointing to the sky; perhaps a few greyed and laceless shoes, a dead dog, and, without fail, the graceful patterning of turds upon the sludge. The town's offerings to its capricious god. Because the tidal river which had brought the wealth of the place, had brought ships and brigs and shallow-keeled cutters with cargoes from the remotest corners of the world, had also brought, from the limestone caverns in the fells, from the stones stirring in far-off streams, from the eroded banks of watermeadows, more and more alluvial mud, which it deposited here, on the tide's turn, and all the way out along the channel to the sea. The saltmarshes and the mudflats inched themselves out, slowly pushing the sea further away. The channel grew ever more shallow and treacherous, strangled by sandbanks. And Sailortown, which still clung stubbornly on, watched, and cursed, and faded day by day. Traffic on the river had dwindled to the point of non-existence. A few bumboats bobbing on the current as their owners picked through the flotsam, some fishermen bringing in their already stinking catch.

It's not what I had thought it would be. As we'd walked (in my mind's eye we were still crossing the schoolroom map, the dust rising, a dot dot dot line from there to there) he had described the place so vividly that I had thought I could almost hear, smell, see, the sounds, scents, sights he was talking about, the unfamiliar words bursting through the darkness like fireworks as we walked. Cutters, clippers, sloops and pinks, moored along wharves of golden stone. Wind whistling faintly through rigging, stirring reefed sails. The aching creak of sea-tired timbers, the smell of canvas, and the fresh salt scent of the sea. And above that, heady and insistent, the scent of spices, the musty odours of cotton and of silk, and the clean cold smell of coal. Along the quayside, the bustle and crush of crews and dockers, windtanned, salt-cured to a general reddish brown. Voices loud with argument, barter or friendship, the words themselves unfathomable; a welter of jargons, pidgins and creoles. And yes, he'd said, there were always mermaids about the place. They were ten-a-penny in Sailortown, he'd said.

Now his stories somehow seemed more real than the town, more vivid than the life I'd found myself living.

They left me with a faint sense of melancholy, with a nostalgia for something that I'd never known.

I hadn't seen a mermaid yet.

It was only a couple of weeks after we'd got there. He'd gone out early, before dawn, and came back to our room with a bundle of cloth. He handed it to me. Blue sprigged with white flowers. I shook it out.

'It's a dress,' I said.

'Put it on.'

'But it's a girl's dress.'

'I know. Put it on.'

I held the garment out at arm's length, looked at it. I'd never worn a dress. Somehow it didn't appeal.

'I thought I was your boy.'

'You're not making any money as a boy.' He took the dress out of my hands, began to fold it to slip it over my head. 'Anyway,' he was saying, 'what does it matter? Boy, girl, what's the difference?'

The waterfront's dark hinterland. I'd never liked that part of town. Half-rotten, verminous, staggering drunkenly up the hillside from the quays. A place eerie with empty warehouses and decaying factors' offices, wormed by dark, dripping alleyways and stinking ginnels. Populated by the meanest thieves, the cruellest pimps, the poxiest of whores. One of whom had been beaten half to death one bitter night last winter, and dumped unconscious in the street to freeze the rest of the way. A score of people must have passed by her that night, seen her slumped against the wall, skirts tangled, hair straggling over her bruised face. Some of them must have stepped over her blotched bare legs.

She was only young; she was still pretty. I used to see her about the place, once in a while. She had a nice smile, I remember.

I heard she'd kept some money back. I'd heard that was why he'd done it.

At least it was morning, now, and daylight. Though you'd hardly know it back here. This room would look the same any hour of day or night. Smoky, dark, the windows shuttered, a circle of smudged and pallid faces caught in the light cast by a soot-dirty lamp. I was aware of the landlord at my back, watching from the doorway. Joe was seated at the table, his chair drawn back, his face turned up to look at me. In the dim light, I could see his skin was smutty with exhaustion, his eyes red from overnighting it.

'How much?' he asked.

'Not much.'

The night's takings had, in fact, been paltry. I dropped a brace of coins into his palm; he looked at them, then up at me.

'And the rest,' he said.

'There is no more.'

'That's it?'

'Yes.'

'You wouldn't lie to me now would you?'

'Of course not.'

A pause.

'I hope not.'

He looked down at the coins again, and after what appeared to be a moment's thought, his eyes began suddenly to brighten, his expression lifted. And I found my spirits lifting too. Everything would, of course, be fine. All the petty scams and cheats, the gambling, his long absences; they would all be over soon. He would win, and we would have enough at last to leave. He turned back to the table, shunted the night's earnings towards its centre, ran his eyes over the circled faces. He swept the dice up in his cupped hands, lifted them to his mouth. I watched for a moment the lines of concentration on his brow, the round of his mouth as his hands came up towards it, and I felt the excitement swell, bubble inside me. His eyes flicked back to me.

'You still here?' he said.

'Yes –'

'Get you off home,' he said. A moment, then he smiled. 'Go on, run along. Don't want you jinxing it, now, do we? Go and get some sleep.'

And, in the circumstances, all I could do was turn and leave him there, rattling the dice in his hands, my earnings scattered among the other coins in the centre of the table. Ready to sprout, take root, and grow into something extraordinary.

As I passed through into the main bar room, the publican turned and followed, drawing the door closed behind him. He stopped me, a hand resting heavy on my arm. His fingernails were rimmed with dirt. I looked up at his face. Blackened pores, a sheen of oil, a briny crust at the corner of his mouth. He must have fallen asleep on a table at some point during the long night, and drooled.

'There's still,' he said, 'the small matter of his slate, of course.'

'Of course,' I said.

'We'll settle that right now then, shall we?'

I breathed.

'If it's not inconvenient,' he added.

So, when I emerged from the public house on to the bright and cool quayside, blinking in the daylight, it was to the stench of foul water and black mud, and with the taste of semen in the back of my throat. We couldn't go on like this much longer, I thought. It was unpleasant. It was insanitary. We were getting nowhere.

When he came back it was evening. The room was almost dark. I'd been dozing, curled up under the blankets in just my shirt. A moment passed, and he didn't come over, didn't slide in beside me, put an arm around me. Puzzled, I dragged myself up on to an elbow and looked round for him. He was standing at the window, staring out. I followed his line of sight through the smutty pane, across the street, to the blackened sandstone wall opposite, the dripping gutter. He turned and paced across the room, three paces, and halted at the door. He stood and chewed a fingernail. I'd never seen him do that before. I sat up fully, looked at him a long moment.

'What's the matter?'

'Mnh?'

I pulled the bedclothes up around my knees, leaned back against the wall. I felt the plaster flat and cold against the knots and ridges of my back, felt the damp press through my shirt on to my skin. His forehead was creased, his teeth still working at a sharpness on his nail, but I couldn't help but notice the moistness between his lips, the way they pressed around his finger.

'Are you all right?'

He tugged his hand away from his mouth, crossed the room again, three paces, and halted at the window. Same view. Dark wall, dripping gutter. Certainly nothing worth that much interest.

'I'm going out,' he said.

'You've just got in.'

He turned to face me. He didn't speak. I pulled the covers back for him. He just looked at me.

'Don't go out again,' I said. 'It's filthy out.'

'I won't be long. It's just a bit of business.'

'I'll go for you.' I made to get up. 'Just tell me what it is: I'll deal with it.'

He held my gaze a moment longer, then looked away.

'I won't be long,' he said again. He came over and kissed me on the mouth. 'Once I've got this all sorted out, we can head on. Go somewhere else.' He smiled at me. 'Anywhere you like. Think about it. Anywhere at all.'

Then, before I could even ask if I could go with him, he left, dragging the door shut behind him. I heard his footsteps on the stairs, then the streetdoor slam, then the scrape of his boots on the cobbles. I crossed over to the window. He was already at the end of the street. He turned right.

I went back and sat down on the bed, pulling my knees

up close to my chest, tugging my shirt down over them. I clasped an arm around my legs, hugging them close. I slid the smoothness of a thumbnail back and forth across my lips, remembering that kiss. Just this last bit of business and we'd be ready. We'd have enough to leave. I felt my heart begin to beat a little faster. We'd go anywhere I liked, he'd said. Anywhere at all.

His coat was lying in folds, slung over the back of the chair. He'd gone without it. His hat was there too, sitting black and pristine on the chair's fraying straw seat. He'd catch his death.

I'd have to be quick if I was going to catch him. His spare shirt and britches were lying on the same seat so I pulled them on: it was quicker than buttoning myself into that dress. I gathered up his coat and hat and made for the door. If he was already too far ahead, if he was going too fast, if I had to just follow a while and see where he went and who he met, well, that wouldn't be my fault. It wouldn't be spying. I was just bringing him his hat and coat.

I slipped out through the front door and hurried down to the end of our street. At the corner I caught sight of him going uphill, his head down, hand to mouth. I followed.

After climbing about half a mile, he turned abruptly and stepped into Bashful Alley. I ran up to the corner and peered round. He was just reaching the far end, was just turning to the right. I ducked down the passageway, trying to run softly on the flagstones, and stopped at the end to peer after him. The lane was steep and cobbled.

He was climbing slowly: he looked tired. And I was getting breathless too. Clutched to my chest, his coat was bulky, cumbersome, and his hat was getting crushed. I slipped his jacket on over my own, tapped the hat down on to my head. It sank down low over my eyes. If he glanced round, he'd hardly recognize me. He wouldn't stop and send me back. I slid round the corner, followed him.

Each turn he took was dragging us further uphill, each narrowing street bringing us further round in a shallow curve from our lodgings towards that dark and threatening quarter, that rat's nest of dives and dens and brothels up behind the quays. He'd been there all last night, and he was already going back. Despite the extra layers of clothing, despite the exertion of the chase, I felt cold.

We were coming to the brow of the hill and a cross-roads. Ahead of us, Hope Street sloped down towards the waterfront. The cobbles were thick with filth, the street overhung with dripping, carious tenements. The darkest, most notorious of slums. I felt anxiety rise inside me, like sickness. He turned down a sidestreet and I followed.

Thirty yards or so ahead of me, on the far side of the street, he'd stopped. I slid my back up against a wall and watched. A trick of the town: at the end of the street was a view out across the rooftops to the world beyond. A slice of saltmarsh, fading evening sky, and river. Sailortown's speciality, these sudden perspectives, glimpsed at the turn of a mildewed street, at the brow of a hill, or through a cavity left by collapsed tenements.

Cut against this backdrop, his silhouette looked crooked, his head slumped forward from his shoulders like an old man's. Anxiety rose again inside me, but I swallowed it back.

He'd made it rain, I told myself. He had made it rain.

We both stood there a moment longer, me pressing myself breathlessly back against the wall, and him standing, not moving, just staring at someone's shut-tight door. Its paint was peeling, blue.

Slowly, he stepped up towards the door. He lifted a fist, then hesitated, his hand suspended a moment in front of the boards. Then he knocked and immediately stepped back. I couldn't see his face: his quarter-profile was dark against the brightness beyond. He waited just a moment, not really long enough for anyone to answer, then stepped forward and knocked again. Impatient, I realized, wanting to get it over with. Whatever it was.

I heard bolts being drawn back, watched as the door was scraped open on darkness. Inside, a figure; substantial, paler than the shadows. Joe moved forwards, lifting his right hand, extending it to be shaken. The figure didn't move. A moment's awkwardness. Joe's hand fell back to his side.

'All I'm asking,' I heard him say, 'is that you give me one more chance. Just one. That's all I'm asking.'

'It doesn't work like that.' The voice was dark; it brought with it a sense of bulk, of heavy strength. 'You played the game, and you lost, so now you hand over the goods. That's the way it works.'

'I'll pay you double what you'd get on the open market.'

A low-pitched growl, indecipherable.

'I can get the money. No problem. That's what I'm telling you. It's no problem.'

'You made the stake. You honour it.'

'I'm offering you a better deal.'

'I'm not interested.'

'I can understand that,' Joe's voice sparked with animation. 'I understand what you're saying. You're right to be suspicious, you've every reason to be. Because what I'm offering you is pretty much unbelievable. What I'm offering you is the best deal you'll ever –'

For some reason, my mouth had gone dry. He was still speaking, but all the energy seemed to be slipping away from him as he spoke. His voice began to take on a failed, husky quality.

'I mean,' he said, 'when it comes down to it, what's the kid worth, really, anyway?'

The press of cold stone against my palms and shoulderblades.

'You saw last night's takings,' he added. 'A pittance, it was. Just pennies. And to be honest with you, that was one of the better nights –'

There was acid rising in my throat.

'I'm a fool to myself, but that's why I'm saying – the only way you stand to make any money out of this –'

The other man's voice was low: 'There's always a market for young flesh,' he said.

I found myself sliding back along the wall, slipping into the darkness of a narrow ginnel. I still remember the smell of the place: decay and emptiness. I stretched out a hand to the wall. The stone was sweating. I leaned over, and, quietly as possible, vomited.

For a while I was conscious of little more than that: the heave of my guts, the choking feeling in my throat, the sick in my mouth. When the sickness passed and I was able to wipe my lips, and spit, and then peer out of the ginnel's shadows, he had gone and the street was deserted. I came back out and leant against a wall, breathing.

What was it he'd said, that first night on the valley road, when he'd agreed to take me with him? *It's not what you think it is, you know. It's never what it seems to be.* Everything, everything that had ever happened since I met him seemed to have become loose and shifting. Memories slipped and tumbled like coins, like dice. I wanted to go after him, to confront him, to make him explain, to make him tell me what it was that I had so far failed to understand, but my legs felt weak beneath me, and I didn't know where he'd gone, or how I could possibly string half a dozen words into a question if I caught up with him. I found myself gazing out across that view of river, land and sky. I knew that from here my feet would take me down into the dark streets, towards the gantries and the mud, back to men's gaping flies and unwashed dicks and the scuttle of rats and the stink of shit. I felt my stomach churn again, put a hand to a wall, head reeling. If I could sail straight out there above the rooftops, over the smoking chimneys and rain-greased slates, gliding out towards the clean clipped saltmarshes and the sea; alone – something went solid in my chest, choking me. My eyes squeezed themselves shut, my face contracting. He had lost me. He had lost me in a game of dice. No skill, no foresight, no pattern of play: nothing but pure dumb luck with dice. He had run out of money, the money that I'd brought him, and so had placed my life on a single cast.

He lived by chance. I could see that now. Everything was luck. I found myself thinking of the phials of pills, the stories he had told, the way his hands had darted like spiders as he dealt cards across a table. And the first drops of rain thwacking on to the dusty road that night, and the downfall's sudden stop on the cusp of the hill. And me turning round, stretching out my hands, and turning to him, alive for the first time with the wonder of it all. *It's not what you think it is,* he'd said. *It's never what it seems to be.* He'd told me there would be mermaids here, but there were only whores.

Something was forcing its way out of me, something uncountenanceable, something that hadn't happened in what felt like a lifetime. I buckled in on myself, I choked. I began to cry.

I don't know how much later it was that I blinked away the tears, rubbed the back of a hand across my face. I'd already given myself a headache and my eyes felt raw, but for some reason I'd become suddenly self-conscious. I sniffed, glanced round, half-expecting trouble. I blinked and wiped my eyes again. I stared. Because, rounding the bend in the river, against the evening blue of the water and the green of the saltmarsh, its colours snapping silently, sails bellying, rigging and deck alive with tiny figures, steering a precise path between sand-banks and shilloe beds, came, at last, the unexpected splendour of a ship. Which changed everything.

I'd been wasting my time, I realized. I would go and find my mother.

Nine

The agent glanced up from his ledger, looked at me, then narrowed his eyes and said, 'Do I know you?'

I'd already begun to shake my head before I realized that in fact we had met before, in rather more intimate circumstances. Which was why I hadn't immediately recognized his face. His prick, on the other hand: that might well have been a different matter, but he didn't happen to have it currently on display. I'd been in the dress then, and now I was wearing Joe's clothes. It made things easier for me, being a boy; but it obviously made things uncomfortable for my former customer. To put it frankly, he was no longer quite sure who he'd paid to suck his cock. A slow blush rose up his neck, flushed his cheeks.

'Perhaps you've met my sister?' I suggested.

He tugged at his collar.

'No, no, I don't think so. I must have been mistaken.' Flustered, he picked up his pen, put it down to straighten his ledger, lifted it again.

'Name?' he said.

He signed me there and then, scratching my name on to the page with a sputtering pen. As he reeled off the questions I answered him as well as I could.

Name: Malin Reed.

Age: Unknown.

Father's occupation: Ferryman.

And then, without asking me, he scratched out the words:

Engagement: to the slaver *Sally Ann*, five years.

Position: Boy.

He dipped the pen again, held it out to me, and spun the ledger slowly round. An inky finger tapped at an empty column.

'Sign here,' he said.

I took the pen and wrote out my name. I looked at it a moment, inscribed there in black and white by my own hand. It didn't look like me.

He pushed a coin across the desktop. 'Most of that,' he said, 'will go on your kit. Next door; the chandler's office. They'll sort you out.'

And then later that same day, the ritual humiliation of getting on board. I struggled up the gangway with my kitbag dragging heavy on my shoulder and the planks swaying and buckling underneath me as, at the bottom of the gangway, two sailors jumped up and down on the boards, laughing. Then I crossed the deck. The agent had told me I was to report to Mr McMichaels, the captain, but I had no idea where to find him, and when I came to the middle of the deck, I realized I didn't have a clue where to go next. If I kept on going the way I was going, before long I'd be all the way across the ship and off the far side and into the river: overboard before I'd even made it out to sea. I slowed. Clustered here and there on deck, men were standing in their shirtsleeves, chewing on tobacco. A bad impression made now would stick like pitch, and I was, I realized, already making one: despite the fact that we were docked, and on the river, the deck seemed to be lurching beneath me, and I found myself teetering from side to side like a drunk. Someone laughed. I turned towards the noise. I squared my shoulders.

'I'm looking for the captain,' I said.

Behind me, someone said something which I didn't quite catch, and then everybody laughed. I flushed with anger. I'd wanted to leave complications and entanglements behind. I'd wanted to start afresh, to be someone quite new, and already it was going wrong. I opened my mouth and was about to speak, was about to call into question the virtue of their mothers, their sisters, of all their female relations young and old, and suggest that they themselves had picked up something unpleasant, itchy and ultimately fatal in some foreign port. I was lucky I didn't get the chance.

'That's enough,' someone said.

I hadn't noticed the higher deck, the flight of steps behind me. A man was coming down them, an account-book tucked beneath an arm. He came to the bottom of the flight, stopped. He flopped open the book in his hands, looked down at it.

'Reed,' he said.

'Yes.'

'Come with me.'

He turned and disappeared through a doorway beneath the stairs, and I followed. Behind me, someone spoke again, and though I missed the words, the inflection was unmistakably jeering. A general, breathy snickering followed me down the dark passageway.

The room was warm, it smelt of wood and oil. One wall bellied outward like a sail; a glazed window looked out across the river towards the crumbling Exchange building on the far bank. There was a writing desk, a narrow bunk, a washstand. A book lay open on the desk. McMichaels scraped back the chair and sat down, looking at the text in front of him a long moment before laying the marker ribbon down the gutter and closing the book. He set it to one side, drew his account book to him and opened it again. He picked up a pen, scratched down a few words, did not look up.

'So, this is your first time at sea.'

I nodded. His pen stilled. He looked up.

'Speak when you're spoken to,' he said.

'Sir.'

'This is your first time at sea.'

'My mother was a mermaid,' I told him, by way of explanation.

'What?'

'She was a mermaid, sir, and my father was a ferryman, so . . .'

He stared at me a moment longer. He placed his pen

back in its holder. And then he spoke.

'I don't care about you, Reed; remember that,' he said. 'I'm not interested in you. You are nobody. Do I make myself clear?'

'Yes,' I said.

'This is not about us getting to know each other,' he said. 'I don't want to get to know you. I don't want to even think about you. I don't want to have you cross my mind again until I pay you off. All I want to know is whether you've been to sea before because I need to know if that crook of an agent has gone and landed me again with some useless soft kid still smelling of his mother's milk.'

'Yes sir.'

'And do you, Reed?'

'Do I what sir?'

'Do you still smell of your mother's milk?'

'No, sir.'

'And have you been to sea before?'

'Born to it, sir,' I said, which I did not consider to be quite a lie. 'It's in the blood.'

After that, down the hatch to steerage, and the duck and scramble across the low and cluttered smoke-blued space, tripping on kitbags and trunks and outstretched feet. The conversation was impressively obscene.

Away from hatch's pale spill of light, oil lamps hung from the beams, and the air was warm and foul. I came at last to the remaining free berth, located unfortunately in the farthest darkest corner of the space, near the bulkhead. But then came the embarrassment of getting into the hammock. I was buggered if I knew how to and reluctant to experiment. I couldn't afford to make a fool of myself. Standing there with my kitbag at my feet, I observed the rest of the lower deck out of the corner of my eye, in the hopes that someone eventually would get in or out of their hammock so that I could see how it was done. But no one it seemed was moving. Or at least, not shifting from their berths. A couple of whores were doing great business, but I didn't like to stare and so never got to see how they managed to get up and down from the hammocks. The men themselves were either lying back smoking, or enjoying a whore's exertions, or both; or they were sitting below on their seachests playing cards. Next to me, just at chest height, hanging there quite peacefully, a man lay with his eyes closed. One hand was behind his head, a clay pipe was cupped in the other, its stem in his mouth. His shirt sleeves were rolled: his arms were brown, and lean, and strong.

I'd been looking at him too long. One eye flicked open. It was blue.

I wasn't sure what to do, so I didn't do anything.

He opened the other eye too, looked at me a moment longer. He took the pipe from between his lips, opened his mouth, and blew a smoke ring up towards the ceiling. My eyes followed it. I watched it drift, disperse.

'Arse first,' he said.

'What?'

'The hammock. That's how you get in.' He shifted himself up on to an elbow, gestured with his pipe. 'Stand with your back to it, grab the nearest edge and stretch it out tight, then hitch yourself up, arse first.'

'Oh,' I said. I looked round at the hammock. 'Right. Thanks.'

He lay watching me. The blueness of his eyes was unsettling. I gritted my teeth, hitched myself up and perched on the canvas. The hammock swung giddily back and forth: I must have looked uneasy, or just stupid, because the man laughed.

I looked at him.

He shrugged, lay back, put the pipe in his mouth, but I was aware of him still watching me obliquely, and with half a smile. The hammock's swing subsided, and I drew my legs up on to it. I lay back, gently rocking, conscious of the decking below me, hard, black. It was an uneasy feeling. But not half as uneasy as the sense of the space around me, populated, alive with the mutter and scuff of men.

It was John Doyle, captain of the foretop, the man in the berth next to mine, who was assigned to show me the ropes. On our watch, he walked the tops like they were country paths, climbed the shrouds like a squirrel. Later, I would see him come down fresh-cheeked from reefing the topsail in conditions which had bigger men sliding back to deck from half as high, green and sick with fear. And when the other men indulged, between watches, in drink or talk of wives and whores, or in who-could-piss-the-furthest competitions, or in sniping about McMichaels, John Doyle kept his own company, would lie in his hammock and blow smoke-rings, and take his rum-and-water, and was never, it seemed, insulted or mocked for his behaviour.

And I was with him, on the mizzentop, with the wind in my face, swallowing down great lumps of air as if I'd been hungry for it all my life, when he knocked a hard hand against my upper arm, pointed, and I watched as Sailortown sank into its river banks, was swallowed, at last, by its own mud.

'You'll not be seeing that again in a while,' he said.

I looked round at him, almost ready to laugh out loud, but his face was serious, his mouth a dry hard line. He shook his head slightly, seemed to be about to say something and then change his mind.

'C'mon,' he said, shifting his grip on the rope, turning himself back to the work.

The first two weeks were the hardest: my body had forgotten what real work was. My muscles were constantly tight with fatigue, my hands raw with ropeburns and blisters, my lips cracked and peeling. Like all the topmen, I went barefoot, and my feet grew strong and hard and brown, and developed a dexterity of their own, gripping and clinging almost as adroitly as hands. Like the other sailors, I tied my hair back into a queue.

I played cards, and threw the game. It made me a little more welcome. From the players' conversation I learned about the working of the ship. McMichaels was pretty much despised: it was felt that he cut corners. In Sailortown, when he should have been mustering half a dozen men, he'd only signed on me. He wouldn't appoint a mate or a boatswain or a purser. He considered them too expensive. Luxuries.

I learned my knots, I learned my ropes, I learned I had a head for heights. I learned, from John Doyle's teaching and example, that there was joy to be found in a job well done, and pleasure to be gained from the quiet and proper practice of a skill. And all the time I felt, glowing in my chest like a lantern, a sense of satisfaction and excitement: I was, at last, under way.

I remember quite clearly one evening towards the end of that first fortnight, perched on the foretop as the sun was setting to starboard. John Doyle was just beside me, showing me the working of some block and tackle. Above us and below, the sails were taut as pregnant bellies; everything was bathed in pinky-golden light. My skin was glowing from the day's sun, and the air was moist and clean. I could feel the heave of the ship beneath me, perfect and balanced as the muscled strength of a horse. I had already come to know, almost to the point of forgetfulness, the precise geometry of our pitch and sway above. I looked up from the movement of the rope, the easy skill of John Doyle's fine fingers, and watched his face for a moment. His expression was contented, he looked entirely himself, and at ease. He glanced up: caught unawares, he smiled straight back at me.

'There's no beating it,' he said, his eyes returning to the work. 'There's nothing better in the world.'

It wasn't long after that the storm hit. A week, maybe two. I'd noticed, perhaps, a shift in the wind, the cloud massing behind us, gaining, but I'd been aware of it without any sense of foreboding or apprehension. Then a slap of cold air hit me on the cheek, I looked up from the knot I was practising, and at the same moment heard John Doyle calling the topmen together. The first of them were already swarming up the shrouds. My eyes caught on John Doyle's: he called me over to him with a jerk of the head. I was on my feet and across the deck in an instant.

'Good lad,' he smiled at me. 'On up you go.'

I began scrambling up, and he called after:

'Watch yourself now. Stay sharp.'

Aloft, the wind was squally, argumentative. It tugged at our shirts and hair, slapped at us unexpectedly from this way and then that. My eyes streamed with water, the breath was tugged right out of me. It was as much as I could do to hold on while older, more seasoned men tackled the reefing of the sails. Through wind-blurred vision I watched and marvelled as John Doyle swung about with perfect ease and confidence, moving along the yards as if he'd been born out there. By the time the full rig had been reefed the storm was fully on us and we were being tossed about like spit on a flat-iron. I slid and scrambled as best I could back down to the deck, shaking and clumsy with fear. I remember clinging to the base of the mast, spray lashing my face, salt in my mouth and eyes, squinting up in wonder as John Doyle tied the last of the reefpoints and then calmly, methodically, picked his way back down.

Below decks, the lanterns and hammocks swung wildly, crazy shadows skidding across the room. The boards pitched beneath me and the foul air of steerage made my stomach churn. I held on to the bottom of the ladder, blinking, swallowing down bile, not daring to go any further. Then a wave hit, and a shower of spray fell over me. John Doyle came down, slamming the hatch shut behind him. He stopped at the base of the steps.

'All right, lad?'

I was watching, in disbelief, as the men sat on their seachests, playing cards, smoking. Here and there a mug or shoe had come loose and was rolling back and forth with the pitch of the ship.

'Don't they care?' I asked him.

A shrug.

'Shouldn't we be *doing* something?'

John Doyle laughed. A little spurt of sound.

'We've done it. Sails are reefed and there are three men at the helm. Standard practice for these parts.'

I looked round at him. 'We're not going to sink?'

'No,' he laughed again. 'We're just going to make pretty good time.'

I staggered after him, across the cluttered space, lurching from seachest to hammock to sailor's shoulder. John Doyle planted his feet down on the boards like they were suckered. In our dark corner he swung open his seachest, dragged out dry clothes. I looked away, began to undo my buttons. I ducked to rummage in my kitbag and found a dry shirt. As I crouched there facing the bulkhead I pulled the wet shirt off and put the dry one on. I slipped off my lower garments underneath. I straightened, pulling up dry britches. When I looked back round, John Doyle had changed and was lying back in his hammock, smoking.

My Da had been a sailor, way back: he'd met my mother when he'd been at sea. He'd've been like John Doyle: competent, accomplished, a good teacher. I clambered into my berth, lay back. The ship moved, and I, it seemed, lay still within its pitching hulk, slung there in my hammock. I watched smoke rings rise towards the ceiling.

By morning the gale had settled into a strong following wind. We were up in the heavens again, spreading a little canvas, when I heard a shout from below. Abrupt, harsh, not the usual sailors' birdcall. We looked down from our perch.

'McMichaels,' John Doyle said.

His face was a blurred oval; I could see the tops of his shoulders, one outstretched foot. He called again, his mouth wide and dark. My name. Reed.

He'd been watching me for days. Every time I'd turned round he'd been there, watching. Waiting for me to slip up.

I looked round at John Doyle.

'What does he want?' I asked.

He shrugged.

'Did I do something wrong?'

'You'd best just get down there. Look lively.'

'Sir!'

I lobbed the word down at McMichaels, scrambled after it.

He was already walking away when I got to the deck. I followed, my skin prickling with apprehension. He came to a halt at the cargo hatch. It was lying open.

'Right,' he said. 'Down you go.'

My mind flailed about, searching for something to say, for a lie that might still save me. He was locking me up and I had no idea why. I leaned over the rim, looked down. The hold's dark inverted arch reminded me suddenly of the pitched roof of the village church. I'd sat with my head tilted back against the pew, looking up. There had been the faint buzz of a sermon then, the gentle mutter of rain, and I had decided to be good.

McMichaels was still speaking.

'Make sure it's all in order,' he was saying. 'You'll find plenty of fresh straw down there – spread it out on the shelves, report any repairs.'

'Yes, sir,' I said, perhaps too keenly, because he glanced at me, his eyes narrowing. I met his gaze, looking as blank as I could, then turned to look back down into the hold.

And the smell hit me. Coming up from the hatch, sharp and dry in my nostrils. I stepped back from the edge, blinking. I realized suddenly that the same odour had been there faintly, permeating everything, all this time.

'What are you waiting for, Reed? We have a cargo to pick up. You want to spend the rest of the voyage down there?'

'No, sir,' I said.

'Then get to it.'

*

I hitched myself into my hammock, lay back. The stink seemed to hang around me like a guilty secret, but I knew that everybody knew. I was aware of John Doyle looking at me, knew he was leaning up on an elbow, was turned my way, had watched me ease myself down on to the canvas. I looked blankly up at the boards above me. I thought of the cramped storeys of shelving padded with musty straw below, the salt-rusted chains, the dark-stained boards. The stench. I hadn't realized what it had meant, *to the slaver* Sally Ann, *five years*. But now it was beginning to come clear.

We didn't disembark. We watched from the deck as they grounded the boat and walked up the beach. McMichaels had taken just a few of the bigger crewmen with him. There wasn't much to carry, just a few bags of beads and sequins, a couple of rifle caskets swinging from rope handles, a crate of chain and shackles. I remember the smell of the forest, the harsh cry of the birds, the dark figures emerging from the treeline to welcome McMichaels and his men. I remember the numb, broken faces of the slaves as they were herded on board, the clank and scrape of their chains, their awkward stumble down the steps into the dark.

On the long haul for the Western Isles, towards the setting sun, they died daily, and every evening McMichaels sent two of us below to bring out the corpses. I don't know why it was always in the evening. There was, perhaps, a slender vein of compassion in

McMichaels, that he would not leave the dead lying there, packed tight as weft among the living, all through the night.

It was always on my watch. It seemed it was always me who was sent below. All day I tried not to think of it, but as the sun sank ahead of us, scattering gold across the water, it became impossible to ignore. I would try, fiercely, to hold the sun still in the sky, to suspend it by sheer force of will, so that the time would never come when McMichaels would call my name, or his hand descend upon my shoulder and steer me towards the cargo hatch.

Down below, holding up the lantern, I would stare into the shadows, catching only here and there the glassy sheen of eyes, the oil of sweat on skin. The more usual sounds of the ship were muffled beneath the sigh and moan of the captives and the cries of their children. The stench was more overpowering even than the fierce flush of shame that hit me every time. Shit and piss and sweat, and then, like an afterthought, the faint sweet smell of blood. The dead, and sometimes the nearly dead, would be unshackled and hauled out on to the deck, and McMichaels, standing by, would hiss slightly, it could not quite be called a sigh, and scratch another note into his account book.

We had just heaved her over the side. The last one on my watch. Heavy, naked, her belly swollen with pregnancy or disease. The ship had pitched just as I'd let her go: she knocked against the keel as she went down. A shoulder was disarticulated, the head thrown back. The body crashed through the water, resurfaced, and then was pushed away by the wake. The sun had set, leaving a clear sky, a brilliant moon. I leaned over the rail, watching as we left her behind, a stain on the sky-reflecting water. Incriminating, inescapable, that trail of darkly bobbing bodies in our wake.

The bell sounded and I turned towards the stern, watched McMichaels' retreating back as he headed for his cabin. He came back with his Bible, and the watch gathered while he read to us and led prayers. I couldn't listen; I could barely mumble along with the familiar words. Afterwards I went below, climbed into my hammock and turned my face to the bulwark. The sounds and smells rising up from beneath wrapped themselves around me, leached into my skin, my hair, my blood. I would never be clean again.

We would carry it with us everywhere, through the bright water, to wild untainted places, this darkness cupped in the ship's hold. This cargo of shadows.

What woke me was a shift in balance, a sense of weight.

'You were crying.'

Little more than a breath, soft on my ear. A hand's weight on my arm. The hammock swung, weight shifted, and he was lying there behind me, his body fitting into the contours of my own. So agile. So slight. For a moment I'd thought that it was Joe.

'I knew you were asleep, but you were crying.'

I raised a hand to my face and found that it was wet.

'I wasn't.'

A moment in the darkness: the sense of him warm behind me, the populated space around us, the boards above us and below. The aching hollow inside me. I shifted myself clumsily, turning over to face him. Close up, his eyes caught a speck of light. A hand came up and touched my face, swept away the wetness and brushed back my hair.

'I know,' he whispered, the words low and warm on my skin. 'I know. It's all right. I know . . . don't fret.'

I reached up, touched his cheek. It was smooth as risen dough.

'I'm not –'

'Ssh.'

Somehow, in the darkness, our mouths met. The tenderness of inner lip against inner lip, the catch of a broken tooth. His hand in my hair, and mine at his throat, pushing back his shirt a little, smoothing round the strong cusp of his shoulder. Utterly alert to the sounds of the ship, the thud of footsteps on the deck above, a barked-out order. Pushed up close against each other in the tight folds of the hammock, his mouth leaving mine, his lips grazing my cheek, jawbone, throat. His teeth pressing gently into the flesh, making me shiver.

'Malin –' the word was just a shape in the air, noiseless, 'don't be afraid.'

'I'm not afraid.'

A moment's scuffling as he tugged at his shirt, then he took my hand, laid it on hot, dry skin. His belly, strong and lean. I ran my fingers up over the ridge of his ribs, brushed my knuckles across his stomach, but he took my hand again and guided it down, underneath his loosened waistband, into the soft furze below. I slid my fingers down further, searching, and found –

'Oh,' I said, almost out loud.

'You,' she breathed into my ear, 'didn't fool me for a minute.'

Sweating skin stuck to sweating skin; our necessary silence was like a lid pressed on a pot to boil. Around us, the synchronous sway of row upon row of hammocks. Rhythmic snores, the occasional low and thunderous fart, and once a cough which stopped us dead, listening, electrified like hares. From above, the indistinguishable voices of the watch; faint but constant noises from below. Beyond, the stilled ship: the creak of timbers as they eased themselves, the incessant soothing lap of waves against the hull. I had never been with a woman that way before. She tasted like the sea.

The bell was sounding. I heaved myself over, looked up. John was sliding off her hammock, stood tucking in her shirt. I smiled at her. She half-smiled back.

'Don't say a word,' she said.

I slipped down from my berth. She stood there, tying back her hair, her head turned to one side as if she was absorbed in what she was doing.

'You're young, you're new to this, you can start again,' she said. 'But this is all I know. I'd lose everything if they found out. I'd never sail again.'

'I promise,' I said. 'I won't tell anyone.'

She nodded, smiled at me, and turned to go. I followed, weaving between seachests and kitbags and waking sailors. John put a foot on a rung and began to climb. I just stood there at the foot of the ladder and watched her, watched the wiry strength of her muscles as they moved. The daylight caught her hair, tinting it gold.

Someone shoved me from behind.

'Get a fucking move on.'

I gripped a rung, scrambled up.

I came up into the sun. John was standing there. I hitched myself up on to the deck.

'Dead calm,' she said.

That night, as our limbs had tangled together, as we'd wrapped ourselves up in each other, the wind had caught its breath and held it, the waves had stilled and settled. The sea was now flat, a sheet of opaque water. Above us, an empty blue sky and the sun as fierce as fever. Not a breath. Not a ripple. Not a sound. I glanced back at John. Two deep, parallel creases had formed between her eyebrows, a precise line was drawn from each nostril to the corners of her lips.

'What does it mean?' I asked.

'It'll be all right,' she said. 'It'll be fine.'

The hairs stood up on the back of my neck. McMichaels was standing on the foredeck. He was watching me.

He wouldn't let us keep the shackles on the bodies, and for want of weight they resurfaced quickly. They hung there in the water motionless. Their eyes shrivelled in the sun; their tongues swelled, forcing their mouths open. The ship stank, we stank, the very sea was rotten with humanity. And every day, there were more of them, their number increasing, I began to think, at an even greater rate than we were throwing the bodies overboard. Every night as I lay with her I tried to think only of her, tried to immerse myself entirely in the scent and taste and textures of her. And every night I could not forget the bodies floating just beside us, their sightless eyes, the silence of their open mouths. The ship's hull was rendered thin, had become just a fine membrane between the living and the dead. The woman with the swollen belly, her shoulder breaking, the crack of her skull against the keel. She and all the others, congregating, gathering round the ship, watching us with sun-parched eyes.

There was nothing to do. That was the worst of it. Just dragging out the bodies, heaving them overboard, watching them watch us from the water.

'You'd think there would be sharks,' I said to John.

She turned her head. She had her knife out, had been chipping away at a bit of something.

'Maybe they don't like it dead –' she said.

I slumped down beside her on the deck, swallowed dryly.

'How far is it, once we got a wind?' I asked. 'How long will it take us?'

John looked at me a moment, then snapped her knife

shut and slipped whatever it was into her pocket.

'I'll get the men together. We'll go over the rigging again.'

'Why?'

She was on her hunkers, about to straighten. She stopped, a hand to the deck.

'You've got to do something,' she said.

Underneath our feet the rope swung slightly, shifting with the rhythm of our movement. The sun pressed down on us, headachy, mesmeric. Not a breath, not a whisper of a wind. Out along the yards, to my left, someone was chanting a faint, half-hearted song, '. . . *he was young, but he was daily . . . growing . . .*' and then the rope bounced beneath my feet. My stomach lurched. I gripped tighter to the yard, turned my head. A man gone. He'd fallen backwards: his mouth was open, arms and legs flung wide, fingers rippling like anemones, his cry fading as he fell. No chance to grab the rigging, to catch at a fold of sailcloth. His hair blew back around his face. He hit the deck. Silence. His body settled into death. Down below, figures moved towards him, hunkered down. My head swam; darkness began to curl in around my vision.

'Malin.'

A hand on my arm, gripping round the muscle. I blinked. Her face was near mine, deeply lined.

'Stay sharp,' she said. 'Stay clear.'

She led us down from the ropewalks in silence, kept me always just behind her, just above. I felt giddy, sick, for the first time in ages terrified by the distance between me and the deck, by the precariousness of each foothold, each grip. As we descended, she would glance back up at me, touch my ankle, guide my shaking foot down towards the next hold. Finally we reached the deck and my knees gave way beneath me. John caught me under my arms and held me up. A moment's darkness and the smell of her skin as I was pressed against her.

'Can you stand?'

'Yes.'

And she pushed me away so that I stood swaying, blinking in the sun. A crowd had gathered round the fallen man.

'Who is it?' someone asked.

'Hannigan,' said John. 'It's Hannigan.'

He at least was granted the dignity of rotting in private. We weighted his body with ballast, wrapped it in sail-cloth, dropped it overboard. We stood and watched. The body slid beneath the surface, gave off a volley of bubbles, then sank slowly until it was obscured by depth and murk. All around, the rotting corpses of the slaves still hung in the water, like uneasy distant cousins at this makeshift funeral. Here and there, their lips had peeled back, exposing teeth and desiccating gum.

McMichaels turned away from the rail, hissed his not-quite sigh. He was about to go past me, but stopped mid-stride. He shifted his weight on to his back foot, looked at me.

'Reed,' he said.

'Sir?'

'Come with me.'

He walked away.

He couldn't blame me for this. However much he wanted me to slip up, I couldn't see how he could make this my fault. I glanced at John, but she didn't meet my eye. I followed McMichaels to his office.

The room was tight and airless. The Bible lay shut on the desk; another book I hadn't seen before was splayed open beside it. I caught a glimpse of an engraving, grey lines and shapes and patterns on the page, but could not make out the picture. McMichaels scraped back his chair and sat down. He placed a hand on the Bible, but he was looking at the other book. He kept his eyes on the picture as he pulled open a desk drawer, drew the Bible towards him, and slid it into the drawer. Then he looked up at me. His eyes narrowed.

'Right,' he said, pushing the drawer shut. 'What's going on?' He couldn't punish me for something I hadn't done, I told myself. And I'd had nothing to do with Hannigan's death.

'Sir?'

'A calm sea. No wind. John Doyle, captain of the foretop, one of my most experienced sailors, decides to lead the men aloft, and one of them ends up dead. What do you make of that?'

'Nothing, sir.'

A pause. He watched me, waiting.

'It was an accident,' I said.

'Do you think I'm stupid?'

'No.'

'Do you think I don't know you're laughing behind my back?'

'I'm not laughing,' I said, feeling my face begin to burn. 'It was an accident.'

'Before I signed you John Doyle was an exemplary crewman. And now – now I am just about this far away from having him dance on nothing, and hanging you alongside him for good measure.' He held up his hand, thumb and forefinger held half an inch apart. 'This far.'

'Because Hannigan lost his grip? Because he was careless?'

McMichaels' fist hit the desk. I jumped. The pen rattled in its holder, ink slopped in the inkwell. His face flushed suddenly red, he spoke through gritted teeth.

'D'you know what I think? I think he'd seen something he shouldn't have. I think he saw something and was going to report it.'

He knew. McMichaels knew.

'I'm sorry that he's dead,' I said, 'but I really don't know what you're talking about. I barely knew him.'

'It doesn't matter about him,' McMichaels said, and the words seemed to come with a sickening inevitability, as if he was just repeating something I'd already heard a hundred times before. 'People die every day,' he said. 'This is not about Hannigan. This is about you. This is about John Doyle.'

She'd spent almost a lifetime at sea, unsuspected, until we met. *This is all I know. I'd lose everything . . . I'd never sail again . . .*

I couldn't let that happen to her. I couldn't let it be my fault.

'No –' I said.

But McMichaels was still speaking.

'He's been a good friend to you, John Doyle has.'

It seemed like a complicity between us already; McMichaels' use of that word 'he', and my refusal to correct him.

'Sir, I don't know what –'

'You wouldn't want anything to happen to him.'

So here it came. The bargain.

'No,' I said.

His fist uncurled on the desk.

'Well then,' he said.

'Sir?'

A pause. He glanced down, ran his fingertips over the open page of his book.

'Have you ever seen a book before, Reed?'

'Sir?'

He looked up.

'Ever seen a book?'

'In church, sir – and the Bible when you read.'

He laughed. An uncomfortable sound.

'You'll like this one much better. Come and have a look.'

I hesitated.

'Are you going to keep making me repeat myself?' he said.

I moved round the desk, stood at his shoulder, looked. Fine grey lines and dots picked out loose folds of clothing, the smooth curve of skin. A three-quarter profile of a young woman leaning back upon a couch. Her bodice was unlaced, her shift loosened, and her breasts spilled out over her stays. Her raised skirts revealed crumpled stockings, garters, and the neat dark fold between her legs. A soldier in full uniform stood between her thighs. His britches were loosened, and he held his prick in his hand, was looking down at it. Underneath his moustache and whiskers, his face was serious. My own face felt hot.

'What do you think of that, then, Reed?'

'Um –' I said. 'That's um –'

I watched McMichaels' hand reach out and stroke the page flat.

'Do you like it?'

'Sir – I couldn't say.'

'Do you like girls too, or is it just men you like?'

'Sir –?'

He was fumbling with something. Unbuttoning his fly. Stupid: I should have realized much sooner. Suddenly memories of Sailortown were around me like a bad smell. McMichaels reached inside the folds of clothing, dragged out his cock. It was swelling, its head purple and glossy.

'D'you like *this*?' he asked.

It was almost instinctive. An acquired instinct, if you like. One I'd picked up in back streets and back rooms and in the shadows under bridges. Lucky I hadn't picked up something worse. I reached out and took his cock in my hand, then sank down on my knees in front of him.

On the desk, in the corner of my eye, the inkwell was a third full. Where the ink had slopped with the ocean swell, it had stained the glass like smoke. Beside it, in its holder, was McMichaels' pen, its wooden stem worn dark by his fingertips.

His hand, on the back of my head, was almost a tenderness, but he pushed himself too far into my mouth and my eyes watered and I gagged. When he came, he pushed still further, and his spend was thick and sudden. A moment, then he released my head and I leaned back. His prick slipped out of my mouth, and I swallowed.

I don't like recounting this, but it's what happened, and I promised you the truth, or at least my version of it. If it hadn't been significant I would have left it out. I did it for John.

I pressed the back of a hand to my lips. I put the other hand on the desk and pulled myself up on to my feet.

Nothing was said. I stood there a moment looking down at the picture of the girl and her soldier. They seemed happy, I thought. Maybe they were in love. There was a blot on the page, then another, landing on the tumbled petticoats, making the paper dimple. I rubbed a fist over my eyes. Stupid, how it made your eyes water, doing that.

McMichaels had rearranged his clothing, was standing at the window, looking out. Out over the heads of the dead, out towards the horizon.

'You know the punishment for sodomites on board?'

'What?'

'Death,' he said, but that hadn't been what I was asking. He hadn't known about John Doyle and me, I realized. He'd just thought he had.

'Breathe a word of this,' he was saying, his back still turned towards me, 'and I'll have John Doyle keel-hauled. And I'll have you flogged to ribbons. Just give me an excuse.'

'Sir,' I said.

'Ever seen anyone keel-hauled, Reed?'

'No sir.'

He cupped one hand inside the other, behind his back. His fingers curled up towards the ceiling. He turned away from the window, looked back round at me. I met his eye.

'It's a nasty way to die,' he said.

I remember two things: the taste of him in the back of my mouth and the certain knowledge that everyone I passed knew exactly what had happened. I crossed the deck without looking round, caught the afterburn of smiles in the corner of my eye. Someone laughed; a low, rattling sound, and I felt my ears burn to their tips. I didn't know where to go, didn't want to stop anywhere because there was always someone, someone who would catch my eye, and look away, and smile.

He'd be on edge, now. He'd be watching my every move. He wouldn't give me a chance to betray him.

'Are you all right?' I'd ended up in steerage, amongst the resting watches, down at the far dark corner where I slept. John was crossing towards me, weaving through the trunks and seated sailors, pushing empty hammocks swinging out of her way.

'What happened?'

'Nothing,' I said.

She came up to me, stopped, searched my face a moment. 'Did he beat you?' I looked up at her. *Breathe a word of this to anyone* –

'Does he know about me?'

'No,' I said. 'You're safe.'

She breathed, reached out to touch me. I moved away.

'Don't,' I said.

I was lying back in my hammock, looking at the boards above. I knew she was perched on her seachest, still scraping away at that scrap of something. I could smell her tobacco, had been watching the smoke-rings fade as they rose towards the ceiling. I tried not to think of the scent of her throat, or of the press of her hands on my skin.

I heard movement, and she was standing by my side, looking down at me. I shifted myself up on to an elbow.

'What is it?' I asked.

There was something pinched between her forefinger and thumb. She said:

'A present.' She held it out towards me.

I watched my hand reach out, watched my fingers uncurl. She dropped the thing into my palm. It was warm from her hand, hard and dark. I brought it up close to look at it. A triangular shape carved into the figure of a mermaid. Her tail, curling up against her, formed the base, her hair falling down over tiny torso, breasts, belly,

made the sides. A minute hole was bored into the apex.
The work was delicate, fine, the whole thing no bigger
than my thumbnail.

'What's it made of?'

'Shark's tooth.'

She took it from my palm and pulled a thread from her
pocket. She slipped thread through the hole and handed
the pendant back to me.

'It's supposed to be good luck,' she said.

I took it from her fingers, turned it round. She had
carved the back too, the flowing hair and tiny scales. Its
beauty made my heart beat faster, left me breathless. I
looked up at her, held out the carving.

'I can't take it.'

'Don't talk shite,' she said. She took the thing off me
again, lifted the string. It glinted gold in the lamplight, a
plaited strand of her hair. 'Course you can.' She reached
round my throat and tied the thread. A reef knot. Simple
and neat. She tugged it tight.

'It's to keep you from harm,' she said. 'To keep you
safe.' She looked at me a moment longer, then she kissed
me, quickly, on the mouth, before I could move away. I
reached up, took the pendant between my thumb and
forefinger. I rubbed the shape between my fingertips, felt
the rib of flowing hair, the stippled scales. I tucked it
down inside my shirt.

'Thank you,' I said. 'I wish I had something for you.'

Days later and the calm was still upon us: the stench of
bodies rotting into soup, the sun scowling down, the

pendant resting warm against my skin. Constant thirst and heat. Below decks the air was stinking, unbreathable. Above, we sought out the shade. Sometimes I found myself dreaming while still half awake: my mother was talking to me but the words were tangled together and all I could make out were syllables here and there; coloured lights swam before my eyes like fishes; someone would lay a hand on my shoulder, and only then would I realize that they'd been speaking to me for some time. I seemed to dream that I was back in the village, getting down on my knees to suck cock in the back room of the pub. What was real, what I wanted, and what I was trying to escape from were no longer distinguishable. They were all around me, all happening at once.

Someone was calling my name. I shook my head clear. John was sitting in the shadow of the ship's boat, beckoning me. I moved over to her, stood at her feet, in the sun.

'Yes.'

'Sit down,' she said. 'We're going to go over your knots again.'

I crouched down at her side. I watched the loop and twist of the rope.

'A Carrick,' her fingers moved precisely, strong and deft. The cords knotted neatly, were released. 'A reverse Carrick, an Anchor Reef.'

'I know all those.'

She looked up at me.

'I know,' she said. A curl fell down over her eyes. 'I miss you.'

She pushed back the fallen strand of hair, her hand

sliding slowly over the crown of her head and coming to a rest on the nape of her neck, where the hair was curled tight into ringlets, damp with sweat. She looked up. Something had caught her attention: she searched the empty sky, the rigging.

'What is it?' I asked.

She shifted herself on to her hunkers, one hand to the deck.

'I better go and tell McMichaels,' she said, and straightened up.

'What?'

She was already heading away.

'He won't have noticed yet,' she called back to me.

'Noticed what?' I asked, scrambling to my feet. 'What is it?'

She stopped in her tracks, looked round. Something made her face soften, made her almost smile. She came back the two paces to me.

'Can't you feel it?' She lifted a hand, and I felt the faint ribbing of her fingerprints brush against my cheek. 'Can't you smell it in the air?'

'No,' I said. I moved away from her touch. 'What?'

She let her hand fall back to her side and was brisk again, turning to go.

'There's a wind, thank God,' she said. 'At last there's a wind.'

The sails dropped, filled, and the ship began to move. The gentlest of breezes. It had come out of nowhere, and unexpectedly, but it was fair for the Western Isles, and we were in no position to find fault with it. But there was no cheer from the crew, no sense of jubilation. Rather, there was disquiet, as I recall: a faint unstated intimation of unease.

As we ploughed out through the dead, the wake made them roll and shift, so that different bits would surface: water-bloated flesh, or a picked-white bone where the fishes had been eating. For the rest of the afternoon, if you glanced astern, you could see them, clustered into a low dark island on the water. By the following morning, we had left them behind. They had slipped over the horizon, out of sight.

I, for one, could have done with a gale. I wanted torrents and tornadoes to boil up the seas, storms to tear the sailcloth into tatters. I needed the distraction. But instead, constant, steady, gentle as a sigh, the wind continued. The ship clipped along, seemed daily to gather speed, but there was never a bluster or a gust, no shift in course with this wind. And all the time the sea remained implausibly flat: our progress was continuous, frictionless, like a skater's. I found myself shivering in the sun. it became more and more difficult to shake away the dreams, the lights, the colours, the tangled voices. I took to holding my pendant between my fingers, bringing it to my lips to kiss. My little bit of luck. Made for me.

We may have been a week like that, a fortnight: it passed in a blur, the sun skimming daily overhead like a thrown stone. I don't know how long it had been in my head before I heard it. A dark sweet sound, wordless or filled with unknown words, gathering itself, becoming surer. Then suddenly it came clear to me, clearer than John's face in front of me, clearer than my own voice when I said to her:

'Can you hear that? Can you hear them singing?'

'What?' she said, 'I can't hear anything.'

'Reed! Reed! You feckless bastard. Where are you?'

McMichaels. My skin prickled. Something cold coiled itself tight around my stomach. The mermaids' song was tugging at my thoughts. I turned to go to him. John touched my arm.

'I'll go.'

I shifted away from her.

'No.'

A hesitation, then a slight nod, her lips tight.

'Watch yourself,' she said.

'Reed!'

I moved across the deck, conscious of the line I trod from John watching me as I walked away to McMichaels glaring down from the steps of the quarterdeck. Every step a pull against desire. I came to a halt at the foot of the steps. McMichaels was on the third rung, his midriff level with my eyes. He looked straight out over my head.

'Sir,' I said.

'My desk drawer, left hand side, there's a lump of beeswax. Fetch it and take it round the men.'

I found that I was examining the folds of cloth, the buttoning of his fly. An uneasy feeling. I'd brought it with me: my own cargo of shadows. I looked up at his face.

'Are you listening, Reed?'

'Sir.'

'Make sure you get everyone, mind. Below decks, too.'

The song was growing thicker, more palpable. The sounds hung in the air, soft and entangling like spiders' webs, like the travelling-lines that sweep across your face in autumn, invisible till sun-caught. A memory resurfaced: an intimation of nettle-stings, the smell of vomit and of piss, and the reeling heady joy of recognition. On deck, in the hot sun, the hairs stood up on my arms, on the back of my neck. So close. They were so close.

'And the cargo, sir?' I found myself saying. 'What's left of them, I mean?'

He had been turning to go, had lifted a foot to the next rung. He turned back round to look at me.

'They're hardly in a position to desert, are they?' he said.

He didn't follow me to his room, though the back of my neck prickled with apprehension all the way down the corridor. The book still lay open on his desk: a different page. The soldier wasn't there, and in his absence the young woman was consoling herself with the intimate attentions of her maid and a small tabby cat. I dragged open a drawer, found the beeswax. A lump the size and shape of an otter's head. I lifted it out, began warming it in my hands.

I brought the last of the wax to John Doyle. A ball the size of a cob nut. She took it, began rolling it into plugs. She blinked, and her eyelids showed white against her weather-tanned face. She didn't speak. Maybe she thought I'd already taken my share. Or maybe she'd noticed McMichaels nearby, watching.

We went about our tasks in silence, in dumb show. At first, I mugged and gestured along with the rest of them. Someone dropped a deadeye: it landed with a noisy clatter on the deck. I flinched, but no one seemed to notice. I worked briskly, moving through the ritual patterns of my tasks, my eyes turning at every chance towards the water, straining to catch a glimpse of something. Then all at once a tailfin broke the surface of the ocean, and across the ship a sudden cry went up. And the only one who heard it was me.

I heard, but was no longer listening, and no longer had to pretend my ears were stopped. The mermaids' song had wrapped itself around me, thickening, taking form. The ship's noises began to fade. I watched everything through a veil. The music was a paleness and a softness in the air, and I could swim through it, wrap myself up in it, be held and lifted and carried along and never have to think or work or worry again. My mother. I would be with my mother.

They were slipping through the water, diving, breaking the surface. Moving through the ocean like currents, streams. Their tails were translucent; some green, some grey-blue; here and there was a touch of luminosity, a glimpse of gracefully articulated spine. Eyes dark as seals' eyes, they were turning to me, calling; one raised a pale arm in a flash before rolling, slipping down through the bright water and away. Then another curl of foam, a splash of tail fin, a curve of diving back. Dozens of them.

Scores. I clambered up on to the railing, raised my arm towards them, called:

'I'm coming! Wait for me!'

But was slammed down on to the boards, the breath knocked out of me. There was weight on my back, legs, arms. My nose was pushed askew, my eyes watering, my cheek pressed hard against wood. I heard shouting. And still above it and beyond and all around me, stronger, thicker, was the mermaids' song. As I writhed and twisted under the sailors' weight, I thought I could hear the battering of delicate cold hands against the keel. They were calling for me, coming for me, demanding that I join them.

'Let me go!' I shouted. 'Let me go!'

I was hauled up and held, thrashing like a fish. Suddenly I found myself face to face with McMichaels, standing between me and what I'd crossed half the world to find. I didn't think twice about it. I heaved myself forward and slammed my forehead into his nose.

He staggered back, blinking, brought his hand up to his face. There was blood on his lip.

He hit me. A crack to the jaw as if the bone had burst open. My head flew back; I staggered and was held. I blinked, slid my tongue round my teeth, tasted blood. I looked up at him. His eyes were thin. It was inevitable now, I remember thinking. I'd given him his excuse.

I almost welcomed it. It would simplify things.

Then his fist landed on the side of my head, and everything collapsed into darkness.

*

I'd been dreaming, swimming, weightlessly twisting through the green water. My mother was swimming there beside me, translucent, just out-of-sight, and when I turned my head just gone. Then light crashed on to me like breaking glass. I peered up, squinting. A dark shadow against the sun.

'John?'

She crouched down beside me, began helping me to my feet. There were shackles round my wrists and ankles. Plenty of them to be had on board the *Sally Ann*. They were cold and heavy and cut into the skin.

'I'm sorry–' she said.

'It's all right, I'm fine.' This came as something of a surprise. My jaw ached, I was very thirsty, and there was a sting and tightness at my temple where the blood had dried, but I was, all things considered, fine.

She led me into the sunshine. The wind was buffeting the ship a little, like a bully. Taking us away. A sharp sun overhead. Sharp as a needle.

'I'm sorry,' she said again.

I shambled forwards, chains clattering.

'S'all right,' I said. 'It's all right.' I was thinking, I'll find them again. Now that I've seen them, and they've called out to me, it's only a matter of time before I find them again.

We moved slowly, awkwardly, John's arm under mine, supporting me. There was a cluster of men, a crowd on deck. I looked at them, vaguely puzzled. A few faces turned to look at us. We came up towards them. I turned to John, asked:

'What's going on? What are they waiting for?'

'I'm sorry.'

McMichaels was there. And the whole crew. Even the other watches, those who should have been below, who should have been sleeping. Everyone. Every last man jack of them.

I stopped dead. I straightened up, looked round at John. She held my gaze a moment, then looked away. She swallowed. Tell-tale, of course, the smoothness of her throat; no roll of Adam's apple, no grey stipple of growth on her tanned flesh. I wanted, suddenly, to kiss her there, where her skin dipped over her collarbone and caught the light.

'I'm sorry,' she murmured.

I looked away from her, looked round. McMichaels' eyes were as thin as the wind. From his hand, twitching like the tail of an excited cat, hung the lash.

'Tie him, Doyle.'

'Sir–'

'Have you got a problem with that, Doyle?'

A pause.

'No, sir.'

'Then tie him.'

John Doyle released my shackles, brought my hands around the mast. With my cheek pressed up against the wood, I couldn't see her, but I sensed the movement of her hands, the deliberate precision of her fingers. I felt the rope loop and twist and tug itself tight. A Carrick bend. Workmanlike. Unshiftable. A final twist, a tug, and the knot was finished. A breath. She came round the mast. I looked up at her, the skin tingling down my back, jaw clenched tight.

'John?' I managed.

Nothing.

'John?'

She looked at me, her head bent, her face in shadow.

'I loved you,' I hissed at her, and realized that it was true.

She reached out, took hold of my shirt and tugged at it, as if straightening me against the mast. Her face near me, turned away from the assembled crew, I felt the words on my skin as she breathed them.

'I'm sorry,' she said. 'I am so sorry.'

Then she turned away.

'Take the lash,' I heard McMichaels say.

'It's not my job,' John said.

'Nevertheless,' McMichaels said, 'take the lash.'

The flogging was worse than the one Uncle George had given me. It wiped away those scars as if they'd never been.

Occasionally, even now, I get a twinge from a spot between my shoulderblades where the nerves were flayed and will never, it seems, quite recover. As John Doyle lifted the lash and whipped it across my back, peeling away linen and skin, it seemed that I was being born again, this time through my own pain. I bit at my lips and tongue to stop myself from screaming, as if by this slight self-inflicted discomfort I could control the agony of the scourge. I passed out before she'd finished, my mouth full of blood, my mind dissolving into black, but I knew in that moment of dissolution, with a miraculous clarity like nothing else but the certainty that sometimes comes to me in dreams, that the person that I had been was gone for ever, had now been peeled entirely away. If I was to live, I would need to grow a new skin, a thicker one.

Night. The steady pitch and roll of the ship, the creak of timbers. A pallet beneath me: the prickle of horsehair on my cheek. The smell of smoke and men. I lifted my head; my back screamed with pain, a lesser ache throbbed through jaw and temple. I lowered my cheek down again on to the mattress, exhaled. A slow burn down my whole back, from nape to coccyx. Someone hunkered down at my side.

'Malin?'

Hands were cupped round my head; it was lifted, turned. The movement made my flesh sing out at me again. I sucked in a breath. There was something cold and hard against my lips. I flinched.

'It's all right.'

Again, the cold hard rim against my lips, and something wet in my mouth, burning broken lips and swollen tongue: automatically I swallowed. The bottle was tilted again and I drank, the fierce liquid making my eyes water, my nose prickle. My head was gently lowered back down upon the mattress. I closed my eyes. Everything had gone slightly fuzzy, slightly soft. The burning of my flayed skin seemed just a little further away.

She said it softly, quickly, so that I couldn't even make

the words register before the pain came. *'Be brave,'* she said.

She poured something on to me, over the whole open wound of my back. Cold at first, and then stinging, and then burning worse than before. I gasped, in too much pain even to protest.

'I'm sorry,' she said. 'I'm sorry. It'll help you heal.'

And then the drink took over, and the pain, and blackness covered me again.

When I was able to move about again, I was assigned to light duties, shuffling round the deck on my knees with a bucket and brush, or hunching over bits of old rope, splicing them or unsplicing them according to instructions. It was all I was fit for. The scabbing was still so tight across my shoulders that it made climbing an impossible agony: it made any movement at all an act of will, of sheer bloodymindedness. But I was determined. I had been beaten, but I would not, I told myself, be crushed. And I was healing, day by day. I would live. John's ministrations had seen to that.

She had poured salt water over the raw wounds, and when they began to heal, gently stroked on sharp-smelling ointment to give the skin some suppleness, to try to ensure my future mobility. She had made me drink rum and water, and helped me swallow crumbs of biscuit, and suck on limes, and had kept death from me, but every moment was an agony to add to the pain of my wounds. To be touched by those hands again, so tenderly. To feel their strength and skill again. I could not speak a word. I could not find a single word to say. And beyond the slight instructions of her nursing, neither could she. The one time I had met her eyes, as she helped me raise myself to my feet for the first time since my thrashing, there had been tears brimming there, ready to spill, and I had looked away, had watched instead my toes spread on the boards as my feet took my weight. A drop, warm and wet, had landed on the knuckle of my second toe, and I still could not find a word to say. The clumsiness of a swollen tongue, of lips bitten to ribbons. My misery was overwhelming, incommunicable. It left me mute.

At night I would lie awake, face down on a pallet, the hammocks swinging row after row above. Parched with exhaustion, I would rise and climb the steps to the deck, breathe cool night air, sense its moisture on my skin. I would watch the moonlight on the waves. Sometimes sleep would descend on me unexpectedly, and I would wake, cold and shivering, hunched against the cathead or the rails. The other watches must have got used to me trespassing on their time, but no one spoke to me, no one came near. A superstitious inkling, perhaps, that my bad luck might be catching.

Stooping over my work day after day in total silence, my eyes heavy with fatigue, the only pleasure I took was in the smudged and fevered memory of the mermaids. The elegant community of their shoal swam past my vision, its movement instinctively synchronous as starlings' flight. I could almost hear the keening of their voices, the faint clamour of their fine cool hands beating at the keel. I had been recognized. I was wanted. I belonged with them.

The voyage could have gone on for ever. I was ignorant of the distance to be travelled, of the speed we were making, and of signs that we were nearing land. Time itself had unravelled, the days and nights shredded by fatigue and sudden sleep into a perpetual moment, a patch of hours. Wrapped up in my misery, I noticed nothing. My tasks were completed mechanically, unthinkingly. I did not, could not allow myself to think.

Then, one morning when the air was still cool and I had already settled myself down to some repair, there was a cry from above. I glanced up, instinctively looking for someone in difficulties aloft, and the movement sent a ripple of pain down my back. There was no one up there, but nearby a white gull was gliding along on the same wind as us, wings spread, steady as a kite on a string. The bird gave another cry, pushed twice against the air current and came to rest upon the rigging. I watched it settle itself, watched its shit fall and hit the deck, watched a man walking towards me from the bows. One of the topmen. Davies, his name was. Slowing as he approached me. Coming to a halt. He crouched down to speak to me.

'McMichaels wants you,' he said.

He was standing by the window, facing me, but dark against the tropic's glare. I tried to straighten myself, stood as best I could before his desk.

'It's amazing what a little discomfort does to a person's

appearance,' he said. He moved over towards the desk, planted his hands on the wood, leaned forward to peer closer at me.

'Not such a pretty face now Reed, eh?'

It had been gathering inside me all this time. Now it was making my fingers tremble, making my jaw clench tight. My hands curled themselves into fists. I don't think I've ever felt hatred like this.

'Still good friends, are you, John Doyle and yourself? Still great chums?' He gave a little uneasy laugh. 'Look at you. No one in their right mind would come anywhere near you.'

He moved away, back towards the window, and looked out. My lips almost moved, my tongue instinctively attempting to form an answer, but no words came.

'This is a sorry state of affairs I find myself in. A sorry state. Here we are,' he said, 'no more than a day's sail from our destination, and I find myself burdened with a troublesome, corrupting crewman who won't do the decent thing and die when he is flogged to mincemeat. And that leaves me in something of a dilemma.' He paused a moment, lifted a hand to glance at his nails. 'I've been mulling this over for days now,' he continued, 'and I still can't quite make up my mind. Tell me what you think. Should I keep him by me, keep this bad apple to his contracted five years, just under my eye, so that I can be sure that the rot won't spread, because we can't let vice and slander and rumour go unchecked now can we? Or,' he paused, cupping one hand inside the other behind his back, his head swivelling round to look at me. 'Should I just sell him at the Western Isles and see what I can get?'

His face was a shadow against the light.

'What do you think, Reed? What would you do in my position?'

Underneath the bold words there was an uneasiness of tone. Even in my fury I could detect it. No matter that he'd had me flogged, no matter that he'd almost broken me, no matter that he could be rid of me tomorrow, there was something in him that was afraid. Afraid of me, or of what I might say, or afraid that he still wanted me. It didn't matter.

I opened my mouth. I was going to tell him that I couldn't give a shit where he found himself, tell him how wrong he had been about John Doyle and me, tell him that he was a coward and a fool and that before he could get rid of me I'd tell everyone on board that he'd made me suck his sweaty cock.

But my lips moved soundlessly. My tongue was clumsy. Not a word. I brought my hand to my mouth.

He came closer to me again, looking into my face.

'What is it, Reed? Cat got your tongue?'

The rest of the day, to all outward appearances, passed much as any other. When the watch was over I lay awake for hours, face down on my pallet, listening to the ship. The birdcalls of sailors up above, the creaking timbers, the muffled sounds from the cargo hold below. And closer, John Doyle's breathing, soft and dry. There had been land on the horizon: as the sun had set, there had been a slender thread of dark against the glare. A day's sail away, McMichaels had said. No more than that.

He'd never feel at ease, not entirely at ease, until he was rid of me. I might not be a threat to him anymore, but I'd always be a reminder. Desire and jealousy and pleasure and guilt: he could never quite feel comfortable with me nearby.

I listened to John Doyle's breath above me. I remembered cool hands battering the keel.

It was hardly a decision. I didn't seem to have much choice.

The ship was growing quiet. All day we had been running before a fair wind. Easy going. Above, in the darkness, sailors would be dozing at their posts, slumped forwards on to folded arms at the tiller, lolling back against top rails with eyes fast shut and mouth fallen wide, or with a cheek pressed against a spar, dreaming. In steerage, the sleepers' collective breathing was like the sea, patterned, multifarious. And just above, in her hammock, the soft and quiet breath, the gentle rise and fall of John Doyle's breast. Cautiously, I eased myself on to one side, then up on to my knees. I crouched, then stood up, uncoiling slowly. She was sleeping, lying there suspended at chest-height. A curl had fallen down over her forehead. I stood a long moment, just looking. Then I bent down, opened my kitbag, and drew out my Da's old clogs.

The moon was half-hidden by cloud. The lookout was dozing: a spindle of drool hung from his open mouth. No sounds from the watch. No one called out to me. I would hardly attract much attention, even if I was seen. Just another of those many nights without sleep.

In the darkness, the lid of the cargo hatch looked more solid than ever, unshiftable as a tombstone. I knew this was going to hurt. I lowered the clogs onto the deck by their laces, then crouched down and tucked my fingers underneath the rim of the hatch. I heaved. My back seemed to catch fire. The hatch lifted an inch, a handspan. The pain was incredible. A gap appeared between the deck and the lid. I knocked one of the shoes into the gap to wedge it open. I heaved one more time and shunted the clog along towards the hinge. I released my hold: the hatch stayed open, held up by the bulky wooden sole. A space of two hands' spans, no more. Just enough to slide a body through. And not enough, I hoped, to draw attention to itself. I lifted the other clog, took it round the far side of the hatch, wedged it tight into the gap. I'd have to leave them there, there'd be no getting them back now. But Da would have understood.

I took a breath. And then I eased myself down into the darkness.

Ankle-deep in filth and straw. Something furry brushed against my foot: I trod on something that wriggled then crunched under my weight.

They weren't packed as tightly as they had been at the start of the voyage, so it didn't take me so very long to free them all; men, women, still a handful of children left alive. I could barely see them, just got a sense of different bulks and shapes in the darkness. Mostly they just lay in silence, their eyes catching whatever glimmer of light there was, but one of the men took a swing at me the moment his hands were free, landing a right hook squarely on my chin. As I stumbled away to the next set of shackles, the next pair of wrists tacky with sores, I was faintly puzzled to find that he hadn't knocked me out, or even knocked me over. Even in the dark it was clear he was a big man. My chin hurt: I would have a bruise there, but a right hook from him should have sent me flying halfway into next week.

One by one, as they were released, they moved to the base of the ladder. I saw them standing there, looking up at the sliver of blue night above. Someone put a hand out: the fingers gripped a rung and a figure began to climb. Others followed, heaving themselves out through the gap. I came to the furthest corner of the hold, the last bunk. There was a child lying there. When I touched her, her wrists were thin and damp, sticky where the irons had chafed her. From somewhere in the darkness a woman's voice was calling, urgent, low, but I barely noticed until I felt the child shift under my hands. The same word was repeated, and I turned to call out *she's over here*, but the words wouldn't come.

As the shackles came away in my hands the woman was beside me, leaning in to lift the child past me and away. I felt them brush by me in the darkness, turned to look after them. For a moment there was only darkness, then the hatchway cleared briefly and I watched as the child was lifted, hoisted to someone higher up the ladder, passed to the next pair of open arms. At the top of the ladder, she was slipped through the opening, into the night air. Someone stood aside to let her mother pass. The last few remaining people followed after.

Silence in the hold. I wiped my palms down my britches, swallowed, then picked my way back to the ladder. I began to climb. I had half expected the hatch to be slammed down, to find myself stuck down there: there would have been a certain justice to it. But as I slipped my hand out through the opening another hand closed round my wrist and I was hauled up and through the gap, biting my lip against the pain. I was set down on the deck. Hunched and gasping, I stood there in the moonlight, my wrist still clasped in the man's hand. I couldn't look up at him. He didn't speak. I wanted to say something, but I knew it was useless. We stood like that a moment longer, separated by languages and silence. I realized I was shaking, and that my lips were moving continuously, as if of independent will, as if desperate to fulfil a duty of communication. My wrist was released, I felt the lightest touch of fingertips on my head, and when I looked up, he had turned, and was moving away.

A moment passed. I could hear the sounds of stealthy movement round the ship. A muffled cry: the lookout woken from his doze and at the same moment silenced, a hand pressed tight over his mouth, another round his throat. I turned and walked across the deck, hitched myself up on to the rail. What chance would they stand as freed slaves, a day's sail from the Western Isles? I swung my legs over the side, looked down at the water. Black as ink. Another cry, abruptly cut off. A crewman's neck snapped in the darkness, before he could even register what was happening. I took a breath. I dropped down into the water.

I'd like to say that, as I swam out into the dark, I heard the flurry of ropes through pulleys, the crash of one of the ship's boats hitting the still water, and the splash of oars as the slaves rowed themselves away to some kind of new life on a deserted or a friendly island, leaving the ship's crew relatively unmolested, but I still can't quite convince myself of that. There were screams, I know, I couldn't help hearing the screams. There must have been many deaths, one way or another. I know I heard the crash of bodies hitting water, and thrashing noisy panic as my crewmates floundered in the calm sea. I heard familiar voices crying out to God or mothers or to sweethearts. But I also heard the neat dive and strong slow strokes of a practised swimmer somewhere nearby: whoever it was, they would most probably make it ashore. John Doyle, I imagined. John Doyle or McMichaels.

I've wrestled with my conscience ever since that night. It wakes me in the small hours, descends on me out of the blue when I'm doing something quite normal, eating, perhaps, or smoking, or just watching the ripples on the river. A tangle of panic tightens in my chest, my hands begin to shake, and the meal, the pipe, the river is no longer there, is blotted out. It is unresolvable, this sense of guilt. What I did was right. I freed the slaves. What I did was wrong. I sent those other people to their deaths. I can't make this fit, can't make my way around it, can't even figure out if there was any point at which I could have done something else, could have made a different choice, could have circumvented that whole situation. But even if I'd never left the village, if I'd let the stranger make his moonlight flit alone; if I'd grown old and bent rubbing down the doorstep of the Anchor with generation upon generation of donkeystones, there would, surely there would still have been that ship, those slaves, such cruelty.

But enough of that. At the time, all I thought about were my chances of getting clean away. I knew I would not be missed. I knew that there would be no search parties. With the sounds of thrashing and floundering, the cries and shouts still loud behind me, I swam away, straight out to sea. They would come for me, I was sure of it. My mother's people would come for me.

Ten

They didn't. By dawn there was still no sign of them, and I was growing weak.

A wind had gathered overnight, whipping up the sea into madness: just keeping my head above water all this time had been a battle; a battle which, I was beginning to realize, I could no longer hope to win. The waves slapped into me, crashed over me, tossed me high and dragged me down into their troughs. Gasping for air, seawater slopped into my mouth, making me cough and retch. Again and again I lost my grip on the surface and sank beneath it. The water burned my eyes, ate at the lining of my nose. It was entering me through every pore.

To just give up, I thought. To just let go. To be claimed by the water and become one with it. Perhaps that was what I had to do before they'd come for me: perhaps that was how I could become truly one of them. Another wave hit me, dragged me down. My arms still flailed instinctively, my legs still kicked as if tangled in wool, but I was aware of this only distantly, and without much concern. My eyes were wide open on stinging, misted submarine blue, but my head was exploding with light.

What I first noticed was the smell; musty, sharp, yellowish. I was lying face down on something hard, and I could tell by the ache in my ribcage that I had been lying there for some time. My left hand was lolling over an edge, hanging in clear space.

I was alive then, I realized. I hadn't really expected it.

I breathed in, felt my ribs expand against the surface, felt a catch in my lungs. There was a faint trace of music in my head, an afterthought of colour. They'd come for me. My heart began to race. I opened my eyes, pushed myself up on to an elbow. My sight was blurred, my eyes stung on contact with the air, stung still more when I squeezed them shut. I'd caught a vague impression of underwater dimness and of space. I raised a hand to rub at my eyes, and the movement shifted a cover which had been placed over me, had been tucked in round me as I'd slept. A gentle swell, a creaking timber: I was aboard ship. I gasped, heaved myself upright, blinking. The mermaids had not come for me: I'd been caught.

But the sight that met my eyes, once my vision had come clear, was not the brig of the *Sally Ann*, nor even steerage, and now I came to think about it why would I be dry, and covered, and, I noticed, wearing someone else's (someone much bigger than me's) shirt, if I was back on the slave ship and in danger of my life?

McMichaels was hardly going to make sure I was warm and comfortable before he had me flayed to ribbons, before he had me keel-hauled. And of course, I remembered, he was in no position to come looking for me: there wouldn't be anyone on board the *Sally Ann* who would have the slightest interest in coming after me by now. Either they'd have far more pressing concerns of their own, or they'd be dead.

I had been lying on a table. My head had been pillowed on a book, and around me on the tabletop were towers and ziggurats of books, marking out the space where I had lain. I pushed back the coverlet and eased aside an unsteady stack of volumes to swing my legs round over the edge. Every muscle ached, was stiff with exhaustion. I was at once nauseous, hungry and desperately thirsty. Where was I, I wondered; what was this place?

The room was high and long and dim; it bellied outwards at the sides, tapered into shadow at the ends. I noticed that there were doors let into the end walls, and narrow windows let into the sides, but apart from these slight interruptions, every inch of the place was covered with books. Bookshelves lined the walls. There were books piled on the floor, books heaped on to the seats of chairs; books had been shifted aside for me to lie down, by the looks of it more must have been placed around me as I'd slept.

And I was below the waterline. Blue-green brine pressed against the portholes, supplying a gentle underwater light; from higher up sunlight shafted through the windows, catching the aimless drift of dustmotes, marking out trapezoids on the floor. A pair of wheeled ladders rolled gently to and fro along the shelves with the motion of the ship.

I slid off the table and landed barefoot on something soft. There was a carpet beneath my feet, patterned with a faded intricate design in red and green and blue. I had never trodden on a carpet before. I spread my hard-skinned toes into the pile. I couldn't feel much at all. The shirt hung around me in loose folds. It was thin with age. The cuffs hung down long over my hands; they were frayed at the edges and none too clean. I reached behind me for the coverlet and wrapped it round my shoulders. The movement released a miasma of dust which caught in my throat, making me cough. And once I'd started coughing I found I couldn't stop. I must have inhaled a bucketload, a bathful of seawater; it now came ratcheting back up from my lungs. I crumpled in on myself, spluttering, one hand to the table for support, the other cupped over my mouth.

'Ssssshhhht.'

There were hands underneath my arms. I was guided across the room, books were shifted and I was seated on a chair. The coughing subsided, leaving me feeling breathless and raw. I wiped my face with a sleeve, blinked away the wetness from my eyes, looked up.

The man seemed very old. His face was on a level with mine: underneath bristling grey brows his eyes were pale; his mouth looked blurred around the edges. There were crumbs of eggyolk and clots of what looked like gravy clinging to his moustache and beard, and streals of something similar down the front of his long garment. His sleeves hung low over cold-looking, freckled hands. Not a sailor, manifestly. But not like anyone I'd known in the dry either. I blinked, opened my mouth. He brought a long and dusty finger to his lips.

'Sssssshhhht,' he said again.

I was about to ask why, but as my lips parted there was another, more furious repeat of the shushing, accompanied this time by a shower of spit. He turned and moved away, but didn't straighten up. His back was so bent that his neck and shoulders were almost parallel to the floor, though he held his head up to peer ahead. That's why, though I was seated, we'd been face to face. I watched as he picked his way across the book-strewn floor. Like a heron, I thought; hunched, wild-eyebrowed, intent.

I sat there, wiping away the spray of spit from my face with a knuckle, tugging the coverlet tighter round me. I was itching to call out after him, to ask him his name, how I'd ended up here, and what kind of ship this was, but it would obviously get me nowhere. I watched him reach the far end of the room and dissolve into the shadows. It seemed to be his natural habitat: camouflaged as a peppered moth against a lichened tree, his dark vestments and straggling hair faded entirely out of sight.

I swung my legs, glanced round the room again, then looked back towards him. Though the room had seemed empty when I'd woken, he must have been there all the time. I spent a moment or two half-heartedly trying to pick him out, but soon lost patience. He was invisible, uncommunicative, and apparently busy, and as I was patently not going to be getting any information from that quarter, and could not sit there swinging my legs indefinitely, I slid off the chair and walked over to the bookshelves. The books were obviously significant: after all, from the shape of the room it was clear that it took up the majority of the vessel's tonnage. They must be the ship's main cargo.

They were of many different colours, rich and soft and deep. Burgundies, purples, blues, browns and greens. I ran my fingertips down their spines, traced the letters embossed there in gold and black: I recognized the individual marks, and here or there could put them together to make up a word, occasionally a phrase: *the book of* something, I read, and *the life of* somebody, and someone else's *thoughts*. I found myself wondering if I was still contained within the schoolroom map, bobbing around on the green waves near the corner of the frame, or if I had by now slipped underneath the wooden rim and was off somewhere across the bulging plaster of the schoolroom wall.

A sigh issued from the far end of the shelves. I turned to watch the old man shuffle from the shadows. He came to one of the stepladders and hitched his skirts up for the climb. I caught a glimpse of thin and hairy ankles, of greying canvas slippers. There were three or four books tucked beneath his arm. As he climbed, the ladder rolled along the shelves with the motion of the ship. Unperturbed, he slotted the books into their places as he rolled past. The ladder stopped, then slid back towards its original position, and he climbed carefully down to alight just at the point he had got on. He shambled back into his corner, leaving the stepladder to roll back and forth on its own. He didn't even glance my way. I was obviously not of any particular interest to him: he wouldn't notice if I left. And I had to find out what was going on. I headed aft, towards the door set into the bulkhead. As I moved, every joint, from neck to ankle, seemed to grate as if it had been dusted with fine sand.

I pushed my way through the door. It fell shut behind me. In front of me there was another door, to my right a steep staircase. What little light there was came from above, spilling itself down over the stair-treads like milk. An opening on to deck, I thought: otherwise, the stairwell was quite windowless. I was in no rush to climb the stairs. Instead I tried the doorhandle.

A little light came in through a porthole, alternately white and green as the vessel pitched. The cabin was plain and spare: a slung cot, a trunk, two or three piles of books, some crates and boxes piled up in the corner. One of the boxes had been opened: scrolled manuscripts and sheaves of paper strayed across the floor, slithering and rolling with the ocean swell. I stooped, picked up a sheet, held it to the light. Line upon line of tiny spidery writing crossing the page without a break. The same hand filled the margins at right angles to the main text, the writing even more crabbed and compressed. I released my hold upon the paper, watched as it descended, in abbreviated arcs, towards the floor. It landed near the others, immediately rejoined their drift back and forth across the boards. I went back out into the stairwell, pulled the door shut behind me, and began the climb.

Daylight and a cool fresh breeze, the blood singing in my ears, my breath harsh in my throat. We must be way past the tropic. How long then, I wondered, had I been unconscious? How far, for that matter, had I swam? I glanced up, my neck stiff and creaking: the sun was to my right, and it felt like afternoon, so perhaps we were headed south, but I couldn't be sure. I felt the wind tugging at my coverlet. My legs bristled with goosepimples, hair blew into my eyes. I wrapped the cover tighter round me. That deep, flesh-shifting shiver rippled through me again. I looked the length and breadth of the ship. She wasn't big: nothing like the size of the *Sally Ann*. A lightweight, shorthaul, coastal vessel. For day-tripping, I thought, for summer jaunts: I wondered where we were headed.

I leant upon the railing, scanned the horizon for other ships, for land. Nothing. Just the cool slate-grey ocean stretching as far as I could see. So if we were heading south, we were cruising at some distance from the coast. The major trade, if I remembered right, was a kind of leaf, sometimes dried, sometimes refined to powder. Useful stuff to a captain with an exhausted crew. Crumbled into a sailor's tobacco, it could keep him up and awake and working for days, have him scrambling up the main topgallant shroud in a hurricane without a moment's misgiving. Which was why, when bad weather was approaching, sailors would sniff suspiciously at their tobacco, watch each other for the first signs. It was dangerous to feel invincible on board ship. Sometimes the only thing that kept you alive was a keen sense of your mortality.

No bad weather approaching for the time being, though, as far as I could tell. A following wind, no squalls, no stormclouds massing. The common creak and strain of shipsounds, but otherwise silence. No calls or shouted orders. No human sounds at all, I realized. I looked round: no one at the helm. I turned to glance up, caught sight of the bare rigging, of ropes flapping loose and untrained in the wind, of tattered shreds of rotten canvas, and I knew that we were drifting.

I had a sailor's instinctive horror of being left adrift. It went against everything I had become. I was on the verge of running down to him and demanding that he tell me what was going on, when a noise caught my attention, a soft burbling coming from somewhere nearby. A familiar backyard sound that brought with it instantly the smell of blackcurrant bushes and the texture of dried earth between my fingertips.

The ship's boat was just beside me. Inside, a dozen bantam hens were nesting, crooning, tucked into straw between the boat's ribs. The cockerel flapped his wings at me and clambered on to a rowlock. I realized suddenly that I was ravenous. I had no idea when it was that I'd last eaten. I decided I would reach under one of the broodier-looking birds and tug out a still-warm egg to suck. I stretched out a hand; the chickens began to caw and flutter, the cockerel cocked his head and glared at me with a button eye. I dropped my arm back to my side, turned and walked away, leaving the bantams to settle back to their contemplative maternity.

I could not, I realized, go below and accost him, could not demand to know why we were drifting, just to satisfy another, less vital, impulse on my part. Having been rescued, it was not my place to question the manner of my rescue. I would find out what was going on soon enough, I told myself. In the meantime, I went looking for the galley.

Dark came slowly, creeping up on the ship like a child playing tin-can-lurky. I descended the stairs carrying a platter of cheese, sausage, greyish bread and a handful of soft pickles. On the edge of the platter I had balanced a jug and two cups. In the galley I'd found a strange contraption of pipes and vessels that bubbled and hissed, heated by a little flame. A jug stood underneath, filling slowly as water dripped from the mouth of a canister. I'd lifted the jug, sniffed it, then held it to my lips and drank. Clean, unbrackish water, about a pint of it, but not nearly enough to still my thirst. I found a cask of beer that had been broached and drew off about a quart, then gulped it down without thinking twice. The beer went straight to my head, giving everything a pleasant fuzz. I decided then that I would take supper down to the old man. We'd eat together, we'd have a few cups of beer, we'd get to know each other, and then I'd ask him what the hell was going on.

Platter in hand, I came to the bottom of the stairs, knocked the door open with a foot, and stepped over the threshold.

The old man was sitting at the table. He had been reading. Hearing me come in, he looked up, frowned, closed over the book and pushed back his chair.

'No food or drink,' he hissed, stalking over towards me. His voice rose as he came nearer the door. 'Rule number two. No food or drink.' He took the platter from my hands, swept past me and out through the door. 'No respect these days,' I heard him mutter, 'No respect for the rules.'

I followed him into the stairwell: he was flying up the stairs, his skirts flapping. I climbed after him, back on to the deck. He was heading forward, to the galley. I was surprised to find he could move so fast. When I came to the galley door, he'd placed the platter on the table, crossed over to the water-purifier and was peering into the empty jug. He glanced up at me. I looked straight back.

He sat down at the table and began to eat. I pulled back a bench and sat down opposite him. He looked up at me through his eyebrows, continued chewing. I reached out and took a piece of bread, peeled off the crust, and was just formulating my first question, when he spoke.

'What are you doing here?' he asked.

What am *I* doing here? I wanted to say. What are *you* doing here, and where is here, and what the hell is going on? But when I opened my mouth, nothing came out. I'd forgotten. Somehow it had slipped my mind that I could no longer talk. I hadn't needed to, for so long. The last words I'd said were 'I loved you', and it seemed that it was someone else who had spoken them.

'I suppose you take me for a fool?'

I looked up. I was going to have to say something, or at least try to. Something uncomplicated, to start with. I took another sip of beer.

'No,' I said, a faint and draughty sound.

The old man frowned.

'You think I'm just some credulous old pedant with his head buried in his books –'

Again, I had to settle for just saying 'No,' though by this stage I wasn't so sure what I was denying. But the word came out a little clearer this time. A smile began to pull at the corners of my lips.

'Who sent you? Hamelius, was it? De Outremeuse?'

'Nobody,' I said. 'Nobody sent me.' The words were coming back. My smile broadened. But the old man wasn't listening, he wasn't looking at me. His eyes had glazed over. I lifted my cup, took another gulp of beer. It seemed to be helping.

'It isn't too much to ask, is it? A little privacy? No one looking over my shoulder. No one sneaking in at night and rifling through my manuscripts. A little professional courtesy?'

'I don't want to seem ungrateful,' I said, each word coming easier than the one before, 'After you saving my life and all; I can tell you're quite worked up about something, but to be honest with you, I don't have a clue what you're talking about.'

'What?'

'I mean –' I swigged some more beer. 'I mean, what the hell is going on? There's no crew, you've spread no canvas, you're going nowhere. You're just drifting. In the middle of the ocean.'

He reached out to the platter and picked up a lump of cheese. He pulled it in two between his dusty fingertips, replaced one half.

'I do not consider it drifting,' he said, putting the cheese down, picking it up again. 'And I am not, as you put it, "going nowhere". I am closer than I've ever been. It's all coming together – that was the problem, you see – they knew it, they saw what I was about to achieve and – that's why I had to get rid of them.'

Them? Did he mean his crew? Had he killed them? Was I drifting in the middle of the ocean with a murderer? Suddenly, my regaining the ability to speak did not seem so important. How would he have done it? Poison? I dropped my crust back on to the table. He was still eating, though.

'You're a scholar, then, I take it?' he said through a mouthful.

'What?'

'A scholar. You must have studied.'

'No. I'm a sailor.'

'You would say that.'

'Yes, I would, because it's true.'

I looked down at the almost empty beer-cup, realized I must already be half drunk, and tried to call my thoughts together. I remembered the soft cold feel of a slate against my palm, the smooth glide as I guided my hand round the loops and dips of the alphabet, the smell of chalkdust. 'I know my numbers one-to-ten,' I said, putting down the cup, my fingers instinctively counting out the numbers as I spoke. 'And I can write my name, I can read a little, but that's all.'

'Of course you'd say that. If anything, it's evidence against you, saying that.'

I looked down at my hands, palms up and fingers curled from counting. There were calluses on my palms, yellowed hardnesses on the pads and along the fingers' edges. I turned them over, looked at the sundarkened skin, the scars that laced and pocked their backs. I blinked, held my hands out towards him.

'Look,' I said. 'These aren't scholar's hands.'

He took them between his cold dry fingers, held them for a moment palm up, then turned them over. The lines on his face shifted and looked uncomfortable for a moment, like hair combed the wrong way. He let go of my hands and looked up at me. 'It's not *proof* of anything,' he said. 'Evidence, perhaps, but not proof.' A pause. The water-purifier gave off a hiss: he stood up and moved across to fiddle with it. Then he turned back to me. 'If you weren't sent here to spy on me how did you end up here? You say you're a sailor but where's your ship? There's no sign of wreckage, no corpses, no other survivors, not even a spar for you to cling to: just you, drowning all by yourself in the middle of the ocean. Just where I'd happen to be passing. I find it very hard to believe it could just be coincidence.'

'You weren't passing. You were drifting.'

He narrowed his eyes at me. 'I know a spy when I see one.'

I narrowed my eyes back at him.

'If I'm a spy and you know a spy when you see one, then why did you pick me up?'

There was a long pause. He pursed his lips. When he spoke again, if it hadn't been for the beer, and for the unfamiliar words, I would have realized that what he was telling me was not quite the truth.

'I should never have started on the *Nichomachean Ethics*. I knew it would only lead to trouble. How could I let you drown after that?'

I just looked at him.

'Wha'?'

He waved the question away.

'It's beside the point. The point is, you have yet to tell me why you are here.'

I sat back and considered this a moment, my mind grown flabby and unwilling with drink and fatigue. I remembered the slaves I had set free: I brought my hand up to my chin and touched its tenderness. I remembered the lash peeling the skin from off my back, and before that, McMichaels at his desk, and the way the light was refracted by his cut glass inkwell. I remembered John Doyle; I could almost feel her teeth grazing my flesh, her hands on my body. I could almost smell her skin. I remembered, before that, Joe's lean body on mine and the smell of heath and heather. I remembered the rain falling on my face the night we left the village. I remembered the foul taste of drought in my mouth, the pain of Uncle George's belt across my back. My father had died, and I had tucked a blanket round his toes. The circus had left a circle on the green, where the grass caught the light at a different angle. I had heard a mermaid singing, had watched her in the moonlight as she painted her nails.

'I was looking for a mermaid,' I said.

He nodded.

'Then you're a fool,' he said. 'They don't exist.'

I leaned forward.

'Yes they do. I've seen them.'

He looked at me. 'And what's it worth, the word of a self-confessed semi-literate deckhand? I'm a scholar, and I am telling you, they don't exist. It's a myth.'

By now I was barely listening. I was boiling with hostility.

'My mother was a mermaid,' I said.

'I'll hazard a guess that you never knew her? Someone told you she was a mermaid?'

'My Da –'

'Well there you are then. It's a euphemism.' He leaned back, a fingertip placed on his upper lip. 'Or maybe it's slang.'

'What's a euphemism? What are you saying? That he lied to me?'

'It's like a lie. He might have said your mother was a mermaid, but what he really meant was that she was a whore.'

It was then that I decided he was the enemy. I'd have nothing more to do with him.

And it was also then that the old man decided that I was not a threat. Now that he considered me a fool, he became suddenly loquacious.

He informed me that his name was Jebb, that his ship was called the *Spendlove,* and that I would be allowed to roam the vessel at will, so long as I stayed away from the library and did not distract him. If I should happen to stumble in upon him at his books, I was to be sure to observe the four cardinal rules of the place. He explained them slowly, as befitted my idiocy, counting them off one by one on his fingertips: Rule One: no talking; Rule Two: no food or drink; Rule Three: no inkpots, and Rule Four: no livestock. I nodded along as he spoke, but was barely listening. The fact was, I had no intention of disturbing him. I had no intention of going anywhere near his library. I was going to be far too busy.

There was a great deal of work to be done. If there hadn't been all the time in the world, and nothing else to do, I would have thought that it was hopeless. As it was, I decided not to think about it. I just started work on repairing the *Spendlove.*

If Jebb had enquired, and he didn't, why I was doing it, I would probably have said that it was some kind of reparation for his hospitality, for fishing me out of the water and accommodating me on board. It wouldn't have been entirely untrue: I was looking on it as a prophylactic against meeting the same fate as his crew. But when I think about it now, I realize that it was in part instinctive, a defence against the solitude in which I found myself. I needed something to console myself with. I needed to lose myself in something. And I knew, I was reminded every time my hand raised itself to touch the pendant at my throat, that there was joy to be found in a job well done, and pleasure to be taken from the quiet and proper practice of a skill.

But even that was an effect, rather than a cause. I needed to repair her because I was going to sail her. I would get her shipshape, then I would turn her round and sail back the way I'd come. I was going to find that shoal of mermaids. I was going to find my mother.

The idea of sailing her singlehandedly was daunting, but it seemed so far off that it didn't seem worth worrying about. Even the simplest of tasks seemed to take so long. I just didn't have the vigour that I'd once possessed. It had worn me threadbare, my time at sea.

But I began to get things done. I took stock of the state of the rigging. Cautiously, dizzily, I climbed. Not nearly so high as on board the *Sally Ann*, but I lost my nerve nonetheless, and clung like a treemouse to the yard, eyes shut, swallowing back the sickness that was rising up my throat. I managed to cut the remaining shreds of canvas away, but came back down shaking, slowly, with no one there to guide my foot from stay to stay. I found spare sails, rolled up and stuffed under a table in the cuddy: some of the canvas had rotted into dark patches, holes: I cannibalized a spritsail and began repairing them.

The days confirmed that we were drifting south, carried only by the ocean's pull. The sun rose to port, sank starboard: by night the stars grew unfamiliar. With every passing day the air was growing colder, drier; the sea had taken on a jewelled, translucent blueness, like a summer evening. Leaning over the rails I sometimes saw dark, vast shapes moving beneath the surface of the water, heading south. Purposeful, going faster than the ship.

It was quiet. Always quiet. The slop of waves against the hull, the hiss of wind through the bare ropes, the creak of the undirected ship served only to reinforce the utter isolation in which I found myself. Leaning over the rail, I watched those dark leviathans moving through the water, heading ever south in their ceaseless, companionable procession. It was infuriating, the knowledge that every day was pulling me further away, was making it more difficult for me to get back to where I'd come from. I tried to drive myself harder, to work more quickly, but I kept making mistakes, making more work, hurting myself. My body was like a tired child: it could not be persuaded. I had to give in to it and let it rest.

Not that I could sleep, though. Not normal, eight-hour, night-filling sleep. Perhaps I had slept too long already, used up months' worth of my nightly allocation lying there on the reading desk while Jebb piled mounds of books around my sleeping form. As we drifted ever further south, the days seemed to stretch themselves, grow transparent at the edges. The hours of darkness dwindled to an eyeblink, to a twilight blueness.

I found boots, leggings and a sealskin coat in among the stores. Muffled from feet to chin, hood pulled tight against the cold, I watched my breath cloud the air, was distracted by grains of ice on my eyelashes. On the horizon there was whiteness, like mist on a river.

Buried in the shadowy corner beneath the gallery,

hunched into the antipodean chill, Jebb emerged only to
shelve or reshelve a volume, or to shamble over to the
reading desk and pore over a page for hours, making
notes in his scratchy, ugly handwriting. And he slept,
still: in spite of the extended daylight he never seemed to
have any trouble sleeping. A creature of habit, the hours
could still be measured by his actions when they could
no longer be determined by the sun and stars. I knew that
it was morning when he came up from his cabin, ate
breakfast, squatted on the glorybox, and then went down
into the library. I knew that it was evening when he
emerged blinking and abstracted, ate dinner, and then
promenaded round the deck, smoking his pipe. I knew
that it was night-time again when he went back down to
his cabin to read. He would yawn once, twice, and then
his lamp would snuff out. A rhythmic rattle would start
up: he would snore until the morning.

It wasn't that I was spying on him; at least, not in the
sense that he'd imagined. It was just that I'd come to feel
so lonely, so utterly bereft, that even though I'd told
myself I would ignore him, I found myself shadowing
him for the illusion of companionship it gave, for the
ghost of structure and meaning it added to my day.

It was during one of his evening walks, though the sun
was as high and the sky as pale as midday, that I watched
him notice, for the first time, that there was something
different about the ship. At first he moved as usual, head
down, hands behind his back, watching, if indeed he saw
anything at all, his own feet in their grey canvas slippers.
Without probably having ever been conscious of the

clutter of tackle and gear, he must have nonetheless become gradually aware that there was now nothing to trip over, nothing to snag at his feet as he took his walk. I watched him stop, glance around where he was standing, then lift his head to look beyond, at the rest of the deck, at the masts, rigging, sails. Then he turned back to look at me. I crossed over to him, wiping my hands on the seat of my trousers.

'You did all this?' he said.

'Yes.'

He looked round the ship again. 'You're not altogether stupid after all.'

'Is that so?'

'At least,' he said thoughtfully, reassessing his statement, 'you seem to be possessed of some kind of instinctive capacity, a practical cleverness that, while it is not without its uses, has almost certainly got nothing whatsoever to do with intelligence.'

'Oh really.'

'It's some kind of learned instinct. Conditioning, if you like. After all, you're a sailor,' he said, turning away to resume his circuit of the ship. 'It's what you do.'

I watched as he continued his walk, head bent, hands clasped behind his back. He didn't look my way again: I had already been dismissed from his thoughts. His exercise concluded, he went below. I waited for a moment, then picked my way down the stairs after him. Like every other night he would lie in his cot turning the pages of his dusty volumes, running a dry finger along the lines of script, though outside the sky was still as blue as a harebell, and the sun was just poised above the horizon, and would not, this evening, ever set.

An arc of lamplight spilled across the floor. I curled myself into a corner of the stairwell, wrapped my arms around my knees. It was draughty, cold: a deep shiver rippled through me, leaving an afterswell of warmth. Punctuating the silence, I heard the dry rustle of old pages being turned. Then, after what seemed like hours, I heard the old man yawn. So his eyelids would be drooping: he'd be struggling to focus on the page. The book would teeter in his grip. He yawned again. He'd slip the marker between the pages, slot the book on to the shelf beside his bed. I heard a sigh, then the sound of bedclothes being moved, then the arc of light was gone like a fan snapped shut. I sat on in the darkness until I heard the first snore. Then I straightened up, put a hand to the wall, felt around for the library door.

I'd show him who was stupid.

The blue light of the southern summer night streamed in through the high windows, the icy green of the seawater pressed up against the portholes. And along the walls and piled on the floor and heaped upon seats and stacked on the desk, were his books.

This was what made him think he was so clever. This was what made him think he had the authority to pronounce sentence on my mother, my Da and me.

Any fool could read a book, I told myself. Even me.

At first I selected them without thought or reason. My hand kept stretching itself out towards the books with the most alluring bindings, the richest colours. The first volume I pulled off the shelf was bottle-green with gold lettering embossed along the spine. I leafed through the pages, stopping every so often to try to pick out the words, to put them together into sense. But it wasn't as easy as I had expected. The words were often long and unfamiliar, and there were no pictures. Still, I thought, there were plenty more to choose from. I placed the book back into its niche between a claret and a blue and walked on down the shelves. I ran my fingers down the books' spines as I moved along. I half expected them to ring out as I touched them, each volume chiming clear and different, according to its content. But it was not, I'd begun to realize, going to be as simple as that. I picked out another, then another, and another, but couldn't make anything of them.

How to get through the dark mesh of those black and scratchy marks? My schooling had been at best sketchy, and it seemed a lifetime since Miss Woodend had battered the basics into us. There hadn't been much call for reading since. I remembered the agent's ledger back in Sailortown, and writing my own name, and how it hadn't looked like me.

I had come to the end of one shelved wall and was about to turn the corner, when my fingertips seemed to snag on something. A dark and worn-looking spine. I pulled the book out, turned it over in my hands. It wasn't like the others I had chosen: no gold lettering, no coloured binding, but something seemed to be drawing me to it. It was almost warm to the touch, its skin soft against my palms, and it seemed to fit into my hands as if made for them. I lifted back the cover, I turned the leaves. It had pictures.

A lithe beast with a curling mane and tail, with cruel claws hooked from each of its four feet, glaring out at me with the features of a man. I flicked forward: men with horses' legs, men with goats' legs, one creature that was half-bird half-beast. Every one of them caught between two natures. There was even a blank-eyed young person blessed with both breasts and a prick. The images were coarse, unsubtle, unlike the suave engravings in McMichaels' book. The artist had drawn savagery into these beings' features, but despite the cruelty of their expressions, I thought that they looked sad. Where, I wondered, could they belong, in this world? Where would they find peace?

I turned another page. The picture was like all the others, depicting a half-formed thing, a creature at once fierce and sad. I looked from engraving to text, from text to engraving, desperate to make the words make sense. Because I could see from the picture, though it was crude and harsh, though it did not capture the ineffable grace of their being, or the community of their kind, though it was monochrome while they were brilliant, and coarse though they were fine, that the artist had seen, somewhere, a mermaid.

The rigging sang with ice. My breath fogged the air in front of me. Everything loose had been battened down, everything broken had been fixed; the ship, which had been teetering on the brink of decrepitude, had been nudged back, had settled into order. There was nothing else to do. Up ahead, there seemed to be white clouds massing low on the horizon.

Inside my skull, a whole world had unfolded, flowered.

It had taken me the entire darkless southern night to pick out the sense of one paragraph of that book. Before I'd even finished to my satisfaction, I heard Jebb moving about in his room, then climbing the stairs for his morning walk. I stuffed the book back in its place and crept up the stairs behind him, crossed the deck unseen. I sparked a flame in the galley. Salt water boiled, steam hissed and condensation trickled in the purifier. I set a pan to heat, broke eggs on its rim. The smell of cooking quickened his footsteps, even brought him a little early to his breakfast.

The following night, slowly, my finger smudging the print, I spelt out the rest of the page. Some patterns were repeated again and again, with variations, like a melody: I began to detect refinements of emphasis, changes in nuance. Some words only appeared once, and were bold and black and difficult as iron bars. But sometimes whole phrases and sentences which had eluded me for hours would suddenly come clear, the letters melting away before my eyes, and I was beyond the black barrier of ink and into colour: I saw places, peoples, fabulous animals. I was elsewhere.

Once there, there was no stopping me. I would read all night, and only stop when I heard Jebb's feet hit the deck in the morning. Then I'd stuff the book back into its place, rush up the stairs, dive into the galley and make a start on breakfast.

At first I read everything, fretted over every word, sounding out the syllables over and over, desperate to miss nothing, to make every little thing blossom into sense. But before long I became confident, reckless: I skipped phrases, letters, guessed at things. I put down books if they did not, after some little effort on my part, open themselves up to me. Unbeknownst to Jebb, I read my way, in a somewhat haphazard and capricious fashion, through a good part of his collection.

Morning. I was still vague and blinking from a long night's study, though Jebb of course was completely oblivious. We had eaten breakfast wordlessly, his eyes barely leaving his plate. Now he was on his way below, trudging down the stairs to the library. I always made sure to put everything back where it belonged down there: a book out of place was one thing he'd be sure to notice. Though if he went straight to the desk, he might find that the seat was warm, I thought, so recently had I left it.

I finished rinsing off the crocks, dried them and put them away. Then I hefted the washpot on to my hip and went out on to the deck. He would already be buried in a book by now, I thought, and then found myself wondering which one, and what he thought of it. I leaned over the side, watched the washing-water crash into the ocean's surface, watched the lighter patch disperse into the denser blue. I put the pot down on to the deck and leant on the rail a moment. I could feel the ghost-weight of the volumes in my hands. When I closed my eyes, my eyelids swam with words. I recalled the electric shiver I'd felt as I realized the incremental weight of what I'd found, these past few nights, down there in the library. There was no dismissing it. It was mentioned time and time again, in all the best sources, in travels, bestiaries and cyclopaedias. The centre of it all, the hub of their world: where they came from, where they departed to; where they were born and bred and went to die. In the centre of a great ocean, a sea as white as milk. The mermaids' home. His books hadn't just confirmed that they existed, they had told me where to find them.

The discovery had left me glowing. I'd been smiling ever since.

But I would wait till evening, I'd decided, until he came up from the library, before I told him. For now, I would just savour the knowledge. I'd enjoy the fact that he was wrong.

I looked down at my hands resting on the rail. The fingers were raw and pink. I brought them to my mouth and blew on them. Must be getting pretty far south by now. I glanced up ahead. That could not be right, I thought. That could not be right.

Ice. Cliffs towered above the ship. Up close, undeniable, cold as Hell's ninth circle. Surf was crashing and thundering against the cliffs, sending spray high up into the air. This was what I'd taken for mist, for clouds on the horizon. I glanced up, around, but could see nothing beyond, nothing but the spray and the ice. We were ploughing straight for it.

I'd read about this. The world's end. All the oceans of the earth must flow underneath this ice and cascade

down into infinity. And they would carry us along with
them.

I ran down the stairs and burst through the library
doors.

Jebb was sitting at the desk, hunched in on himself
like a crumpled sock. His fingertip had been moving
across the page, but it came to a halt at my entrance. He
looked up. His face creased, his eyes narrowing. I went
over to the desk.

'I need your help.'

'Ssshhhh.'

I planted my hands on the desk, leaned in.

'I need it now.'

'Get out of my library.'

'Listen –'

'I will not listen. If past events are anything to go by,
you've probably just mended some idiotically-named
piece of equipment and you're looking for praise.' His
eyes flicked back up at me. 'Well done,' he said. 'Now
run along. I have work to do.'

He gestured to the book. I leaned across, picked it up
and flipped it shut.

'You can read that any time,' I said. 'I need you now.
We're coming up on ice. If we don't act now the
Spendlove will be smashed to pieces. All your books, all
your manuscripts, everything you've ever worked for,
gone. In an instant, for ever.'

I was aloft, struggling numb-fingered with the reef points
I'd tied not so long before. The wind had shifted round. I

felt it stir my hair, touch my face; it smelt cold and clean and peppery. I had to get at least one of these sails unfurled, but the knots had got wet: they'd not only tightened, they'd frozen solid into little twisted blocks of ice. I found myself glancing ahead every couple of seconds, I couldn't help myself, even though I knew each glance was costing me time. That peppery smell on the wind was the smell of the ice, I realized: it was making my nose prickle, my eyes water. Finally, one of the knots came undone between my fingers, the canvas shifted, settled, and I moved on to the next reef point, glancing up again as I slid myself along. A lurch in my belly: the cliffs were already so much closer; closer than I'd counted on. Another knot came undone between my fingertips and I shuffled on to the next. Just two more to go, three including this one. I tugged at the neat tight arcs of cord, trying to tease in some slackness, but these last few seemed even more unshiftable than the others: they had been pulled still tighter by the weight of the canvas hanging on them. They would not budge. I glanced up at the cliffs. Stupid to think that I could do it. No one in their right mind would think they could unfurl this mainsail single-handed, let alone make the turn I was attempting. I wrenched harder at the rope and a fingernail peeled back and away. The flesh was raw and began to bleed, but the knot had loosened. I pulled at the loops, teasing them apart: the knot came undone. I moved on to the next, tugged at it, another nail and then another tearing off below the quick. By the time I had loosened the final reef point my hands were running with blood. I swung myself back to the mast and scurried down the shroud like a rat, without any fear of falling. I ran over to the halyards, unhitched them, and let the canvas fall. The satisfying rush of air as it spread. It caught the wind, the boom jibbed, and the ship began to slow. I looked ahead, beyond, towards the ice. I would never get the full rig spread in time. I glanced round towards the helm. There wasn't even time, I realized, to spread another sail.

I'd told Jebb to man the helm, but he was just standing there, doing nothing. His gown fluttered round him, his hair and beard were lifted, tugged at by the wind, but otherwise, he was still. I dashed past him, grabbed the wheel, began heaving it round.

'I told you,' I shouted at him, 'I told you to heave hard for port.'

I pushed my weight against the momentum of the ship, the mass of water beneath, the determination of its current.

'My books –' Jebb said.

I shifted myself to hang from the wheel, pulling down on a spoke with all my strength.

'Here,' I said, 'just catch hold of this –'

'My life's work – everything I've ever –' he said, and still didn't move.

'Take hold of it and push down–'

'I can't look – I can't – Oh my God.'

Then he sat down on the deck, put his face in his hands, and didn't say another word.

Through the thrum of blood in my ears I could already

hear the breakers on the cliffs. But there was something else. I could feel it, in the timbers of the ship, in the touch of the wind: the *Spendlove* was beginning, ever so slightly, to turn.

A shadow fell across the deck. I looked up. The cliffs were looming up above the ship, higher than the bowsprit, higher than the maintop, sheer. Out of the sun, they no longer appeared white: the ice was deep blue, as if the missing hours of darkness had been trapped there and frozen solid. The *Spendlove* was turning, slowly, degree by degree, to sail alongside the base, but the turn we were taking seemed desperately shallow, and I could give her no more helm: the wheel was already at full turn. I shifted my weight again, was practically standing on my hands to keep her steady. I dragged a coil of rope closer with a foot and, still pressing down with all my weight, began to lash the helm.

'Jebb,' I said.

'My books,' he said. 'My beautiful books.'

The wind was favouring us, thank God: the sail was full, pulling her round, but the ship's timbers groaned with the strain, and we were edging ever closer to the foot of the cliffs. I ran up to the foredeck, leaping over ropes and tackle, and skidded to a halt.

Up close, the ice was radiant with cold, its dark blue streaked with paler tones, with veins of green and yellow. Here and there a fracture in the ice had caught a rainbow, frozen it. The *Spendlove*'s prow had nudged past, her flank was turning to the cliffs, and I thought for a blessed moment we were clear, that we would sail round and away, out into the sunlight. But then the ship bucked, the boards beneath me shuddered, and I stumbled, lost my balance, and fell.

There was a sound of groaning, tearing, as if the ship were being ripped apart, as if she were giving birth. A shiver rippled through her. Pressed flat against the deck, I felt it through my ribcage, my fingertips, my palms and cheek. It shook the air out of my lungs. I pushed down on my hands, heaved myself upright. The boards still shuddering beneath me, I scanned around. We were still moving, I realized, but only just. There must have been an outcrop, a reef of ice beneath the water's surface: we had caught it on the cusp of the turn. The hull was scraping along it, splintering, dragged on by the bellying sail. I staggered across the deck, leaned over the side. I could see nothing but rough dark waves and foam; salt spray hit my face. The sheer wall of ice was close enough to spit at. All that spray — of course there would be something under the water's surface. Stood to reason. I should have expected it. Stupid. Damn stupid fool I was, thinking that I'd to get away with it. I put a hand to the rail, bloody fingertips blindly finding the wood's grain and following it. I'd failed. Instead of ploughing straight into the cliffs, instead of being smashed to pieces in an instant, I'd just dragged out our deaths. We were stuck here for ever. As the food and fuel ran out, as the cold clamped down, as the waves and weather picked the ship apart, I'd be trying to hold it together, patching at patches, clinging spray-soaked to the ship's ladder to hammer at the keel, and Jebb would be down in his library, his feet in saltwater and his head in a book. And I'd never find my mother.

There was something cold on my cheek. I plucked it off examined for a puzzled moment a misty gem of ice between my bloodied fingertips. A tear, I realized, and dropped it to brush away another.

The groaning sound had refined into a shriek. Running one hand along the rail, brushing frozen tears from my face with the other, I moved up towards the prow, numb but for the aching knot inside me, the throb of pain from my fingertips. Jebb had been right. He'd been right about me from the word go. I *was* a fool. I was stupid. Even what little sense he'd credited me with, what he'd called my instinctive capacities as a sailor, had proved insufficient the one and only time they had really been put to the test. I was useless, worthless: I was capable of nothing. That's why everybody left me: that's why they always would. I came to a halt at the prow. Soon, we would grind, would shiver to a halt, I thought, and that would be it. Just half a dozen bantam hens and Jebb for company, for ever. I glanced back at the ship's boat, where the bantams nested. Open-topped, single-sailed. Could I get anywhere in that? Could I sail that from the lee of the wreck and just leave Jebb here to continue his work in peace? He should be happy enough. There'd be no one to spy on him here.

I was just moving over towards the boat, just beginning to consider its possibilities, when something caught my attention. I stopped dead, cocked my head, listening. The tearing, grating shriek: had it softened a little? I

crouched down, placed a palm on the deck. Were the
boards a little steadier? I straightened up, looked back
round towards the prow: there was no mistaking it: the
Spendlove was nosing out into clear water. She might just
make it, I realized, my flesh beginning to prickle. She
might just make the turn. I raced back again towards the
foredeck. The cliff's shadows peeled back and I was
suddenly in sun. Overhead, the sails flapped, the boom
jibbed, and beneath my feet I felt the ship shift, lift and
slip free from whatever it was that had held her. We were
clear. We were free. I stood there blinking a moment,
conscious only of the sunlight on my face, of the cold
peppery wind stirring my hair, filling the sails. Then I
shook myself. I had to get the wheel unlashed, get her
out of the turn before she circled back round towards the
cliffs a second time and wrecked herself permanently on
that outcrop. As I ran for the wheel, the tears were
coming thick and fast. I brushed them away, and they
clattered, milky as moonstones, on to the deck behind
me.

Jebb was still there by the helm, but now he was
standing again, and blinking in the light. I skidded to a
halt next to him and hunkered down to unpick the hitch.
My fingers were torn and sore: despite the urgency of the
situation they moved hesitantly, indecisively. Jebb
crouched down at my side and I caught a whiff of him:
dust, the sour smell of old books and unwashed body. He
stretched out his greyed, ink-stained fingers towards the
rope.

'I'll do it,' he said.

I shuffled back a little, making room for his smell, but did not stop picking at the cord. He pushed my hands away.

'Just tell me what to do,' he said. He looked at me. 'I'll do it. Just tell me.'

A moment. I settled back upon my heels and stretched out a fingertip, dark with drying blood.

'There,' I said. 'See that loop there –'

And Jebb's strong yellow fingernails began to unpick the knot. I watched as the cord came loose between his fingernails, watched the shifting grain of his knuckles, the movements of his fingers as he picked apart the rest of the hitch. He stood to unwind the rope through the spokes of the wheel and I straightened up beside him. The wheel began to turn slowly, to find its way towards the following wind. I took hold of it, passed it round through my hands, helping it back towards its line. The sunlight cut across the deck, casting a net of shadows from the rigging.

'What you did there –' he said.

'Yes,' I said.

He just shook his head.

I felt the air fill my lungs, the sunshine warm my skin, felt the continuing solidity of the deck beneath my feet. The wood was warm and curved beneath my palms, it seemed to pulse as my flesh pulsed. I felt that I could almost see the wind, hear the watercurrents flow, taste the time of day.

Eleven

'I don't recall giving you permission.'

I put down my cup.

'You never said I couldn't. You just said no ink, no livestock, no food. You never said no reading.'

He raised a hand.

'Just a little professional courtesy. That's all I ask.'

'That goes,' I said, 'both ways.'

Jebb hesitated a moment, then nodded.

'Fair enough.'

The galley flame was flickering. The air was warm and stuffy. The day had melted round the edges and grown soft. I'd washed the blood from my hands with salt water, tied the worst-torn fingers with scraps of rag. We'd broached a fresh barrel of beer and were a quart gone, both of us, by then. Jebb had produced a spare pipe for me from somewhere and we were smoking. The tobacco-smell had brought first my father and then John to mind. I'd been trying, unsuccessfully, to blow smoke-rings.

The coughing made my eyes water. The tobacco had a taint of mud and mould about it, as if it had been stored somewhere damp. I drank to clear the taste, and my hands shook as they brought the cup to my lips. They'd been shaking ever since we'd cleared the ice. The beer got on the bandages, stung at my torn quicks.

Jebb was talking, saying something about the poor state of the tobacco, then praising the quality of the beer, but it was clear he wasn't really interested in the smoke or drink. He just needed to talk, to fill up the space between us. The day's events had softened him towards me, I realized. It seemed he no longer considered me a fool, or a threat.

'Why did you think I was a spy?' I asked.

Jebb was tamping down the tobacco in his pipe. He looked up at me. He might have begun to trust me, but he still couldn't quite manage to be courteous.

'My collection – over which you have been running your grubby little hands – has been half a lifetime in the building. It contains some of the most exquisite, rare and valuable books in existence,' he said. 'Though I don't suppose you noticed.'

'Wouldn't that make it more likely I was a thief than –' I began to say, but he held up a hand, stopping me.

'I have spent half a lifetime studying these volumes. I could name a dozen people, without any difficulty, who would give their eyes to get the credit for my work. That's if they're still alive.'

'So is that why you're out here, drifting? To stay away from them? You thought one of them had sent me?'

He nodded. 'Though drifting does not adequately describe what I have achieved. My catalogue alone is a wonder to behold. My Grand Concordance, when it is finished, will be a marvel.'

'So if you spent half a lifetime gathering the books,' I said, 'and half a lifetime studying them, shouldn't you be dead by now?'

'That depends on whose lifetime we're talking about.'

I drained the last of the beer from my cup, refilled it.

'So who's this work for, then?' I asked.

He paused a moment, leaned back, and looked me in the eye.

'For posterity,' he said.

While Jebb talked on, I sipped my beer and tried to listen.

His suspicions hadn't fallen on me alone, it transpired: he hadn't trusted his crew, but he hadn't killed them either – he'd cut the anchor rope when they were off foraging on shore. They'd rowed after him a while, he said, but the *Spendlove* still had sails back then, and there had been a wind. Before long the words began to smudge in together and become as meaningless to me as the bantams' sleepy crooning. I settled back into a warm fuzz of drunkenness. I felt exhausted and content. I had a ship now, I had my freedom, and I knew what I was looking for.

After a while, I noticed that he had fallen silent. The only sounds were the flames crackling in the stove, the water bubbling and dripping in the purifier. I looked up, opening my mouth to speak. He was watching the water condense, drip, and as I looked at him a droplet gathered on the tip of his nose, and fell.

It was then that I realized that he hadn't quite told me the truth. It wasn't ethics that had made him save me. He had been alone for so long that he hadn't known how lonely he was until he'd found me. Floating broken and half-drowned in the middle of the ocean, I must have seemed like a miracle to him.

'The white sea? You thought I didn't know about that?'

We were in the library. Jebb was leaning forward over his book, finger marking the point where I'd made him break off. For him it was the following morning. For me, drunkenness had turned into hangover without the benefit of sleep. Chin on folded arms, I was looking at him gritty-eyed underneath the green shades of the reading lamps.

'I just assumed that if you'd been aware of it, and had the opportunity, you would have investigated it. Being a scholar and everything,' I said.

He leaned back and folded his arms, looked at me.

'Why would I want to do that?'

'Because you'd want to get your facts right before you pronounced judgement. Before you went and called someone a liar.'

'I don't need to. I know that it's a myth,' he said.

'There are dozens of accounts. Some of them are centuries old.'

He snorted.

'It's the nature of myth to be old. And anything recent

is just a reworking of the old stories. I can't believe you've been wasting your time on this nonsense, when there's so much else you could be –'

'There must be a germ of truth,' I said. 'You can't be sure, you can't *know* unless –'

'I know. Believe me. Save yourself the trouble and take my word for it: the white sea does not exist. Mermaids do not exist. It's all just fantasy and fabrication.'

I leaned back, folded my arms and glared at him.

'Prove it,' I said.

Underneath his eyes the creases shifted a little. Something like the beginning of a smile.

'I am entirely satisfied in my own mind.'

'Yes, but you can't prove it.'

'I can tell you now you'll never find anything.'

'It still wouldn't mean it didn't exist.'

'You could spend a lifetime searching.'

I shrugged.

'Maybe,' I said, 'but I can't just drift.'

I had no crew, no charts, and no training in navigation. And even if I had had them, I still wouldn't have known where I was starting from, or where exactly it was that I wanted to go. What seemed to be the earliest account placed the white sea in the middle of an ocean. So, looking at it one way, I wasn't doing too badly. It was the one thing I knew for certain, that we were drifting around in an ocean. But looking at it from any other perspective at all, the situation was hopeless. It wasn't necessarily this ocean. And the writer of this account hadn't even seen the sea himself, he'd heard tell of it from an ancient sailor, and could only repeat what he'd been told. Another, more recent account contained a very similar description, but in this case the writer claimed he'd seen the white sea for himself. He had, he said, been on board a ship that had passed too close to it and one of the crew had been maddened by the mermaids' singing. He had dived overboard to be with them, and on hitting the water's surface had been turned, in an instant, into stone. The seabed all around was littered with statues of diving, leaping figures. Having closely studied this account, Jebb concluded that it was an appropriation of and embroidery on the earlier story, which was itself a piece of sensationalist nonsense. Another version dismissed the notion that the place was inhabited by mermaids, but considered the sea itself an interesting topic for enquiry. A mineral in solution, the writer suggested, or excessive salinity, or the suspension in the water of millions of tiny bubbles from volcanic activity beneath the surface, were possible causes of the water turning white.

It wasn't much to go on.

The only map that Jebb possessed was unfathomable to me: its script was crabbed and obscure, and I couldn't make out a word. On vellum traced with the veins and arteries of its donors' flesh, it showed a disc of land riddled by seas, ringed by a strip of island-dotted ocean. I spotted a red sea but couldn't find a white one. But near the bottom of the map, at the edge of the world, was a tiny thick-nibbed sketch of a mermaid.

'See,' Jebb said. 'There's no white sea.'

'But there's a mermaid, look.'

'That's just decorative. It's marginalia.'

'So you're saying the mermaid's not real?'

'Of course it's not real.'

'It's not real, but it is on the map. Then the map's not reliable.'

'What?'

'The map. You can't trust it.'

'Well, no.'

'Then that explains why there's no white sea on it.'

He drew the map away, began to roll it. Another of those smiles that just creased the corners of his eyes.

'You might have to satisfy yourself with drifting after all,' he said. 'Given the situation, it could be the most effective strategy.'

But I was thinking back to the school of mermaids I'd seen flashing through the water like herring. So many of them in one place, and with such an air of purpose and direction. If I could just get back there, back the way I'd come to the point where I'd encountered them. But it wasn't possible. The winds were now taking us east and north, and there was no way I could pitch the *Spendlove* against them. A nerve twinged between my shoulder-blades. If I could get back to that moment and make it all happen differently.

I shook the thought away.

'We'll go with the prevailing winds,' I said. 'We'll follow the ocean's pull. It's better than nothing. At least we will be sailing. We will not drift.'

When the sun shone, the water became as blue as

forget-me-nots and the waves sparkled. I put away my
sealskin and from then on worked in shirtsleeves. The
sun creased my eyes, drew the cold from my bones.

I'd find myself resting a hand upon the ship's timbers,
feeling the sun's radiated warmth as if it were the
Spendlove's own life. I'd stroke the curve of the helm
wheel, would cup a palm around the camber of a mast as
I was passing by. I couldn't help but feel that she was
mine.

Sometimes, in the corner of my eye, I could almost see
a trace of land on the eastern horizon, but when I looked
directly, it seemed to melt away. I paid it little attention.
I wasn't interested in land.

It grew too hot to work in the middle of the day, in spite
of the breeze. I would sometimes let her ride at anchor at
these times, strip off my shirt and britches and drop down
into water. Sometimes I would just leave a line trailing
from her stern, dive off the prow and swim her length to
catch the rope and haul myself back on board.

Underwater, I'd run my hands over the belly of the
ship, over the scar where she had caught on the ice,
where the barnacles and algae had been scraped away.
Sometimes shoals of silver-sided fish flickered past. Hair
clouding the water, I would stretch out a hand towards
them, and maybe one, and then another, would turn,
pause to mouth at the hardened skin of my palm. And all
the while, beside me, just separated by the boards of the
hull, Jebb remained inside at his books, sweating, the
dust sticking to his sweat.

Jebb never seemed to care much about his physical

comfort. He treated his body as if it were merely a conveyance for his faculties: he provided it with the most basic of maintenance – plain food, the glorybox, his evening perambulation – but he didn't seem to see a need to indulge it in any way, apart from the occasional smoke, the odd cup of beer. His needs were few, and he seemed to have no wants. I certainly never caught him watching me, not even when I was swimming. But then, he must have already seen me naked when he rescued me. I can't have been a pretty sight.

Every time I peeled off my shirt, every time I raised my arms to dive, every stroke I made through the water, I was reminded of the thrashing, of the damage that covered my back from nape to hip. Skin like citrus peel, like elephant hide: it would not, I had come to realize, ever be the same again. Scars slinked over my shoulders and round my ribs; I caught sight of them if I turned my head. My new skin. My carapace.

Once when I was swimming underwater I noticed something floating above me, dark against the rippled mirror of the surface, round as a buoy. I kicked up to it, cupped it in my hands and lifted it above me. It was hard, hollow and fibrous; liquid sloshed around inside. It was difficult to get back on board, kept slipping from my grip.

'It's a coconut,' Jebb said.

'Oh?'

'I've seen pictures.'

'Can you eat them?'

I took a swing at the nutshell with a cleaver. Milky

juice sprayed into the air, spattering our faces, and the two halves of the nut rolled apart, cool white and fleshy, and smelling, irresistibly, of gorse flowers.

'Apparently,' Jebb said. 'But I have no intention of doing so.'

He wiped his face with a sleeve. I dug a knife into the flesh, pulled away a chunk, lifted it to my mouth. It tasted sweet and dense and rich. Its fibres lodged between my teeth.

Evening. The water dripping in the purifier. A stream of successful smoke-rings rising towards the ceiling. The same old arguments rehearsed again.

'Poppycock. You were hallucinating.'

'No, like I said, it wasn't just me – they all saw them, the whole crew.'

'Then either they were hallucinating too, or, more likely, you were deluded. You wanted to believe in it so much that you imagined they saw them too. You interpreted events to suit your view of things.'

Once more the ululating song was thickening the air around me, and I saw myself dragged back from the ship's rail, felt the grip of hands holding me, saw McMichaels' face uneasy and afraid, his fist swinging through the air towards my cheek. And then I remembered the rain falling the night we left the village. I'd believed that Joe had made it fall. I'd been wrong about that.

'Or you're lying to me,' Jebb added.

I shook my head.

'I'm not lying.'

'Well, in that case I bow to your superior wisdom,' he said. 'I'm obviously in the wrong. Please accept my apologies.'

I picked up the jug, sloshed beer into his cup.

'There are any number of references and pictures, you know there are. That little drawing on the map. A scholar such as yourself –'

'Doesn't mean a thing.' He shook his head. 'You can't trust books. You must have seen it yourself, they contradict each other, they obfuscate, they lie. Books are crooks.'

'And yet you love them.'

He looked up at me.

'They're beautiful,' he said. 'They're just beautiful. You must admit: the way they smell, the feel of them in your hands –'

'There's nothing worse,' I said, smiling at him, 'than a beautiful liar.'

He smiled back.

'I am not so easily seduced.'

And then he took out his pack of cards, and began to deal. He was still convinced, against all evidence to the contrary, that some day he would beat me.

Still no sleep. I spent the hours of darkness in the library, filling up the gaps. I studied languages and scripts as obstinate as rock; glossaries, indices, concordances. Pipe-smoke spooling up into the shadows, I leafed through astronomy and history, medical texts and missals, books of hours and books of natural philosophy. The nights passed by in a moment; dawn always came as a surprise. I got myself an education.

Other nights I'd watch the stars. Looking for familiar patterns, for brighter markers in the sky, listening to the creak of the *Spendlove*'s timbers, the faint hum from the rigging. The stars faded with the dawn. I'd walk up to the prow, unbuttoning my clothes as I went. At the rail I'd slough them off and dive out into the dark. The sea was warm by night, cool by day; always at odds with the dry world. I'd swim the length of the ship, each time toying with the notion that this would be the one occasion that I'd miss the trailing rope; that I'd have to watch, treading water, as the *Spendlove* ploughed away from me, became just a dot on the horizon. I would pull myself down into the water, long slow strokes into the warm dark, and as my chest tightened and my head began to pound with blood, something, some vague ache of recognition would begin to tug at me. A sense that I was just beyond, or just outside something. I'd want to pull down further, into the deep, to heave myself through this intangible barrier, but instead I'd find myself pulling up; strong, fast strokes I couldn't stop myself from making. My head would crash up through the surface, my lungs angrily suck in the cool night air. I'd shake the hair back from my face, gasping, catch at the trailing rope and drag myself back on board. And all day that ache would be there with me, and would never quite fade away.

It was on one of these dives that I saw the petalling pulse of a luminous jellyfish, and was suspended by a moment's memory. The circus tent. The brush of its fleshy warmth against my fingertips as I walked around it, the burning chill of fever, the smell of urine and vomit. I was suspended there, watching the light ripple and surge through the creature, but was aware only of the scents and sounds and lights of years ago. The creature pulsed, surged away, and I swam after it. Almost as transparent as the sea, its seemed entirely of its element. I would have followed it out of the ship's ambit and away, out of reach of the rope, had not a volley of bubbles rattled from my mouth and nose, my chest squeezing tight and desperate. Defeated, I pulled up towards the water's ceiling, crashed my head once more through into the air.

'Malin!' Jebb hollered my name. I heard him clattering up the steps below deck. 'Malin, have you seen?'

I straightened up, turned towards the hatch. This was new. I took the pipe out of my mouth, scratched at my cheek with the stem. Had he finally found something, some clinching piece of evidence? Had he constructed some devastating argument which would blow me entirely out of the water? I put back my shoulders, eased a crick out of my neck. I wouldn't let him win without a fight.

He came stumbling up on to deck, scanned around for me. His hair was wild, his eyes brilliant. He was empty-handed. Somehow I'd expected him to bring a book, to brandish it at me, to jab at the text with a fingernail.

'Look!' he said, coming up towards me. He could really move when he wanted to. He grabbed me by the arm, spun me round and dragged me over towards the rail. 'I was in the middle section of *De Tribus Impostoribus,*' he was saying, almost gabbling, 'and for some reason I just looked up.'

'Yes?'

He wrenched harder at my arm, urging me on.

'That was when I saw it, through the porthole – I saw –'

'What?'

He heaved me up against the rail, leaned over.

'Look,' he said.

I looked.

The sea was white.

White as milk in a bucket. Miles, leagues of it. Lapping at the *Spendlove*'s hull, pooling out around her, stretching out ahead as far as I could see. My throat tightened.

I turned on my heel and crossed back towards the mast. I climbed the shrouds. I remember the movement of my arms and legs as if I were watching myself climb. I was vividly conscious of Jebb standing beneath me on deck. At the masthead I raised a hand to shield my eyes. In the sunshine, the white water's glare was extra-ordinary, fierce.

'Can you see anything?' Jebb called from below.

'I don't know,' I said. Perhaps something. Something darker than the water, darting through it.

'I think I can see . . .'

'Yes – ?'

'Wait a minute.'

I began clambering back down the shrouds. I stepped down on to the deck. I turned towards him, smiled.

He leaned forward, stood on tiptoe, and kissed me on the forehead.

'Well done,' he said.

The old man smell of him. I still remember it.

There was a sudden, distant crack, like lighting; then a noise I couldn't place, like a swift tear through fabric. And at almost the same moment a dull thud, and Jebb slammed forwards, slumping into my arms. Something hot and wet was pressing through my shirt and on to my skin. I staggered, held his weight, but it made no sense to me at all. He was slack and heavy, his legs limp. I lowered him down on to the deck, knelt beside him, and still it made no sense to me at all.

I rolled him on to his side. Grey-black and bent, bird-bone frail, a wet stain spreading darkly across his chest. His eyes had glazed over. I looked up. Something rent the air above me and thudded, with a burst of splinters, into the mast. Just above my head. I didn't stay to examine it. I hit the deck.

Twelve

They were alongside. I scrabbled across the deck, hands and knees, buried myself in the angle between the cathead and the rails. They were on board in an instant, their tread heavy, their voices loud and rough after so much quiet. I couldn't catch the words, didn't understand the language. A canny little ship she must have been, I found myself thinking: well-handled, to creep up on us so swiftly. Out of the blue. Out of the white glare.

Pirates.

I curled myself up smaller behind the cathead. What could they want with us, I wondered. What could we have that would interest them?

The blood was cooling, drying on my shirt. It was sticking to my skin. It smelt sweet and foul and intimate. I knew from what I'd read that if they found me, Jebb, having died in an instant, would suddenly become the lucky one; that, if they found me, I would never have the chance to find my mother.

But if I stayed there very still, if I held my breath, they might just walk past and not notice I was there. They might just take whatever it could be that they wanted from the ship, and go.

From where I crouched I could see him lying crumpled and broken, like a nestling fallen from a tree. Milling around, the intruders' legs were visible from the calf down: some were barefooted and weatherstained, some wore boots. I watched, I heard the crunch of old bones as a boot was landed in Jebb's ribs. I fought the urge to vomit. I had brought him to the place where, the moment when, a man had levelled a pistol from another deck, squinted along its length, and fired. I had made it happen.

Bickering, a shouted threat. Then scuffling and a volley of angry syllables. And at the same time, there was movement all over the ship. Feet pounding up and down the stairs, hatches being lifted, slammed, the hollow thud of running feet across the boards. And I realized what was happening. They'd taken the *Spendlove* for a trading vessel, for a diminutive merchantman. They'd expected a good haul of spice or opium or tobacco, and were now in the process of discovering their mistake. All they'd find would be stacks of dusty old books to go with their heap of dusty dead scholar.

And then a hand gripped my ankle. I was wrenched backwards, scrabbling for a handhold, for a fingernail's gap between the timbers. I was swung up into the air and held, hanging upside down from my ankle. I had one thought: that's it, it's all over. And then instinct overwhelmed me, and I fought.

And as I struggled to get free, I was strangely, intensely aware of the tiny detail of the world around me. I was conscious of the way the breeze folded and stirred the shadows in Jebb's gown as he lay upon the deck, of the smooth lines of the deck's planking sliding out towards their vanishing point, the masts reaching vertiginously down into the sky, the sails spread like nets to catch birds that might swim by. My shirt was falling down over my face: I smelt on it the scent of my own skin, was vividly aware of the pattern of warp and weft in the linen, the way that tiny squares of sunlight pierced through between them. I was conscious of the plane of my exposed belly, the way the muscles rippled and contracted as I fought, the ridges of my hips and ribcage. Perhaps life is condensed by the threat of death, distilled into instants, into these ordinary beauties.

In my peripheral vision, I saw figures collecting, circling round. I twisted, lashed out more furiously. A noise was coming out of nowhere, a sobbing, wrenching sound. The coughing up of utter disbelief, of misery. It was coming from my mouth. I pressed my lips tight, bit my tongue. I held it back.

Then I was dropped. I landed on the deck, winded. My head knocked against the boards. Next to me, Jebb's pale green eyes were occluded, vague. Behind them, a whole world had flourished, grown, had been wiped out in an instant. His jaw had fallen open; inside were yellowed, peglike teeth, pale curves of gum. There was something inexpressibly sad about the dryness of his lips: I felt, like ashes, the faint ghost of the kiss he'd printed on my forehead, and in that moment all the instinctive fury ceased, and my mind was crystalline and clear. To do that, to kill a man: they could have no notion, no sense at all that he was real.

I rolled myself over on to my back, blinked up at them. They had gathered around me, a circle of dark forms, their faces indistinguishable against the sky. A blunt exchange. I didn't understand the words, but there was no mistaking their meaning. There was no way that they would leave the *Spendlove* empty-handed. They'd want something for their effort. And however worn and travel-weary it might be, there is always, as I well knew, a market for young flesh.

I shifted myself half on to my hunkers, paused. No one seemed to register: they were too occupied with their discussion. From the tone and the quick-fire patterns of their speech, I realized that they were trying to allocate blame for their wasted effort, were arguing over what was to be done now to make the best of the situation.

I drew in a breath. The air whistled through my teeth. I'd sprint for the gap between two of the men, and beyond that, I could just glimpse it, the rail. I would leap up on to the rail and throw myself out into the air, then dive down, sliding neatly through the water's skin and away. And if as I raced across the deck, or as I leapt, or as I made those first strokes down into the milky water, a bullet should sing out after me and thud into my back, a sudden bloom of pain that stained the water pink; if I was to die now, if I made them kill me, at least it would be failure on my own terms: it was better that than slavery.

And maybe I would make it. Maybe they would miss.

Maybe the water would turn me into stone.

I heaved myself up to run. A pistol butt cracked into the side of my head. I'd barely made it to my feet. Through the fug of sounds distorting, of colour swimming into colour, of the acid smear of pain, I knew that I'd lost everything.

One of them crouched beside me, hauled me onto my side, set about tying my wrists behind my back, trussing my ankles. The others dispersed. I could hear the movement, feel the impact of their footsteps on the deck as they walked away. I registered dimly that the man tying me was expert and swift with his knots. I could feel the filthy yellow smell of his breath on the back of my neck. When he had finished he stood up and nudged me with a toe. He left me there.

Sideways, cheek pressed down against the deck, I watched through eyes that couldn't focus, my vision supersaturated with light. The dark shapes of men were moving round the ship. I saw books, volumes almost as rare as phoenixes, being carried up from below, being brought across the deck. I watched as gilded bindings, silver clasps, chalcedony, beryls and carbuncles were ripped off and stuffed into pockets, bags and pouches. I saw pages torn from their bindings, shredded into fragments, flung in handfuls into the air. Such wilful, unnecessary destruction. I had smoothed a palm over those pages, I'd read them by the pale light of the southern night and then later by the warm glow of oil. I'd closed those covers over and turned to see through a window the first light of dawn spill across the sea. Moments earlier I would have shouted out in rage and shame, but I was now winded, heartsore, and could not speak. I watched helplessly, half-blinded with the light, as these scraps of paper and vellum caught, were lifted on the wind, were carried up into the air, were brushed across the deck and away. They would land like mayflies on the water; a word, half a phrase, an illuminated letter, the ink softening, the colours smudging, staining the water for a moment.

Someone grabbed my shirt and hauled me on to my feet. Then I was lifted and dumped across a shoulder. An arm was clamped around the back of my thighs, holding me in place. The jolt of movement. Blood rushing, pounding in my ears; my head throbbing with pain. Pressed close, I felt the breath rasp through his lungs. The sour smell of long-worn leather, of dirty flesh: nausea rose inside me. I was sickened by the sway of the gangplank; I was dazzled by the white glare of the sea.

A different deck. The different sounds and smells of a different ship. Not the ammonia stink of the *Sally Ann*, nor the fusty odour of the *Spendlove*. Something thick and heavy, something animal.

Then something else. I caught it on the wind and felt my heart contract: smoke. In the same instant I heard the snicker of flames catching, running, tearing through hemp, canvas, timber. I raised my head, peered out through swimming aching eyes one last time upon the

Spendlove. The fire raged in her like madness. I watched as ropes burnt, snapped, whipped down in showers of spark and flame. The mainmast swayed, fell crashing on to the deck. Through portholes and windows I glimpsed a hold full of fire. And Jebb's dark form still lay there hunched upon the deck as the flames licked and snapped around him.

A whole world, a whole universe had died.

Thirteen

Dry heat. Sweat ran down my skin like the tiny brush of moths' feet. People dressed in pale robes, in coats and britches, in brightly-coloured evanescent gowns were passing before me. Some had skin the same weather-stained brown as my own, others were as fair as milk, still others as dark as the slaves I'd freed.

I was standing on a dais in a market square, and I was dying for a smoke.

I wouldn't lift my eyes, wouldn't meet a single gaze. Head bent, I watched in my peripheral vision as the people passed before me, stopped in front of me, looked me up and down. As hands were outstretched to try the circumference of an upper arm, or to tug down the jaw and hold it to inspect the teeth, to lift the corner of the shirt and appraise the strength and shape of a thigh. I caught a word here or there. I'd picked up a little of the language, enough to know when it was me that was being spoken of. I knew the word for slave.

I'd thought that I was prepared, that I was in command of myself and would at least be able to acquit myself with dignity. But then I'd been led up on to the dais and I realized that nothing on earth could have prepared me for this.

My mouth was dry: my tongue played continually at the back of my teeth, trying to gather moisture. I was aware of the other captives there beside me, all of us ranged along the dais, mute, our hands bound and heads bent, a community in misery. I was conscious of each one of us alone, probing at our own particular sores of loss and fear. I was wrapped up in the fierce hot consciousness of my own body, of the ghosts of innumerable alien hands and eyes upon my flesh, and at the same time I was dizzy with the knowledge of the people who were passing there before me, the multiplicitous worlds that they were living, each of them bound by the darkness of their own skulls. These universes unfurling, overlapping, thick and plentiful as cherry blossom. And at the same time, contrary and compassionless, flickering, catching, spreading like the fire in the *Spendlove*'s hold, a blind hot fury played within me. That was why, more than anything else, more than fear or shame or misery, I did not look up. If I met somebody's gaze, I was certain that they would see the flames flicker in my eyes.

The smell was extraordinary: cooking spices, dung, sweat, and the pungent stink of frankincense. And above that, and closer, the odour of perfume on unwashed armpits, of hair oil made rancid by the heat, of melting cosmetics. Because beside me, on the dais, was the slave trader. He had painted his eyelids with blue, lined them with kohl, and smeared his skin with greasepaint. His nails were polished. He wore a loose robe in purple and white, billowing over flaccid muscles and softened belly. He had tucked a flashy dagger into his belt. But no amount of ornament or drapery or paint or perfume could cover what he was: rotten at the core.

In his left hand he held the end of the rope that bound my wrists. In his right he held a switch of lithe young wood. He was speaking. And as he spun the words out of himself, threw them in loops across the crowd, I caught a word here or there, a phrase: 'chance', he said, and 'teeth', and 'finest of this', but I couldn't keep my concentration on what he was saying, couldn't snap the words off in the right places from the flow of sound. The words themselves no longer seemed to matter overmuch, but the patterns, the cadences and rhythms of his speech were so familiar. I was reminded of cool grey skies, market towns, close smoky rooms and the clink of coin in my palm. The difference was, back then Joe had been selling his phials of blue pills. This man was selling me.

The trader gave a tug at the rope, thwacked me across the backside with his cane, and I stumbled forward a step. I was aware, without looking, of a haze of upturned faces, a blur of oval shapes in tan and cream and black. The trader was now addressing his audience individually, trying to get the bidding started: 'madam' I caught, and then something like 'domestic, farm labour', and then, I think, 'forty, forty five?'

Among the crowd, a few heads were bent to exchange

a word; there was a mutter here and there. My tongue still played silently behind my teeth, gathering sticky, foul moisture. There were no bids.

Then the trader put a hand under my chin, lifted it, turned my face towards him. A thread of spit joined his upper and lower lip, fattening and thinning as his mouth worked, as he lobbed words over his shoulder to the crowd, pinning me down with a clatter of quick-fire adjectives that I couldn't understand. He would glance towards his audience, gathering up their interest, before looking back at me again to enumerate my virtues as a slave, tilting my head to consider it from a different angle.

For the first time that day, I lifted my gaze. I met his eye. I shifted the moisture to the back of my throat, and I spat.

The gob landed on his cheek, flicked into his eye, dribbled down towards his chin. It was unusually foul; viscous, yellowish and streaky. My own nose wrinkled at the sight of it. He staggered back a step, reached up a sleeve to wipe at his face. There was a ripple of laughter from the crowd. He wiped away a streak of greasepaint with the spit, smudged his kohl down his cheek. Beneath the cosmetic smear his face was red and glistening. He must have seen, in the instant that he met my gaze, the flames flicker in my eyes, because I saw a sudden shift, a slackness, a momentary fear in his. I smiled at him, and his face tightened again, the skin twitching under his left eye. He raised his stick and swung it at me, a stinging line down my right flank. It hurt, but I didn't let my smile waver. Instead, I shook my head. I put the strange words together, gathering phrases that I'd heard on board the pirates' ship, words the drovers had hissed at us on the long march here. Statements that came punctuated by a whip's flick, by a cuff at an ear or the back of a head. I wasn't entirely confident of the sounds, of the nuances of pronunciation: I was new to this tangled, spidery tongue. But I gave it all the energy and emphasis I could.

'Cunt,' I think I said to him. 'Son of a hot bitch. Whore of shit.'

Something certainly got through: I could see that much. Either that or he was excessively startled to find that I could speak. His eyes tightened and he raised the switch again, higher this time, drawing it back as far as he could reach. He swung it forward. It whistled through the air and landed on my upper arm. The fabric was old and soft; the blow cut right through the shirt sleeve and into my flesh.

I'd already made myself virtually unsellable. Now, if I could just provoke him sufficiently – if I could just make him draw that dagger from his belt. I glanced down at the weal on my arm. It was deep, red, and welling with blood. I raised an eyebrow, looked back at him.

'Sucker of cocks,' I think I told him. 'Son of a cunt. Go and fuck your mother.'

Someone, somewhere, laughed. And then he drew his dagger.

I could feel, as a prickle down my neck, the silent buzz, the thrill of fear from the other slaves. The trader grabbed me by the throat, pulled me round and back against him:

the damp of his flesh pressed through my shirt; the taint of his breath was on my cheek. His hand was cupped around my chin, pulling my head back against his shoulder, exposing the length of my throat. He lifted the blade. I felt the cold line of metal pressed against my skin. I'd already made the choice, back on board the *Spendlove*, and chosen death over slavery. This would be the last time I would ever have to bear the unwanted closeness of someone else's body, the undesired touch of another's hands. No one would ever hurt me again.

I closed my eyes. I smiled. My father, the ferryman, would have said a word or two in my favour. He would make the crossing easy.

And I would have died, there and then, my throat cut on the dais of the market square in that dusty little town whose name I didn't know, on the trade route through an anonymous desert in a country I had never heard of; I would have sunk down in a pool of my own blood, and I would have welcomed death, had not a voice called out above the noise of the crowd. And the words were, for that one instant, as clear as water, as transparent as if they had been spoken in my own native tongue. 'Stop,' the voice said, and the slave trader stilled the dagger at my throat. My eyes flicked open.

'I'll give you three.'

For the first time, I looked directly at the crowd. The blade of the dagger was still pressed against my skin: peering down over it, it took me a moment to pick him out. A plump figure, hatted, coated, his face pink and wet in the heat, coming forward, moving through the crowd like a worm through wood. He stopped at my feet, looked up at the slave trader. He took his hat from off his head, wiped his forehead with the back of a hand. And when he spoke again, his speech had once more turned opalescent: I picked out a word here and there, watching his mouth as he formed the sounds.

'I like,' I heard, and 'spirit.'

The trader slackened his grip and drew the knife across my throat, leaving behind a faint thread of pain, a trace of blood.

'Needful,' the strange man said, and then I heard him say a word that I'd heard maybe half a dozen times before, and never aloud or in daylight. A word that is whispered at night between slaves, when someone has been taken unexpectedly away, when a new captive is thrown into their cage. The man said it out loud in the marketplace, and I sensed the other slaves lift their heads, uneasy. I felt myself flush with something like shame. The word loses all its shadows in translation, but it means, roughly speaking, work so terrible and cruel that it kills you, but only after it has first destroyed your soul.

I looked up at the cold gleam of the stars, shivered. Aries low near the horizon, overhead, the dragon and Cepheus. What did that mean? I couldn't remember. Change? But then everything alive must change, if only by dying.

Just a need to find myself a pattern, to link myself to some external presence, to find meaning. Futile. I leaned my head back a little further. Where was the pole star? Was that Venus? Which way was north?

Nearby, tethered a little way from the lamplight's spill, the camels stood morosely, snuffling a little, shifting on their soft wide feet. Camels. The word stretched itself back across the years, snagged on the day the circus came. I'd never known what they were called until today, when I'd heard the men talking.

There had been three of us travelling together. In front of me, the man from the slavemarket was seated bolt upright, his jacket tight and creasing at the shoulders and armpits, his hat pulled down low. A younger man dressed in similar clothing was following behind. I hadn't had the chance to look at him properly. I was perched on the pack animal between them, surrounded by bundles and saddlebags, my hands tied in front of me to the animal's tack. As we swayed and pitched through the trackless desert, the sun pounding down on the crown of my head like a lump hammer, I listened to them talking, batting the occasional word back and forth between them, lobbing a phrase or two right over my head. Their voices were odd, heavily accented. Some of the vowel sounds were elongated and breathy, others were clipped away to almost nothing. But there was no mistaking it, their language of choice (their native tongue, I couldn't help but suppose) was the same as mine. I recalled that moment of clarity in the market, and wondered if the older man had spoken briefly, unthinkingly, in our common tongue, then shifted to the local one to haggle.

They didn't say much, and the sound didn't travel well; it was soaked up quickly by the thirsty desert air. But I gathered that they were not relishing their journey, and that in particular they loathed travelling by camel.

As the dunes' shadows had deepened, lengthened, and the sky's blue began to darken, there were a number of speculative exchanges as to the best time to pitch camp. The place was irrelevant, as every dune was much the same as every other, but if it was left much later they would be pitching tents in the dark. This decided, the older man called a halt, and shouted and kicked at his camel until he'd bullied her into kneeling. She hissed and folded up on herself like a card table. He dismounted and dragged at the other animals' bridles until they too crumpled down on to the sand. He untied my hands, directed me with a pistol to unload the bundles from the pack animal, then to begin the assembly of the tents. From time to time he'd shout a word or two in the local tongue, 'quick quick', or 'stupid', directing me in much the same way as he had the beasts. I remained as wordless as the camels, tried to keep my face as expressionless as theirs.

Once the work was done, my hands were tied again, and my feet were hobbled; I could stand, and walk a little, but not with any ease or comfort. I was parched, chafed, saddlesore and weary, my head throbbing from the day's long sun. I was given a cup of water, a piece of bread, and a scratchy blanket to keep out the desert cold, so that I could sleep. I could not sleep.

They were sitting on little folding stools. Jackets off, shirtsleeves rolled. Each had a pistol strapped into a holster beneath his left arm. A lamp glowed at their feet.

Beside it stood a basket with its lid off, and every so often one of them would reach down, select something from inside, and bring it to his mouth. I couldn't see what it was they were eating, but imagined, enviously, dried fruits and meats and cheeses.

The younger one was wiping his fingers on a handkerchief.

'I don't mean to be awkward, sir,' he said, 'but I'm very uneasy about this.'

I looked more closely. The yellow lamplight picked out the lines of concern on his face.

There was a chink here. I might be able to worm myself into it, might slip right through.

'Don't talk nonsense,' the older man was saying. 'You'd've done exactly the same if you'd been there. It's just good business. Bargain like that? Cheaper than indentured labour, even. And, when you think about it, the advantage of –' he hesitated a moment '– this kind of worker – is that there's no call for compensation or any kind of fuss, should the inevitable happen. No widows or orphans, no grieving parents, none of that palaver. If only we'd thought of it before, we could have saved ourselves a fortune.'

The younger one nodded, just a slight dip of the head. He was reaching down for something more to eat. The older man brushed his hand aside, picked up the basket and slapped the lid into place, securing it with a peg.

'We can't be too picky now, can we, Cunningham?' he added. 'The way things are going, we can't afford to pass up on a fit young thing, bargain price. Anyway, if we hadn't bought it, he'd've killed it there and then. Cut its throat in the market. We did it a favour, if you think about it. We saved its life.'

Then Cunningham glanced my way. I dipped my eyes back down towards the sand. He lowered his voice.

'I wish you wouldn't say "it",' he said. And I thought, there it is. The chink.

'Eh?'

'I mean, sir, after all, she is a girl.'

This was something of a surprise, but I kept my face poker-straight, as if everything was sailing straight over my head. Even in the half-light, even without looking directly, I registered the flick of the younger one's eyes over towards me again. What was it that McMichaels had said? *It's amazing what a little discomfort does to a person's appearance.* I'd had more than a little discomfort in my time. My time had worn me like a pair of weekday shoes.

I hadn't been a girl in ages. But if Cunningham liked girls, I could be a girl.

'D'you think so?' The older man paused a moment. 'D'you know, it didn't even cross my mind.'

He straightened up, hands on his thighs. He picked up the lamp.

'Well,' he said. 'There's only one way to be sure.'

The younger man stood up beside him.

'Really, sir –'

'Come on.'

They came across towards me. The older man hunkered down, set the lamp on the sand and ground its base in to keep it upright.

'Sir – it doesn't really matter, does it.' The younger man was standing a little further back.

'You just hold its hands,' he said, 'and I'll undo these buttons.'

He was leaning forward, going for my britches. I swung my feet up to his chest and shoved him away. He landed on his arse in the sand.

'No you bloody won't,' I said.

Their mouths fell open. Cunningham turned to look at the older man. A moment, then he started getting to his feet, brushing off the sand. He came back towards me, lifted up the lantern, peered at me. I glared back at him.

'Damn,' he said. He turned back to Cunningham. 'Damn damn damn.'

'Where are you from?' Cunningham said. His voice was unsteady. I opened my mouth to speak.

'Shut up,' the older man told me. 'It doesn't matter where it's from.'

He took Cunningham's arm and steered him away.

'She,' Cunningham said. 'She.'

They reached their stools. The older man sat down, gestured for Cunningham to sit.

'Sir, this changes everything.'

'I know, just don't start making small-talk with it. It doesn't matter where it's from. What matters is how we're going to deal with it now it's here.'

Cunningham took his seat. He looked shaken.

'You'll keep mum, of course.'

'Of course.'

When the older man spoke next, there was a shift in

his tone. I heard it distinctly. A step away, a dis-engagement.

'What are you making these days, Cunningham?' he said.

'Sir?'

'What are you making?' He picked up the basket, undid the fastening and lifted the lid.

'Not enough to marry on, at a guess. Not the way the Company pays.'

The young man swallowed. The older one held out the basket towards him, shook it. Cunningham took it from him, looked absently down inside it.

'We can't take it with us, Cunningham. There'd be no keeping it quiet, who knows what kind of gossip would start to fly around. If we took it back, that'd be two days' journey wasted, there and back again. And I doubt I'd get my money back.'

A moment. The basket hanging limply from Cunningham's hand, forgotten.

'So what are we going to do?' he asked.

'We can't take it with us,' the older man said again.

'I hope you're not suggesting – I couldn't kill her, sir.'

Another silence.

'No.' A pause, a breath. 'No. I don't think I could either.'

'Go on, give it a try. You might surprise yourself.'

Their heads slewed back round to look at me. Almost as if they'd already forgotten I could speak, that I could understand what they were saying.

'You shut up,' the older man said.

'You'd be doing me a favour,' I said.

'Keep out of this. I'm trying to think.'

'Something quick and clean would be nice,' I called out. 'I'm not so keen on the idea of dying of thirst, and I've had it up to here with flogging –'

'Shut *up*!'

'All right.' I shifted a little on the sand. 'Got any baccy?'

They conferred in whispers for what seemed like hours, hunched over the lamp, glancing round my way from time to time. The light grew dim and smoky. Eventually, the desert's fierce night-time chill wormed into their bones. They lit another lamp and went shivering and, it seemed, still undecided, to their respective tents.

And then, a shadow-puppet show as they undressed for bed, their bent goblin figures projected by the lanterns onto the walls of their tents. Jackets were shrugged off shoulders, holsters unbuckled and laid over the backs of camp chairs. Shirts were unbuttoned, britches stepped out of, nightshirts dropped down over heads. I watched as, in turn, each of them extracted his gun from its harness and slid it under his pillow. I hunched into myself against the cold, my one blanket tugged tightly round me, and watched as bedclothes were drawn back, and the silhouettes folded themselves away flat into their low beds. A few rippling waves of shadow followed as they rearranged their blankets, then one and then the other light blinked off. I waited. The shadows heaved and shifted as one of them turned upon his side. After a little while I heard the first snore.

I heaved myself up on to my feet, dragging my blanket awkwardly over a shoulder. I shuffled up towards the camels, stroked a neck, scratched a tufty forehead with my trussed-up hands. Intransigent, foul-smelling beasts that they were, I'd rather risk their temper and stink than sit shivering the whole night alone. Anyway, I was pretty sure that I stank too. It'd been a long time since I'd last dropped down from the deck of the *Spendlove* and through the water's skin, a long journey from the milk-white water of the mermaids' sea. From Jebb's body in my arms and the smell of his blood on my shirt. The stain was still there, brown as tea, but the smell had faded away. By now the *Spendlove* would be scattered cinders on the ocean floor.

I could not get comfortable. The sand was hard beneath me. I found myself wondering whether I had been right about Cunningham, whether there had been an interest, a tenderness in him, or if it had just been my imagination. If I'd just wanted it to be that way.

But the camel-smell had a softness to it, a stable-familiarity. Leaning up against her was comforting: her warmth, her heartbeat, the rumble and squelch of her belly.

Something was hanging there in front of me, a ghostly shape in the darkness. I swung my fists out, without thinking. My knuckles hit flesh, a ridge of bone beneath. I heard a muffled yell and someone was stumbling, falling back across the sand. I had been sleeping, I realized. I couldn't remember when it was that I'd last slept. My knuckles smarted.

'Who's there?'

A pale figure unfolded itself from the sand. It moved towards me.

'It's me.'

Cunningham. He'd come, after all. I peered up at him. His face was just a whitish blur in the deep blue night: he was, I realized by the paleness of his form, still dressed in his nightshirt.

'I was asleep,' I said. 'You woke me up.'

He hunkered down in front of me, a hand raised to rub his stinging cheek.

'Sorry,' he said. He was speaking in an undertone. 'What's your name?'

I'd been right. I almost smiled.

'Malin.' I extended my tied hands as if to be shaken. 'Malin Reed, at, it seems, your service.'

He came closer, settled down on to the sand next to me. He leant back beside me, against the camel's warm musky flank. She sighed.

'That's an unusual name –' he began. 'It's not one I think I've heard before – is that Miss,' he said, 'or Mrs, or –'

And then I couldn't help but smile. He wouldn't see, of course, in the darkness; and so he wouldn't, I hoped, realize that I was already three steps ahead of him, and knew precisely where he was going. If anything, that smile, which was not altogether mocking, might warm the words for him when I spoke, might make them sweeter.

'Why do you ask?' I said.

A pause. He said nothing for a moment. Then he sighed.

'I'm so lonely.' A sniff. Deep and wet and, after all that whispering, rather noisy. 'I just get so lonely.'

I watched as his head bent down towards the pale angle of his knees and rested there. Another sniff. I raised my eyebrows, shifted a little on the sand. My blanket slipped away, and awkwardly, with knotted fists, I dragged it back, tugged it tighter round me. The movement pressed my shoulder for a moment against his. He was shaking.

'*I just get so lonely,*' he said again.

'There there,' I said.

A flurry in the darkness as he raised then shook his head. After a moment I reached out towards him and patted his knee. This wasn't what I'd expected. I'd foreseen the eager untying of my hands and feet, and stumbling across the sand into his tent. Once there, I'd do whatever was necessary. I'd seen where he'd left his pistol: he wasn't to know that I didn't have a clue how to use it. But instead of untying me he was shuffling closer on his backside, leaning up against my shoulder, pushing his face into my neck, making it warm and wet with tears. I opened my mouth, but was dumbfounded. I could not find a single suitable word to say.

'I don't know,' he was whispering, stumbling over the words, breaking them apart with sobs, gulping in air, 'I don't know if I can take it any more. I can't bear *him* a moment longer. He's a *savage*. And I can't go back. My mother – they're all, they're all expecting me to make something of myself. And even if I did go back, there's still Rose. I don't even *know* her, not really. I've met her perhaps a dozen times, it was madness to propose – but now there's no way out – I have to – I can't bear it –'

By now the edge of my blanket was getting damp. Whilst he was speaking I'd been considering saying something, something like, 'Pull yourself together, you think you've got problems,' but as his words broke apart and stumbled off, as they collapsed in the dark, something in me shifted and I found myself softening towards him. He seemed so young. He seemed younger than I'd ever been.

Sitting there, with this boy's wet face pressed into my neck, his convulsions shaking me, I found myself flicking back through all the books I'd read on the *Spendlove*; philosophy, history, theology; hoping to catch upon some useful theory or exemplum to console him with. But any concept I could summon was just a grander, more systematized version of the 'pull yourself together' notion which I'd already dismissed: for the time being, he was way beyond pulling himself together.

So I shrugged his head off my shoulder and twisted round to face him. He straightened up, wiped his eyes. His face, his movements, were just vague palenesses in the dark. But I could tell that he was looking at me, I could hear him gulping, stunned by the force of his own misery.

So I kissed him. Not because I thought that he wanted me to, not because I thought that it would make him let me go. I kissed him to console him. I kissed him to quieten him. I kissed him because he was, after all, just a boy.

But the kiss was nice. Soft and warm and slightly fumbly. I found myself leaning into him, my body warming towards him. His hands reached out, touched my waist. I'd thought, I'd been told, I'd believed that no one would ever want to touch me like that again.

'Oh,' he said, when the kiss was over.

'I'm cold,' I said. 'Shall we go into your tent?'

And he reached down and began to untie my hands. I watched the movement of his fingers. The knots came free: he shifted to untie my ankles. I stood up and took his hand. And now things were, at last, going to plan.

Though just a boy, he was twice my size: a big strong well-fed child. No need for him to feel anxious about me. He could have snapped me like a corn-dolly, like a piece of biscuit, if he'd wanted to. If he found that he needed to. In the closeness of his tent, his hands were at once hesitant and over-eager: he wanted to kiss, more than anything else, but he also wanted to touch me so much it was as if he'd never touched another person's flesh before. When his fingers found the scarring on my back, a moment's pause was all the question that he asked, and even though I didn't explain, the fact that he hadn't said a word made me feel tenderly towards him. I'd told myself I would do whatever was necessary. In fact I did a good bit more.

He came quickly, lying back among the tumbled

blankets of his camp bed, mouth a wide dark hole, startled by the heat and wet and convulsive pleasure of it all.

'I'm sorry –' he said.

And I held back anything that might have sounded like teasing, like a joke: I stroked the hair back off his forehead and kissed him, because he seemed sweet. I lay down at his side on the narrow canvas bed. He kept on taking little gulping breaths, as if about to speak, then failing to find the words, or thinking better of it. Part of me just wanted to stay there stroking his hair, comforting him. To fall asleep beside him. To forget about everything else. But I knew I couldn't think like that. I didn't have much choice. I turned on my side, slipped my fingertips beneath the pillow. I spoke softly, into his ear, to cover any sound my hand might make.

'What do you really want, Cunningham?' I asked him.

For a moment he didn't reply. He turned to look at me.

'What do you mean?' he said.

'If you don't want all that, all that you said, that girl, getting married and everything, what do you want?'

Another moment's pause. His head rolled round again to look up at the night-blued canvas above. I slid my hand further beneath the pillow, searching.

'I don't know – I've never really –' he said.

'Because you really should figure out what you want. It's no good just knowing what you *don't* want –' my fingers found the cool touch of gunmetal. I kept on talking, shifting in the bed, rustling the blankets to cover the noise and movement of my hand. My fingers curled around the smooth warm wood of the pistol butt. 'It's none of my business, of course, but it might be worth just sitting down for a while and thinking it through.'

'I suppose –'

'Because it's not fair to marry her you know,' I went on, drawing the pistol down towards me, inch by inch, breath by breath, 'just out of embarrassment. It's not fair on either of you.' I lifted myself up on to an elbow, as if just to look him in the face, and in the same movement drew the gun out from under the pillow to lie beside my chest. 'Because, when it comes down to it, life is brief,' I said, lifting the pistol and pressing its barrel to his forehead. 'Life is cruelly brief.'

He lay there for just a moment, his young soft body pale in the night, the gun pressing against his forehead, the dark blotches of his eyes fixed upon my face. He lay there looking up at me, and then he began again to cry. Which, again, was not what I had bargained for at all.

Not noisily at first, but insistently, and with an increasing intensity and volume, he cried until his whole body began to shake again, and he was shuddering and sniffing and sobbing phlegmily, and I was sure the other one would waken, hear, and come running in to help him.

'Shut up,' I hissed. '*Shut up!*'

'But you – I thought you – how *could* you –'

'Oh sweet suffering fuck,' I said, and pulled the gun away from his head. 'I only meant to scare you.'

'Well you did!'

'I'm sorry. It's just – I need your help.'

'Fine way to go looking for it. You could've asked,' his voice was hissing, furious. 'You didn't have to go and hold a gun to my head.'

He reached up, pushed my hand further away. The pistol hung loosely from my fingers, over the side of the bed.

'I don't suppose you have many friends?' he said.

I thought about this a moment.

'I've had one, or two,' I said. 'Maybe.'

'I'm not surprised.'

I hadn't really known what to ask for. Quietly, as quietly as he could for a man of his stature, he moved around his tent, handing me objects, naming them in a half-whisper, a breath. I accepted everything, inarticulate with embarrassment, shamed by his kindness.

'Compass,' he said, placing a cool metal disc into my palm. 'Quart flask, full. A week's hard rations. Blanket. And a bag to put it all in. And a hat, you'll need a hat.' He rummaged round in a kitbag, tugged out a dark, broad shape. 'Wear it all the time, pulled down low, to keep the sun off your neck. Otherwise in a couple of days your scalp'll peel right open like an orange. I've seen it happen.' He thought a moment. 'And a jacket. Take my spare one.'

It came down to my knees.

He lifted back the tent flap and we stepped out into the night. The moon had risen. The dunes were silver, their shadows black. I had never, even in all my time at sea, seen so many stars.

It was cold. I buttoned up the jacket and stuffed my hands into its pockets, pulling the fabric tight against my body. I cast around, looking up at the sky, out over the moon-silvered sands, feeling the faintest spot of warmth begin to glow somewhere deep in the pit of my stomach. It wasn't quite like excitement, it was perhaps something closer to satisfaction: I was almost on my way again, and on the cold night air I'd caught the scent of possibility, that first breath of change.

'Which way,' I asked him, 'to the sea?'

He gestured. 'I'd say due north would probably be most direct.'

'How far?'

'I don't know. A week maybe.'

I nodded, kept my eyes on the horizon. A moment passed in silence.

'Look, don't go,' he said.

I looked back round at him.

'I'll talk to him,' he said.

'And say what?' I asked.

'We'll find some way –'

'You won't. There is no way.' I shifted the bagstrap up my shoulder.

'Right,' he said. Then a moment later, 'Right.'

I lifted the compass from my pocket, glanced up at the stars, then back down at the neat instrument in my palm.

'How does it work?'

He took the compass from me, shifted it round in his hand. 'You line the arrows up, then that's north.'

'Yes.' I watched the needle flicker, settle. I took the

instrument from his hand and set it on my own palm. I turned it round experimentally.

'What will you tell him?' I asked.

'I'll let him get up first. Let him discover you've escaped.'

I looked up at him. He was shivering slightly. He smiled at me.

'Thank you,' he said. 'thank you for the – er –'

And I knew I should say something, something about how when we'd met I had been numb, that I had been courting death, and that the tenderness that he had made me feel was something new, and I was grateful for it, and for his kindness. That I was glad to have found him. But I felt awkward and suddenly shy. I missed my chance.

'Sorry about the gun,' I said.

He shrugged.

'You weren't to know.'

We stood there a moment, looking at each other. Then he dropped a kiss on my cheek.

'Good luck,' he said.

I nodded, smiled at him. Then I tugged the bagstrap up on to my shoulder, glanced down at the compass, and walked away.

I turned my collar up against the cold. It smelt of him.

If I hadn't been so preoccupied, if I hadn't been running the events of the night again in my head, if I hadn't been so ashamed of myself and at the same time so happy, it would probably have occurred to me to take one of the camels. As it was, I'd been walking for about an hour before I thought of it, and by then I'd gone too far to go back. It wasn't worth wasting the time. And anyway, a week's walk would be nothing to me. I could handle it.

Fourteen

But it wasn't nothing, it was not a week, and I couldn't. After nine days my strength was almost entirely exhausted, as was my water, and my hope. I was nowhere near the sea, I knew it: the air was dry as dust, and silent but for the hiss of wind-stirred sand. It did not make sense.

I tapped the compass-glass. The needle shivered, settled. Maybe it was broken. Or maybe I was reading it wrong.

It was hard going. Long ridges of dunes lay across my path. I had to wade up the face of each of them, slide step-stretched down the other side and cross a narrow corridor of flat ground just to face another ridge of sand identical to the one before. And the one before that. And hundreds before that. And from the top of every ridge all I could see, in any direction, were more and more dunes just like the one I was standing on, humped like a vast school of rising whales. I toyed with it continually, the notion of turning down the corridor between the dunes, the dust rising from my feet, still hanging there hours after I'd passed. It seemed almost contrary to battle on the way that I was going, when this would be so much easier, but I'd glance down at the little disc in my palm, watch the shivering needle for a moment, then drag in a breath, and begin to plough my way up the next slope. A direction, even though I felt I could no longer trust it, still seemed more hopeful than having no direction at all.

At first I went by night, taking advantage of the cool hours to make good distance. The days I spent in whatever shade I could find, sometimes under one of the rocky outcrops that emerged here and there from the desert, sometimes at the foot of a dune, my blanket tented over my head to keep out the glare. I'd shift myself, hour by hour, to catch the last of the morning's shadow, then bear out the midday brilliance as best I could. Sitting hunched there in the stuffy, sticky heat, I would sometimes fall into a fitful sleep, my head dropping forward on to my knees. After so long with so little rest, without the chance to dream, the darkness in my head came instantly alive with vivid ghosts and intricate labyrinthine plots. These would disperse like smoke in the moment that I woke, leaving just a faint hint of story, a sense of words on the tip of my tongue, of colours slipping through my fingers.

When four days had passed without a change in the desert, without a hint of the sea, and my water was almost half-gone, I knew I would have to travel by day as well. I tied my feet with strips of blanket to shield them from the burning sand. I pulled my hat low to shade my eyes. I could sleep later, I told myself. I could sleep when I got to the coast.

The bag knocked against my shoulder. I could hear, with each step, the water slop inside the canteen. So little left.

The wind teased spindrift from the crests of the dunes. The air seemed almost too dry to breathe. When I looked down to check the compass, sand traced the creases of my palm.

Dunes, more dunes, featureless and shifting, melting in the distance to a haze. Here and there a butte of rock. No blue but the sky stretching endless overhead, not a cloud to be seen.

So little water. So far to go. And when I got there, what then? In a place like this, there wouldn't be streams snaking across the beach. And I didn't have any means of turning saltwater into fresh. It hadn't occurred to me, back at the camp. I hadn't known then that it would take so long. I hadn't thought I would run out of water before I reached the sea.

The glass was silver in the moonlight. The cool press of water against its sides as my fingers curled around it. Against my lips, the soft taintless wet. Water knocking against the back of my mouth, rolling down my throat. My belly growing round and hard beneath my palm. Blinking once, twice, drifting into water-softened sleep.

That had been real. Whatever Jebb had said about wanting, imagining, that much at least had been real.

My eyes were narrowed to a line against the glare. The

sand streamed, trailing from each lifted foot. A flake of skin was peeling from my cheek, tickling me: I raised a hand to brush it away and the movement made my head reel. The bag seemed heavy on my shoulder, even though I knew that it was light: the canteen was almost empty.

I couldn't eat. When I chewed, the biscuit stayed dry in my mouth; I couldn't swallow it. I let the pieces fall from my lips into my hand, looked at the dry crumbs a moment before scattering them. Not good. Not good at all.

A little blood on my lips. I licked it away. The skin was sharp and brittle. My tongue felt alien to me, huge.

Rest: just a moment's rest. I sank down to my knees, fumbled in my bag and drew out the canteen. I tugged at the stopper, brought the bottleneck to my lips. The water slid across my tongue and was gone. And that was it. I held the bottle there, upended, a moment more, and one more droplet gathered and fell on to my tongue. I put the stopper back in place, slipped the empty bottle back into the bag, and felt unaccountably guilty and ashamed. I would rest there just a moment, I told myself, before going on. I leaned over, lay down on my side, pillowed my cheek upon an arm.

That perfect cold glass of water. Cold as a beck straight off the fells. Cold as summer rain conjured from a cloudless sky.

But if it was chance that had brought the rain, then who had brought the water?

The sun was slamming down, my breath stirring sand-wraiths before my face, and I remembered the way the light caught in the curls of a woman's hair, recalled the pattern of cracks in her workstained hands, felt the easy weight of an empty pitcher hanging from my fingers as I waited at the village pump.

My eyelashes were encrusted with tiny translucent grains of sand. A slow, sore blink. I remembered the eyes of the dead, parched in the sun. I saw them again, clustering round the *Sally Ann*, their lips peeled back, their mouths open in a silent scream. They would not let me look away. And now I heard them too: a thin wail in the pit of my skull, gathering, growing louder. They were calling for me. In my mouth, I could feel that my tongue was swelling, forcing my lips apart. Soon I would join them, I would be screaming with them, out beyond the reach of living ears.

My existence was now reduced to this: the faint trickle of blood from my lip, the graze of tiny cubes of sand behind my eyelids, the alien thickness of my tongue filling my mouth. The wail of dead men's voices in my head.

And then something else. Faintly at first. I heard, at least I thought I heard, a soft, shambling sound, as if somewhere not too far off the sand was being disturbed, displaced by passing feet. They were coming for me, I thought, all the way from the sea, wading through the dust to claim me. I strained to lift myself, to pull myself up on to my feet, to make one last stumbling run for life. But all I could do was raise my cheek a little, mutely part my lips.

Through the ripple and shimmer of the heat haze,

through the spindrift, under the sun's hot glare, something was coming. Dark, indefinite shapes, moving towards me in a grey cloud of dust. My head fell back on to my arm. The wail was growing louder, clarifying into pain, and I thought, that's it. I am going to die.

And then other sounds. Sparks and flashes of music like the chimes of tiny bells. Then the chink and jangle of something more solid, of horsebrasses, perhaps. I heard the creak of leather, then a dog's half-hearted bark. And then the smell; something I had smelt before, but could not, for a moment, place. The tang of dung, the must of straw and sawdust, and then, perhaps, the scent of cheap perfume, of sweat.

The smell of the circus.

Fifteen

Their dust cloud slipped over me, veiled the sun. A ghostly bag-of-bones horse, his head hanging, his feet barely lifted, was shambling along the dune corridor. His harness shivered and clinked with brasses. Cracked and dusty tack looped back towards the caravan, where glimpses of gold paint caught the light through a film of grime. *Aldobrandi's Circus of Delights*. In the dark mouth of the canopy a hunched figure was grasping the reins and squinting straight ahead though the dust. He wouldn't see me. He would pass right in front of me, not two yards distant.

I lifted my head. Sand fell away from my cheek, poured from my hair. I opened my mouth to call to them, but all that came out was a faint whistling sound, like the wind stirring dry grasses. The first caravan passed by, grew vague in the dust of its passing.

Another followed behind, the horse ghost-pale with dust, her head hanging even lower, eyes half-closed, nostrils caked. Wading through the sand, dragging the caravan behind her, its wheels deep and slow, its old red paint glowing faintly through the caking grey. The reins looped back to another figure sitting hunched in its shadowed canopy.

And all that would come from my mouth was a sound like an old man's breath, like the stirring of leaves in a dried-up pool, and no one stilled the horses, no one slid from their seat and came running stumbling through the sand towards me.

The second caravan had passed. Before my face, my breath stirred the dust-fogged air into whorls and eddies. The acrobats, the dancing girls, the mermaid I'd called mother, slipping through my fingers like the colours of a dream, like sand.

The third caravan was passing now.

I heaved my head up from the ground. I stretched out an arm, yellow-grey in the dim light, ingrained with dust. I cried out to them.

And could not even hear myself. No one stopped, and no one turned my way, and the final caravan was already moving past me. Hunched in their dark canopies, squinting out ahead, the drivers sat contained, oblivious. My hand fell, I slumped forward and lay still, my mouth open, breathing dust.

I would die here. I'd crossed half the world to die here. If I'd had the strength left, I would have laughed.

What a place for a mermaid's child to die.

And then I felt something tickling my cheek. I wasn't even dead yet and the first bluebottle had already come to lay her eggs on me. I tried to brush it away, but found I could no longer lift the weight of my hand. That there should be flies out there. Crossing arid leagues to find each new oasis of flesh. I would have shuddered at the notion of them, of their maggots nosing blindly through my body, if there had been any strength left in me to shudder. I would have heaved, if there had been anything left inside me but the sand.

But then something hot and rough and faintly damp was run across my skin. A puff of air flushed across my cheek, blowing away dust, smelling warm and sweet and slightly rank. I opened my eyes again, looked up.

Something blinked back at me: long lashes swept over eyes as brown and soft as peatwater. Something moved in closer, breathed again, gathering up my scent. The sand was blown away in gusts. Whiskers brushed against my cheek, tickling me again. Not a blowfly, then: a camel.

And then I heard it. A shout from up ahead. Faint, husky, muffled by the dust cloud and the buzzing in my head, but nonetheless a shout.

'Delilah!' it sounded like. Then, after a moment, 'That bloody animal.' My heart contracted. Someone had seen the camel stop, and now they would have to stop too: they would come back for her. And when they did, they would see me. The acrobats, the dancing girls: they would come streaming from the caravans, cluster round me, lift me up and carry me away. I'd slipped inside the circle. I'd come home.

'What is it?' a second voice was calling.

'It's Delilah. Somethin's spooked her.'

Wordless croons and calls, the jingling harnesses falling silent. Once stilled, the horses didn't have the strength left to stamp and blow, to shake their heads.

Someone was speaking, his voice growing clearer, closer: he was moving back along the train of caravans, coming for the camel, coming towards me. I heard the sigh of his footsteps through the sand.

'I told you to tie her to the tailgate.'

A woman's voice this time: 'She don't like it.'

'Can't you keep her alongside then, and keep a friggin' eye on her? This is the last thing we need —'

I sensed the camel lift her head to watch him as he grew close. I heard everything as though through a blanket. I felt my heart begin to flutter faster, higher, as if it were a blackbird caught inside my ribcage. I could not catch a breath.

'She ain't been herself since Sarah died,' this was the woman's voice again, calling out after him.

'None of us have.' He said this in an undertone, hissing. His voice changed in pitch as he grew closer, as he spoke first to himself, then to the animal.

'C'mon old girl,' he crooned, 'c'mon now.'

Soon he would glance down and see me, splayed out like tanning leather on the ground. Soon I would be scooped up into his arms and carried, streaming sand, back towards the caravans.

'C'mon old darling, let's be having you,' he was saying, his shadow falling across me as he reached out to take her bridle. 'What is it, honeybee, what is it?'

And then a pause. I felt the shadow slip over me, felt the movement above as he leaned in closer to look down. I would have smiled, a halved, profile smile, if I hadn't been choking on feathers, suffocated by the beating wings inside my chest.

He called out, 'There's a *body* –'

And then it hit me. He was right. I couldn't speak, I couldn't move. I was a body, just a body, waiting for the flies. I wondered when it was that I'd died. It seemed strange not to have noticed it happening.

'What do you mean, a body?' the woman called.

'That's what's spooking her.' I felt the shadow move across me again as he leaned over to catch hold of the camel's bridle. 'Must've given her a fright, that's all. Don't you worry old girl. C'mon, let's go.'

I felt my eyelid flicker.

'Ach *shite*.'

'What is it Bill?'

'Nothing. Nothing.' He was dragging on the camel's halter, slipping, kicking up dust. I could feel her feet shifting and stumbling on the sand near me: he was turning her too abruptly, forcing her round. She was complaining, yawling and growling in the back of her throat.

'What do you mean, nothing?' The woman's voice was getting closer now.

'It's a body, just a body, that's all,' he said, speaking too quickly. 'It's all covered in sand, you can't see it till you're up close, she must've nearly trod on it and given herself a fright. You come across them sometimes out here, dried out like kippers. It's prob'ly a hundred years old.'

There was a slight movement in the sand as the woman approached.

'Don't look, Marguerite, you'll only upset yourself.'

He was right. I was dead a hundred years, I was parched to leather. The dark open mouths crowded round me, the wailing filled my head like pain or darkness, and I was dizzy now, perched up high and vertiginous: at any moment I would fall, slip between their lips and down into the black, and there would be no river-crossing, no ferryboat, no father there to meet me, just falling, darkness, then black sand drifting, and the sound of high voices wailing, each alone.

There was movement and a shadow passed over my face: someone was crouching down by my side, paired fingertips were pressed into my throat. A moment passed. The fluttering in my ribcage subsided and I watched, vaguely amazed, as a breath stirred the sand before my face. The fingers were instantly lifted from my throat, and as if from the back of a cave, I heard the woman – Marguerite – call out:

'Andre, c'mon over here, give us a hand.'

No other word was said. The dull thud of feet, then a hand gripping my shoulder. I was rolled over to lie on my back. Above, the dust was like dirty muslin across the sun. I blinked once, slow and sore. A dark figure was leaning over me, another standing a little way off, a third just crouching down beside me. A hand was stretched out to wipe the sand from off my cheek.

'Jesus, would you look –' Marguerite said.

A moment's pause.

'Is there any space in yours?'

Hands were slid under the crooks of my knees and under my shoulders. I was lifted up and carried. There were no clustering dancing girls, no acrobats, just three dusty figures with kerchiefs tied across their faces. I felt the warm softness of the woman's body as she carried me; I could feel the regular beat of her heart against me, could smell her sweat. She climbed some steps, turned to move through a narrow gap, and then there was darkness; gentle, domestic darkness; and I was laid down on something soft. I caught the smell of wool, felt its fibres against my cheek.

I could see nothing. The dark swam with chromatic flares, with amoebic plaques of blue and green. I was dimly aware of voices, of shifts in tone and distance. Then there was a rolling sway of movement, and I heard the first faint jingle of shaken tack.

Someone was talking to me, dripping water into my mouth, and my whole body was caught up in that, in the drip-drip-drip of water between my lips, the moisture spreading out across my tongue, the softening of lip and tongue and gum, the sense of wet. And in the relief at being borne along, at being moved, at no longer having to drag myself through every step.

And then, a little later, something was dropped stinging into my eyes, and I was blinking, and streams of tears I had not cried were running over my cheeks, and a cloth was passed across my skin, wiping them away. The stinging subsided, and my eyes felt cool and moist.

I wasn't conscious of the passing time. I became gradually aware of changes, of different shapes and bulks beside me in the darkness, of the different weights and deftnesses of the hands that wiped my face, that dripped the water between my lips. Usually, it was the woman, Marguerite, her shape soft and vague in the unlit caravan, her voice rich and soothing, like toffee. Sometimes I'd be aware of the jingle of tack and the clop of hoofs; sometimes I'd surface on silence, hold my breath until I caught the sound of another breath beside me in the dark. Sometimes I heard a violin. Once I thought I heard the creak of ships' timbers, the slap of waves, but I might have been dreaming. I was dreaming all the time, or remembering, or imagining: a warm slate ferry step against the back of my thigh, swimming with my mother in the fellside pool, rhubarb bubbling on the stove and the view up my grandmother's sooty nostrils.

And with that, I found myself speaking out loud into the darkness, the words coming thick and ugly.

'Where's the mermaid?' I asked.

'What's that, love?' The woman's voice, dulled with sleep. Marguerite.

'The mermaid, can I see her?'

'We don't have a mermaid, love.'

'No – you have – I remember.'

'We haven't had one for years,' she said. 'The last one went a long time ago.'

I couldn't think what to say.

'They never last long,' she added.

'She died?'

'They always die.'

And it was then that I first noticed I was shivering.

There followed a time when I was conscious of no more than the sweatsoaked blankets tangling round me and the bone-shaking shiver that knocked my teeth together, made me huddle up small and clutch the bedclothes close. And then I'd be hot, a desperate flush of heat, and I'd be kicking the covers away, fighting off the hands that tried to pull them straight back over me. And every bone, every joint, every muscle ached and burned. And then after that, there was just feebleness, and acquiescence, and dumb, heart-eating grief.

I'd seen her, painting her nails in the moonlight. I'd heard her sing. And the moment that I'd clambered out from underneath the caravan into a pool of moonlight and the sight of her and the sound of her song, that was the moment when my father's stories had rung true, when my mother, the mermaid, had seemed for the first time possible, and I no longer had to believe in that sugared smutty word my grandmother had used. I'd stood in the gloom of Hope Street, looking out over Sailortown, and seen the *Sally Ann* round the bend in the river, and my world had blossomed into possibility again, and that was because of her. And I was clambering up the ship's rail, calling out to the shoal of mermaids, demanding to be taken with them, and Jebb's lips were pressed against my forehead, and milk-white waves lapped against the hull.

To start again from scratch.

I sat, blanket-wrapped, in the shadow of the canopy, beside Marguerite. I found myself holding, between the pad of my thumb and my forefinger, the lucky charm that John Doyle had carved for me. I could feel the curve of her tail, the snaking waves of hair, the tiny stipple of her scales. It seemed almost impossible that it should still be there, still hanging round my neck from the filament of John's hair, still solid and definite and real, when everything else seemed to have been undermined, emptied, made meaningless.

I sat beside Marguerite and kept my eyes on the horse's bony rump, on the flick of her tail and the shift of muscle beneath her skin. I found myself wondering at her determination, at her continuing willingness to drag herself, us, and the laden caravan along, when she could choose just to give up, to climb down into the nearest ditch and die. Because what was the point of struggling, of dragging yourself on for another day, another mile, when all that you were stumbling on towards all the time was death.

I sat beside Marguerite and thought myself unable to do anything more than sit there, shaken by the jolting roll of the caravan, vaguely aware of her hands holding the reins, the way the flesh hung loose on her fingers, the way the leather strap wove between them, pressing into the soft skin. Sometimes Marguerite's skinny dog would run alongside us, following a scent; sometimes he would hop up and lie behind Marguerite's feet. He would sleep in the shadow of her skirts, twitch and twitter with his dreams. Every so often, Marguerite would talk, her mouth turned upwards in a half-smile, but I never really heard what she was saying, was only half aware of the regular patter of her voice, the rise and fall of intonation. I felt the scratch of the woollen blanket on my throat, the brush of her elbow against me when the caravan's pitch pushed us together. My throat always felt thick and swollen. From time to time I would raise a hand to my face, wipe away with a knuckle the fluid that dripped from my nose and eyes, as if, after all that dryness, I was now somehow overflowing.

In the evening, when someone up ahead called a halt and Marguerite reined in the horse, it always vaguely puzzled me. That they felt the need to stop at all seemed strange: that they had kept going all day seemed, in retrospect, equally strange. There seemed as little point to one thing as the other.

Counting back, I know a long time had passed since they'd picked me up in the desert. I must have lost the best part of two months to sickness and enfeeblement, and that all-consuming grief I couldn't shake. We had come a long way in that time, but I'd barely noticed the journey, barely noticed anything at all until one night, when we stopped, I found myself watching as Marguerite unhitched the horse, her fingers unbuckling and unthreading the tack with an easy grace. I watched the two of them cross the road together, watched the beast's rump and the woman's broad back, watched the horse dip its head and drink from the ditch. I looked round vacantly at the patch of waste ground, the spiny bushes and rank grass. Marguerite led the horse back and pushed a stake into the earth. Tethered, the beast dropped her head to graze. The men ambled over with their horses and the camel. Marguerite gathered brushwood into the crook of her arm, crouched to circle stones into a hearth. I sat and watched her, fascinated by the purposefulness of her movements, by her absorption in the task. It did not occur to me to offer to help.

The two men went back along the track a way, out of sight. Marguerite settled herself down upon the earth, became engrossed in tending the seedling of a fire. I got up from my seat, as if about to do something, but found instead that I just stood there, blanket wrapped around my shoulders, and did not even take a step. My legs began to feel weak and I would have sat down again had not Marguerite looked up from the fire at that moment and waved me over. I moved down the caravan steps, then across the open ground, my feet snagged by the long grass. Crouching at her side I watched as she fed the flames, watched the new sticks catch and spark, smelt woodsmoke. From behind us there was a flurry of shouts and movement, and I turned my head to see one of the men coming towards us, grinning, holding up by the tail what looked like a large rat. He strode over to the fire and handed the creature to Marguerite. She skinned it, gutted it and trussed it to a spit. She caught my eye and smiled at me. I blinked, but couldn't smile in time, and couldn't think of anything to say. She placed the carcass over the fire to cook. The dog sat down between us, eyes fixed on the roasting meat. One of the men had brought out his violin: he stood nearby tuning it. The other hunkered down, swigged something from a dark bottle, then passed it to Marguerite. She upended it at her lips and swallowed, then held out the bottle to me. I caught a whiff of something vitriolic; it made my stomach heave. I shook my head. She passed it on to the violinist, who held his fiddle and bow in the one hand for a moment to take a drink. Marguerite said something, something I didn't quite catch, and the man grinned. He passed the bottle on, tucked the fiddle beneath his chin and began to play. The meat began to cook, dripping fluids on to the fire, making it spit and crackle. Marguerite produced tobacco and pipes, and offered one to me, but my stomach lurched at the smell of it, and I shook my head and tried to smile.

Across the fire, the seated man lifted the bottle again but did not drink. He glanced at me, but spoke to Marguerite, nodding at the cooking meat.

'You're not thinking there's enough for –' he said.

'Yes,' Marguerite said. 'There is, there's plenty.'

I sat, hunched, watching the flames, an uneasy chill gathering between my shoulderblades, and said nothing.

Absences seemed to crowd close, just outside the firelight's spill, massing in my peripheral vision like an army in the shadows. In the corner of my eye I could almost see a child, bare-kneed, cold, desperate to get in; but when I turned my head to look, there was nothing but the dark.

That night, Marguerite lay down in the bed beside me, and it was only then that I realized she had been sleeping on the floor throughout my sickness. She was speaking as she settled herself down, as she rearranged the blankets and her nightgown, and though I wanted to say something in reply, I found myself turning away from her to lie facing the caravan's wooden hull. Behind me, I heard her sigh, felt her move and settle herself finally down into the bunk. I reached out in the dark to touch the boards in front of me, traced the unseen grain as it swelled around a knothole. I swallowed, remembering the *Spendlove,* the feel of her timbers beneath my feet and her helm wheel under my hands; I took my hand from the wood, reached up to touch my forehead, the ghost of a kiss. I felt the sigh of Marguerite's breath behind me as it softened into sleep. And then it came to me that there was another absence here, a space that I was taking up: the bunk was big enough for two. The hairs prickled on the nape of my neck. Beside me, Marguerite slept on, her breath regular and calm, and eventually, despite itself, my mind grew still, and I fell asleep.

When I woke, Marguerite was gone and there was a warm soft space in the bed beside me. I lay for a few moments, becoming aware of my body, of the blanket's weave against my cheek, of its warm tangle round my feet. I heard the single step of a horse moving forward as it grazed. I heard the dog snuffling around under the caravan. I heard a trickle of birdsong. I drew back the covers, slid my legs over the side of the bunk, and moved over to the door. In the morning cool, Marguerite was crouched over the remains of last night's fire: there was woodsmoke on the air. I came down the steps and walked over to her. She had the fire burning well, thick deep embers beneath, bright yellow flames above. A kettle steamed upon it. Seeing me, she wrapped a cloth around the handle of the kettle, lifted it and poured a cup of tea. She handed it to me. I took a mouthful. It was hot and sour.

'Andre, Bill,' she called, and the first sounds of movement came from the other caravans. When I turned my head to look back for them, my eye was caught by movement: the dog was following a scent across the open ground, head down, zigzagging and looping back and forth.

'He won't catch anything,' Marguerite said, 'he never does.'

I nodded, a slow upward movement of the head.

'Bloody useless dog,' she said, and there was fondness in her voice.

One of the front wheels hit a stone, jolting us. The dog trotted by, head down, tail up, going faster than the horses. I swallowed down the lump in my throat. I thought of the space I took up every night, the tangle of blankets, the warm sigh of Marguerite's breath. As I sat there, her shoulder was brushing against mine, her profile was vaguely present in the corner of my eye. I wanted to turn and look at her, but I couldn't quite manage it. Something like shyness. For the first time in what felt like ages, I found that there were words tumbling around inside my head, jostling to get out, but I couldn't quite get them into order. And somehow it seemed inappropriate that I should talk, after being silent for so long. I must have opened my mouth a dozen times and closed it again without saying a word. And when I finally managed to speak, it was nothing like what I'd meant to say, and came out breathless and half-choked.

'Who was Sarah?' I asked, but didn't dare to look round.

'Who told you about Sarah?'

'It was something someone said. Back when you found me.'

'Sarah was the elephant. When she died, Mr Aldobrandi went astray in the head. One last disappearing act, and he took the tent with him. Didn't make her disappear though. We had to leave her lying there, dogs eating out her belly and flies all over her. It broke our hearts. Delilah hasn't quite been herself ever since.'

'I thought she might have been your daughter. I thought she might have slept where I sleep now.'

She glanced round at me. I met her eye for a moment, then looked away. She flicked the reins: the horse raised her head and shook it but did not change her pace. I glanced back round and happened to catch Marguerite's expression in the moment that it shifted: I watched as her face tucked itself up into lines and folds, then watched the creases fade again, as if there had been some sudden pain. I realized then that I hadn't really looked at her before. My eyes scanned over the pouchy soft skin of her throat, her bare weather-tanned arms, the swags of loose flesh hanging from them, and came to rest upon her bosom. Her breasts were low and flattened, they'd settled just above her waistband. The print dress which covered them was baggy: it was much too big for her.

'No,' she said.

'I didn't mean–' I said. 'I'm sorry.'

We just sat in silence for a while as the horse dragged us on. I heard her draw in a breath, felt her hold it for a moment.

'I used to be the Fat Lady,' she said. 'All there's ever been in that bed is more of me, and you.'

She glanced round at me, I caught her eye, and her face wrinkled into a smile.

'There were bad times. Bad decisions, idiotic decisions made. To go touring where there are acrobats in every marketplace. With a camel where camels are commoner than sheep.' She shook her head. 'All Aldobrandi's idea, of course. Expanding the circuit.'

'That's where you found me?'

'We were heading back,' she said. 'One way or another, a lot of ballast has been shed.'

I bit my lip, and for a while there was silence between us. In front, the horse's hooves scuffed on the grit; behind us, the back axle was creaking.

'You should have seen us in our day,' Marguerite said.

'I'm sure,' I said, 'you were wonderful.'

The men were twins. It took until then for me to notice. It took me until then to look at them directly. They were mirror twins: the cowlicks in their red-grey hair swirled in opposite directions; Bill was righthanded, Andre favoured his left.

That night we stopped between settlements, on common land. They caught rabbits and left them, still warm, their fur rumpled, on the caravan steps.

'Keep the dog off them, now, will you?' Marguerite asked me, and I sat down on the bottom step, kept guard.

The three of them moved quickly, slotting together lengths of light pale wood, banging in pegs, uncoiling and knotting lengths of rope. I recognized a running bowline, a bowstring, a half hitch. But there was none of that miraculous fluidity that I remembered from so long ago, no conjured-out-of-nowhere sea of rippling red silk. As Marguerite had said, the tent was gone: instead a stunted bare skeleton was being raised up on the scrubby earth. The twins heaved on ropes and a pole was lifted from the ground. Marguerite was walking with it, steadying its passage to the vertical. She settled its base into the dry earth, and I noticed an unfamiliar sensation growing inside me, vaguely warm and elastic, as if something in me wanted to reach out towards them but could not quite stretch itself sufficiently. The sensation faded, turned into an ache, a knot inside my chest.

I leaned back and felt something soft brush my hand. I looked round and saw the rabbit corpses lying there, warm and glassy-eyed. I caught them up by the hind legs and heaved myself up from my seat, carrying them with me as I climbed the steps. For some reason, I found myself blinking away tears. When I came back out of the caravan, a knife in one hand, the rabbits hanging limp from the other, the dog was sniffing at the spot on the step where the bodies had been lying, the pole was secured with guy ropes, and Marguerite and the twins had moved on to erect the next upright. I pushed away the dog and sat down. I turned one of the rabbits over in my hands a moment, feeling the terrible slackness of its body, the loose articulation of its limbs. I ran my knife along its belly, making a quick cut, then began to peel the skin back and away, sliding my fingers between the fur and the flesh. My grandmother had done it out on the back step: I remembered her saying, if you left them too long, they were impossible to skin. In life they were such slight, vulnerable things, but in death they seemed to gain a new robustness and tenacity. As I pulled out the rabbit's innards, it was my grandmother's hands I saw, weather-tanned and hard, dragging out a hot wet handful of tangled entrails, tossing them to the dog.

The evening was growing cool. The three of them were still moving, still putting the structure together: a cross-piece slotted in, a guyline stretched, a peg hammered into the soil. I took the rabbits indoors and set them on a shelf, out of the dog's reach. Then I went outside again, wandered over to where the animals were grazing. The horses' heads were dipped down to the grass, but the camel looked up at me, her eyes big and impassive, her jaw working slowly round and round as she chewed. I held my fingertips out to her, let her blow and snuff at them, and then reached to touch her on the nose. The skin was downy. I noticed for the first time the peg that had been passed through her nostrils, to harness her.

'Thank you,' I said, under my breath, 'thank you.'

I stood there a moment, hand resting on her muzzle, while she watched me out of one eye. I glanced over to where Andre and Bill were finishing off the frame; they had swarmed up poles, had slung wires across the empty space, and were tightening them with windlasses. They slung swings from the cross-pieces, high above the ground. It looked, I thought, like a ship's rigging, or an unnecessarily complicated gallows.

'Thank you,' I breathed again into the cup of her ear, and the ear twitched. I ran my fingers down her nose and moved away. I began gathering grasses, twigs, and fallen wood. I took them back towards the caravans, then dragged loose stones together to form a circle and sparked a fire. I fed twigs into the flames.

Marguerite came over to me and stopped to stand by the fire a moment, hands on hips. She looked down at me and smiled. I found myself smiling back up at her. Then she moved past me and climbed into the caravan. She came back out with a large cooking pot hooked underneath her arm, the rabbits dangling, tiny and naked, from her other hand.

'Nice job,' she said

I shrugged at her.

'I saw some sage bushes and wild carrot near the road,' she said. 'We'll make a stew.'

The fire burned hot and without much smoke. Steam rose from the cooking pot, fragrant with herbs. From time to time, Marguerite would lean forward to stir the stew, would throw in a sprig of something, or raise the spoon to her lips to taste. Although I was sitting next to her, arms wrapped around my knees, I was transported elsewhere, was absorbed. I was watching the brothers practice.

I had to keep on reminding myself that there were only two of them. The seamless flow of leaps, tumbles, throws, catches and falls, some of which would only be stopped a foot from the ground, with just a hand caught in a rope's curl or on the rung of a cross-bar, transformed the two men into a dozen, a score, a whole troupe of acrobats. As the light faded, they seemed to multiply into infinity, like reflections in paired mirrors. When a seemingly hopeless fall was stopped dead, when a hold seemed to be a hair's breadth missed, I would gasp, and find that I was curled up in a rictus of concentration, my fingers tangled in the hem of my shirt, or my hand clasped around Marguerite's soft-fleshed forearm. She would already be laughing, the loose skin round her face and neck wrinkling and tucking, so that when I glanced at her, her face had taken on the appearance of long-used wood, the grain raised into ridges as the pith between is worn away. The brothers flew among the stars, multiplicitous, indistinguishable, and it caught me with a sudden thrill that I was inside the circle, seeing this.

'You didn't tell me they were acrobats,' I said.

Marguerite shrugged.

'We're all something,' she said. 'Or we were. You have to be.'

The two men were coming over to us, breathless and a

little unsteady on their feet. They sat down at the fire's rim, exchanged wordless happy looks.

'You haven't lost it, lads,' Marguerite said, passing them the bottle. Bill took a swig, handed the bottle over to his brother. Marguerite began dishing up the food. She handed Bill a bowl and he took it in his palm, raised it close to his face, and began to spoon the stew into his mouth. She served Andre, then held out a dish towards me, and as I reached out for it, my eyes strayed over to Bill's and caught there. He had stopped eating, his expression had narrowed and hardened. He was watching me. I looked away and just sat there a moment, holding the bowl cupped in my hand, my thumb pressing down on the rim. The food now seemed irrelevant, faintly ridiculous; my hunger had turned into queasiness.

'Good,' he said, and I didn't know if he meant the food, or was noticing my discomfort, or was just replying to Marguerite. She began filling another bowl for herself.

A moment passed. There were no sounds but those of the flames and eating. I picked up my spoon, looked down at the stew. Next to me, I was aware of Marguerite raising her spoon to her mouth, then hesitating.

'I barely had to lift a finger tonight, you know,' she said. Through a mouthful, Andre made an enquiring sound. 'Everything was done by the time I came back.' Out of the corner of my eye I watched her unfurl a smile, try to catch Bill's attention with it. 'Handy wee thing to have about the place,' she said.

I let my gaze stray upwards. Andre caught my eye and smiled at me, but Bill didn't look up from his food.

I lifted my spoon, took some of the stew into my mouth. I chewed, swallowed. The bottle was passed around again; I shook my head. Marguerite offered me a pipe, but again I shook my head. I pushed the stew around my dish, took another spoonful, looked at it.

'But it's nothing,' I heard Bill say, 'on its own. It's not enough.'

Sitting hunched beside Marguerite, I was aware of her warm softness, of her breath as it came and went. I caught the warm yeasty smell of her skin, the sharp overtang of perspiration, and the musty taint of her clothes. She put an arm around me, but I sat there stiffly and did not lean in against her. Andre lifted his violin, coaxed the strings into trembling with the bow, and the music drifted out into the dark. Bill drank from the bottle, watching the flames. I chewed on the crumbs of flesh, slivers of herb, fragments of vegetable, but they stuck in my throat, like grief.

I lay that night next to Marguerite's warmth, still and straight so that nothing might touch her; not a toe, not a knuckle. Lying looking up at the dark, I imagined myself slipping down to the end of the bunk, sliding out from underneath the covers and into the night and just walking away, anywhere. But fatigue and misery overcame me and I drifted into a troubled sleep, dreaming of winter, and rutted roads, and time an urgent ticking clock inside my belly.

When I woke, I found I'd kicked away the blankets and was lying curled up and goosepimpled in nothing but my shirt. I pulled on some clothes, came out blinking into the daylight. It was late, and there was something different about the place. Nothing tangible, nothing specific, just something somehow knowable about the air, something definite about the quality of the light, as if this was a place that might become familiar. The bare wooden structure they had assembled the previous evening was still standing there; its bones and sinews seemed to root it to the earth.

Marguerite, as usual, was boiling tea over last night's fire. I came up to the hearthstones, squatted down beside her. She poured me a cup.

'Bad night,' she said.

'I was dreaming.'

'Must've been something you ate.'

I glanced round at her. She lifted a plate and held it out to me. A few flat cakes of oatmeal and seeds. She must have baked them in the morning embers of the fire.

'Go on,' she said, 'have one. Do you good.'

'I don't think – I don't want to be any–'

'Go on,' she said again, so I reached out and took the nearest one. I was just raising it to my lips when Bill came round the side of the caravan, buttoning up his fly. I saw the moment that he saw me, watched his expression harden in that instant. As he came up towards us, I just sat there, beside Marguerite, a cup in one hand, the seedcake in the other, motionless and numb. He stood there, doing up his final flybutton, looking down at us.

'Right,' he said, and it was, I realized, the first time he'd ever spoken directly to me. 'Right. I've had just about enough of this. We've brought you all this way and you're a bloody useless, worthless cunt and I've had enough.'

I put down the cake, placed the mug back on a hearthstone.

'Get your stuff together,' he said, 'and go.'

'Bill,' Marguerite said. 'Bill, that's not how it works —'

'No, it's all right,' I said, and straightened up.

'It's not for you to say who stays and who goes —' Marguerite continued.

'No,' I said, 'he's right.'

The memory of last night's dream was a shiver down my back. It had been easy, so easy just to sit there in the haze of Marguerite's warmth, to let myself be carried along, to do nothing. But it could not go on like that for ever.

'This is not,' Marguerite was saying, 'how you treat a guest.' She had stood up beside me, her arm was slipping round my waist, encircling me. I watched, cheeks burning, as Andre came over to the fire, picked up the cup, glanced from Bill to Marguerite to me and back again, then took a mouthful of tea and swallowed.

'Guest!' Bill was saying. 'There's no such thing as guests. We can't afford guests.'

A moment passed. Marguerite's arm was still there, round my waist.

'Andre,' she said, 'say something to your brother.'

Andre inclined his head a little to the left, twisted his lips together, did not speak.

'Just a mouth, eating, all the time,' Bill said. 'Just a great big bloody mouth.'

'That's not true. She's doing all she can. She's not been well,' Marguerite said, and it seemed odd, for a moment, to hear myself interpreted like this, to hear myself described by her. 'But she's getting better now, and I'm sure –' She turned and smiled a thin, uneasy smile at me, 'when she's fully recovered, she'll prove herself to be a real asset.'

'And when will that be?'

Marguerite looked round at me. I watched the soft flesh on her neck ripple as she moved. I glanced back at Bill.

I could just walk away, I thought. I could leave the circus, leave Marguerite. After all, I was good at leaving. Hadn't I left everyone I ever cared about, one way or another? Everyone, that is, who hadn't left me first.

I looked back at Marguerite. I smiled at her.

'Now,' I said. 'I'll do it now.'

From the highwire I could see two pale ovals as Marguerite and Andre tilted their heads back to gaze up at me, their bodies tapering like tadpoles underneath. Bill was standing a little apart from them, nearer to the fire, not looking up. I considered, for a moment, coughing up a fine gob of spit, launching it out into the air in Bill's direction. I'd have a fair chance of landing it on his thinning crown.

'What's the point of me doing this,' I called down at him instead, 'if you're not going to watch?'

I caught the flash of Andre's grin, Marguerite's slow anxious shake of the head. My heart was beating unevenly. The wire pressed into my feet. Not markedly thinner than anything on board ship, I told myself; and here there was no wind to speak of, and I wasn't nearly as high as I was used to. I was good at this, of course I was. Hadn't I walked the ropewalks with the best? Hadn't I re-rigged the *Spendlove* singlehandedly and steered her past the ice? But that now seemed an age ago, and there had always been a handhold, a brace or yard to steady me. And I'd never had an audience before: there had always been a job to do, something to occupy my mind, to keep me from looking down, from the thought of falling.

I set off along the wire.

Don't try any fancy stuff, Marguerite had said as I'd begun the climb, but I didn't have a notion of what would count as fancy, let alone how I would go about trying it. So I just walked, fast, setting down one foot in front of the other at a diagonal to the rope, looking straight ahead at the empty blue sky. I was halfway out across the wire and just beginning to think that I was doing well, that all I had to do was keep my pace steady and my gaze straight, when my foot slipped, the wire thrummed beneath me, and I was back on board the *Sally Ann*, and someone was falling, arms and legs spread, mouth a wide dark O, and John Doyle's hand was on my arm. But she was not here now, and there was nothing, no one to steady me, and the sky swam like a heat haze in front of me and the grass spun up to meet me, and I ran. The wire bounced and lashed, my feet landed anyhow, slipped, skidded; three paces, two, to the end. I leapt for the post and clung there, my chest heaving, eyes closed.

So that was it. I'd failed. Of course I'd failed. I'd be forever what I'd always been, a child left outside in the darkness, desperate to get in. A moment passed. My breath began to calm. I'd go down there, gather my stuff together, and just walk away. It didn't matter. I'd always known I'd have to some day, and at least this way I could still walk. No bones broken. I let go of the post with one hand, wiped the dampness from my eyes. I'd say thank you to Marguerite. She might pull me close for a moment, might just kiss me. I grasped the descending rope, twisted my foot in it and began lowering myself to the ground. When my feet touched the earth, my knees buckled beneath me. And then, suddenly, like an unexpected shower of rain, I heard applause.

'Never seen anything like it.' Marguerite was coming up towards me. She was smiling, shaking her head.

'Not from a first timer,' Andre said.

And everything shifted sideways, was slightly, wonderfully different. I felt a slow grin begin to spread across my face.

'Well, Bill?' Marguerite asked, and turned towards him. 'What do you say now?'

Bill hesitated a moment, half-shrugged. 'Decent balance,' he said. 'Head for heights.'

'That,' I said, nodding back up at the wire, my voice sounding full and strange to me, 'is not a height.'

He didn't look at me. I glanced back at Andre, at Marguerite, my cheeks burning, my chest heaving.

'I want to learn,' I said. 'Teach me everything there is to know.'

*

The land grew rich. The horses put on flesh, their coats becoming glossy and thick. In the evening, when they were unharnessed, they would roll on their backs, legs kicking in the air, like foals. Delilah would dip her head to pull up close-growing plants by the roots.

The evenings began to creep in upon themselves, the twilight lingering on the western rim of the sky. Between us, we would have the structure up in quarter of an hour, would practise until it grew almost too dark to see. Then, in the last of the evening light, we'd strike the frame, unhitching guylines, easing down uprights and pulling them apart, setting the gear out on the grass: lengths of pole, coiled rope and wire, pegs, running blocks. I found myself taking pleasure in the precision of it all; a satisfaction in the way the joints slotted together and came apart so perfectly, in the neat loops of a well-coiled rope, in the orderly stowing of the gear. While the brothers and I would sometimes struggle with the larger pieces, no weight, no bulk seemed to bother Marguerite.

'You're the Strong Woman now,' I told her one evening, and that made her smile.

'I think you might be right,' she said.

The land grew mountainous, the air cold and dry and difficult to breathe. Marguerite gave me an old pair of boots, unravelled a vast sweater and sat knitting pair after pair of woollen socks for us as we travelled. Her breath rose in clouds and her fingers were pink and pinched, twisted up into the wool. Hunched into my jacket, I held the reins with my hands tucked up inside my sleeves. At night the horses crowded close, were buckled tight with blankets. Only Delilah seemed impervious to the cold, loping along all day with the same abstracted calm. And all the time I carried with me a faint sense of nausea, a thread of sickness that was there first thing when I woke and lingered on throughout the day. Just the altitude, the cold, I told myself, and swallowed down the rising bile. But even as I thought it, I knew it wasn't true. It had been hanging round me all this time: something I'd picked up in the desert and never quite managed to shake off.

We came across little settlements, usually just a few low cottages built of logs, a church, a barn. Too cold to perform outdoors, too deep in snow, we'd sling wires and trapezes from the rafters of the barn. Marguerite would begin with a show of strength. She'd lift a goat, its yellow eyes rolling wildly, above her head. Knees buckling, she'd grip one of our horses underneath her belly, lift her four hooves from off the ground. Puffing and blowing, she'd challenge the village men to do the same. They were usually laughing too much to even try.

I'd walk the high wire; Andre and Bill would fly on the trapezes. I did the fancy stuff now, no bother: cartwheels, balances, dance steps, falls. I'd learned quickly. At the end of the show I would just step off the wire into thin air. Andre would catch me as he flew past, his hands strong and safe around my wrists; as we swung across the space he'd release one hand and I would leap to catch a rope, slide down. The gasp the audience gave every time I stepped off into the empty space seemed to be no more than the lurch I felt inside me rendered audible, the moment's unacknowledged fear. And when Andre and Bill slid to the ground after me, and Marguerite joined us to take our bow, the applause and laughter made me glow hot and confused. I would glance along our line, at Marguerite and Andre and Bill. It felt right to be there with them. At the time, it felt completely right. But everything always changes.

We were paid mostly in produce; cheeses, dried meats, the cherry liqueur peculiar to the region; but when we made a little money, Marguerite would count my share into my palm as she did with Bill and Andre. Some copper, some silver. It made me feel at once proud and uneasy. I kept the coins in my pocket, wrapped up in a handkerchief, with the compass Cunningham had given me.

One of these nights, after a performance, we were sitting in Marguerite's caravan, the three of them sharing a bottle of the local drink. I wasn't keen on the stuff: the smell of it made my sickness worse. I'd been drinking tea instead, cup after cup of sour tea, and now it was apparent that I needed, quite urgently, to piss. I pulled on my boots and jacket, went outside. Cold, a clear sky, moonlight. I tucked my hands into my armpits and slipped round the side of the caravan, into shadow. I was just unbuttoning my britches when there was a flurry of movement, a scream, and someone, a woman, dashed past me, skirts flapping. A man was following fast behind.

It was none of my business, I thought. It wouldn't be the first time someone got hurt. And no one had ever stood up for me when I'd been in trouble. Not until I'd met Marguerite. I stood there a moment, hands on my flies. Then I turned and ran after them.

They were heading away from the village, out across open ground, the woman's shape clear against the moonlit blue of the snow, her skirts tangling round her legs as she ran, and it occurred to me how stupid it was of her to run away from the settlement, from any chance of help. The man's dark bulk moved between us, sometimes off to one side, sometimes obscuring her entirely. I stumbled through the dark scars left by their feet, my lungs already sore. I found myself wondering what I would do when I caught up with them, wished I'd thought of calling Marguerite, Bill and Andre before I'd set off. Alone, I wasn't that much of a threat.

The woman stopped. She turned back to face the man, and I opened my mouth to call out to her, to tell her I was coming, but I couldn't catch my breath. She dodged left, and he mirrored the movement. She feinted right. The man moved in front of her, screening her from sight, and I stumbled on towards them. And then she laughed. No mistaking it: she laughed, rich and soft and real, stopping me dead in my tracks. I watched as the man crouched, moved closer to her. I watched as he made a sudden lunge and caught her, and I heard her laugh again. A slow blush spread across my face. They wouldn't have seen me, I told myself as I turned and walked away. They were far too preoccupied to notice I was there.

It would be quicker to turn back towards the village and walk down the street to our camp than to go back the way I'd come. The street was cleared of snow and wood-cobbled; much easier going than the open ground. I ploughed back towards the nearest house, trying to ignore the sounds coming from behind me: giggles, rustling, the creak of snow compressing under weight. I passed a gable wall in shadow; low voices were coming from beneath the overhanging eaves. Male voices. In the darkness I caught the outline of two close-clipped heads, the shape of two entangled bodies. I lengthened my stride, came out on to the village street. Up against a woodpile, soutane hooked up around his thighs, I could have sworn I saw the priest, but I didn't look long enough to see who he was with.

It was quiet when I got back to the camp, the light low from our curtained window. Everyone had gone to bed. I went round the side of the caravan, into the shadow, and at last undid my britches. I closed my eyes, sighed, and pissed on to the snow.

Inside, Marguerite was a hump beneath the covers.

'You'll never guess,' I said, pulling off my boots, 'what's going on out there.'

'At it like rabbits, are they?'

I paused, jacket half off. She rolled over, looked up at me.

'Are you frozen?'

I looked at her a moment. The soft loose skin of her jowls gave her a vaguely canine air. 'How did you know?' I asked.

She shrugged.

'They just get that way sometimes. Just go a wee bit

wild. It's as if, when we're around, it somehow turns their whole world on its head.'

She rolled back over on her side, bringing the blankets up to her ear, and was still speaking, but I could no longer hear what she was saying. I was caught up in a memory that had risen, sudden and stark to the surface of my mind, like a corpse. Miss Woodend had leant up against Mr Metcalfe, was blushing beneath her walnut skin. *Just like the last time*, she'd said. *Always trouble.* And then, *Must be ten years. Twelve.*

Ten years, twelve. How old would I have been?

It had come up on me so slowly that at first I'd barely noticed, but there was something different in me; I couldn't ignore it any longer. There was the sickness, of course, I was almost used to that. But now there was also something else. It didn't feel like a change in my constitution, not a new weakness or the attainment of some new strength. It was just a slight adjustment, a shift: my centre of gravity seemed to have moved forwards and down. It was just because I'd become more aware of such things, I told myself. Practice and performances on the highwire had made me more conscious of my body and my balance. It didn't seem particularly important: I didn't mention it to anyone.

We travelled on, out of the mountains. The valleys were terraced with vines, wintry and bare. Men walked beside their donkeys in dark jackets and broad-brimmed hats, breath clouding the air. We came upon a town, small, tight-buttoned and unwelcoming, and when we trooped through the narrow cobbled streets, cart-wheeling and tumbling, the dog capering on hind legs, Delilah loping along beside us, shutters were slapped tight over windows and children scooped in off door-steps. Our audience that night was half-a-dozen men, all of them drunk, and a young clergyman who scowled at us from the shadows and refused to pay his fee. Up aloft, on the highwire, my head went into a sudden spin, and for a moment I was lost, my balance gone, swaying from side to side thirty feet above the hard ground. The men gave out a drunken hoot, and I caught my balance, flick-flacked back to the wire's end.

'Neat trick,' Andre said to me later when he caught my wrists. Hanging upside down, his face was puffy, the creases all falling the wrong way. 'I almost fell for it myself.' He smiled at me, but from where I was it looked more like a frown.

'So did I,' I said, and smiled back at him.

Afterwards, in the fire's glow, I sat slumped forward, a hand pressed into the small of my back: it was aching, it always seemed to be aching now. When the bottle was passed around it seemed to rest even longer with Bill than usual. He didn't speak a word, wouldn't even look at me. When the bottle came my way, I passed it on as quickly as possible: the slightest smell of it made my stomach heave.

As I lay down beside Marguerite that night, I could feel the vertebrae creak and shift in my back, feel the ache begin to fade.

'It's not my fault the crowd was shite,' I said into the dark.

'No,' said Marguerite, already half asleep.

'So what's the problem then?'

She rolled her head round to look round at me. I felt her breath on my cheek.

'Mnh?'

'What've I done to annoy Bill this time?'

She sighed. 'It's always the same thing with him,' she said. 'Times are hard, we're not making any money, and he's worried that with another mouth to feed – and then when we get to the coast, there's the passage to pay –'

'What do you mean another mouth to feed?' I hitched myself up on to an elbow, looked round at her in the darkness. 'Haven't I proved myself? Don't I pay my way?'

'It's not you I mean, honey,' she said, and rolled her head away again. 'You're extraordinary, you know that; you're a natural. And you know I'm proud of you.'

I hadn't. I opened my mouth, closed it again without speaking.

'But you can't keep on going for ever,' she said.

She'd noticed. That headspin on the highwire, the aches, the nausea: she'd realized I was ill.

'I'm fine,' I said. 'Honestly, I'll be fine. I'm just a bit under the weather, that's all; I'll soon be back on form. And I promise you I won't slack off. You can tell him that. I'll be fine.'

'Of course you'll be fine,' she said, reaching out to turn down the lamp. 'But you're going to have to slack off whether you like it or not. You can't keep on taking those risks. Not now there's the baby to think of.'

*

Marguerite had fallen asleep. I could see her in the moonlight. Her lips were parted, her breath whistling slightly through her teeth. I could not sleep.

He had lain there on the tumbled blankets of his camp bed, his eyes wet and wide. I'd stroked the hair back off his forehead, kissed him, and tried not to laugh.

'I'm sorry –' he'd said. I'd felt a kind of tenderness for him; I'd held a gun to his head. Then I'd walked away into the desert and left him behind. That was when it had begun to tick, this clock inside my belly, though I hadn't realized what the ticking was, till now.

I was not the kind of person who had babies. It was not the kind of thing that happened to me. I placed a hand on my belly, but felt nothing but the muscled curve of my own flesh. A little distended, though. I had to admit it. I thought of the medical books I'd come across in Jebb's library, the difficult script of black scimitars and slashes, and the coloured ink drawings of people with their skins off, the intimacy of nerve and muscle on display. I remembered one of them in which a child was curled up inside the mother's body, his hands grasped around his knees, looking out with old man's eyes. It made me shiver.

'Marguerite,' I whispered. She rolled her lips together, muttered something, but did not wake.

I drew back the covers, slid myself down to the end of the bed. I pulled on my clothes. The shirt that Jebb had given me, patched and laundered by Marguerite, its stain now faded to faint rust. Cunningham's jacket, far too big, and his second best hat. A pair of britches which might have once been Andre's or Bill's. My clutch of coins and compass heavy in a pocket. I opened the half-door, went down the steps, then sat on the middle tread and watched for a moment the way my toes fanned out across the bottom one. Then I pulled on the socks that Marguerite had knitted for me, laced up the boots that she had given me. I reached into my pocket, drew out the compass, watched the finger quiver, settle towards north. There was only one route left open to me.

I took a half-burnt stick from the sleeping fire, and in the dirt, at the bottom of Marguerite's caravan steps, I wrote, 'Goodbye', and 'Thank you'. And then I walked away.

At the time, it was the hardest thing I'd ever done. I didn't even know if she could read.

Sixteen

It was a cold night; the moon set early, and soon the darkness was complete. I couldn't see the road, could only feel the cartwheel ruts beneath my feet. A bramble brushed my cheek and made me jump, leaving behind a faint hot trail on the skin. Something small rustled in the hedgerow. Far off, I heard a fox bark.

Dawn broke, cold and blue, with birdsong. Beside me sparrows fluttered through the hedge, scuffling over the last of the hips and haws. The broad fields were rimed with frost. I walked on through the half-light hours, my arms wrapped around myself to keep in the warmth. When it became fully light I kept off the road and walked parallel to it, behind the screen of the hedge, scrambling over field-boundaries and across ditches, wading through heavy ploughed clay or stepping over the dried stalks of last year's crops. It wasn't that I expected them to come looking for me, but we were all heading the same way down the same road, and sooner or later they would catch up with me.

The sound of churchbells seemed to follow me. Spires stuck up from the dips and curves of the land like thorns. All day the sky didn't change: a high sheet of grey cloud covered the sun. There was no rain or snow, not a break in the grey. The smooth fields, the rows of plane trees, and here and there the copses of woodland took on a luminous, transparent quality, like a watercolour painting. My stomach was hollow, empty. My head felt light.

Around midday I spotted a figure in the distance, walking the fields with a hoe or rake angled over his shoulder. At the next gap, I pushed myself through the hedge and back on to the road, tugged my hat down over my eyes and tried to look purposeful, as if I was meant to be there. I didn't want to get caught trespassing. We passed each other at a distance, too far even to nod a greeting, the hedge a thick barrier between us for most of the time. I doubt he even noticed me. For the hour or so that I was on the roadway, between first spotting him and clearing sufficient distance to go back into the fields, it was hard not to keep glancing over my shoulder, keep turning to look for the keyhole silhouette of a caravan behind me.

The first night I slept beneath the sharp bones of the hedge. Even though I'd sailed to the southern ice and travelled over mountains, I had never in my life been as cold as I was that night, alone, without even a blanket, too anxious to light a fire.

Despite the churchbells and the spires in the distance, I'd come across no settlements. I'd found nothing to eat all day but a half-rotten mangold lying by the roadside. I'd managed to pick out a piece that seemed reasonable enough, but I'd no sooner chewed through it than I was vomiting it up again into the roadside ditch. It was hard to bring up, heavy and dry, and I was spitting blood before I'd done. It left behind a foul taste and a lingering doubt: maybe I couldn't cope. In the past, there had almost always been someone with me who'd decided what would happen next, and I'd either gone along with it, or kicked out against it. The only time I'd had to make my own way entirely alone was in the desert, and that had nearly killed me. In the shallow sleep of that freezing night, I found myself dreaming that someone was handing me breads as soft and warm as human skin, and bowls of hot steaming stew. I cupped them in my hands, inhaled, and melted with gratitude. And when I looked up, I saw that it was Cunningham passing me the food. I woke to find my fingers pressed over my face and an uneasy sense of nostalgia lingering in my belly, a craven doubt that I would now have welcomed slavery if it came with food.

When the caravans caught up with me in the afternoon of that day, it was as much as I could do to stay where I was, crouched in ditchwater, the ice a thin crust round my boot cuffs. But stay I did. Shivering and silent, I let them pass. I watched Marguerite go by. She was hunched forward, looking intently ahead, the dog sitting bolt upright in her lap. She didn't even glance my way, but I knew that she was looking for me, expected at any moment to spot me on the road ahead. I waited until the caravans were just dark shapes in the distance before climbing out of the ditch and moving on.

I still miss her.

Now they were ahead I could continue by road. No more struggling through field hedges, snagging my clothes and scratching my hands. No more wading through ditches of ice-crusted mud. I kept on going all afternoon and into the evening. Around dusk the weather turned and a cold slap of rain-drenched wind hit me across the face. I turned up my collar, wrapped it tighter round my body, tried to ignore the fatigue, the ache in my calf muscles, the grind of my hipbones. The wind grew bitter, squally. I pushed my hat down harder on my head, kept on walking. The light was fading. I watched water drip from my hatbrim. I watched the scuffed toes of Marguerite's old boots swing out in front of me, one and then the other, again and again. My heart beat heavily in my chest.

There'd been nothing for miles, nothing but stands of slender trees and stretches of hedge; nothing to keep out the weather. And as it grew darker I could see nothing but the vague shape of the hedgerow at my side and the paleness of my own hand when I held it out in front of me.

It was fully dark. A nasty, bitter night. My face was stinging with cold. When I looked directly, I couldn't see anything at all: only when I turned away and caught it in the corner of my eye could I make something out: a vague looming shape, paler than the night. Buildings of some kind, on a hill above the road. I moved forward and reached out a hand, touched the smoothness of much-used wood. I pushed and the wood moved forward a little, hinged. A gate. Beyond, there seemed to be a lighter streak which must be a gravel track leading up to the buildings. I felt around for the fastening of the gate, unhitched it and slipped through the gap. The gravel crunched beneath my feet. I walked up the track.

In the shadow of the courtyard I caught the cowbyre's warm stink and turned towards it. There would be straw and the heat of gathered bodies. I felt along rough granular stone, found a windowledge and then a doorframe. My fingertips brushed the cold metal plate of a latch. I unbolted the door, pushed it open. Inside, warmth, the smell of cowshit, hay and milk, the stamp and shift of cattle, the sweet scent of cattle-breath. I pulled the door shut behind me. It was pitch black in there. I reached out a hand in front and there was nothing to my touch. I couldn't even see my hand. I reached out to the left and touched a milch-cow's bony rump: her flesh quivered as if a fly had settled on her. To my right there seemed to be a wooden partition wall: I felt the planes and grooves of planking. I ran my hand along it as I moved down the byre, keeping the other hand stretched out in front of me. A cow shifted, unsettled, as I passed. My right hand knocked against an upright, slipped over it, then ran along a wooden bar. I felt along its length, came to another upright. Above, another bar parallel to the first. And below. A ladder. I felt around with a foot, found a low rung, and heaved myself up. I climbed up into the darkness, came through a narrow gap between wooden boards and was in a sweet summer-smelling drift of hay.

Warmth rose from the cattle below. As I waded

through it, the hay felt soft against my legs. I stopped a little way from the trapdoor, wary of straying over an edge in the dark. I took off my sodden jacket, britches and boots and laid myself down in the hay, dragging armfuls across myself, digging my feet down into the drifts. I lay there shivering, and gradually the shivers warmed me, and after a little while I fell asleep.

I woke to the clank of milkpails, the clatter of wooden shoes on cobblestones, and an argument in a language that I didn't understand. I remembered that I'd left the byre door unbolted: someone else was getting blamed for it. An old voice, a man's, was doing the scolding and a younger woman was defending herself. I lay still, dreading that they would become suspicious and search the place, or just that they would need to fetch hay for the cattle. Although I was pretty much buried in the stuff, my jacket and britches were lying dark and conspicuous on top of the drifts. But the quarrelling soon petered out, and before long all I heard were the murmuring sounds that people make when soothing animals, and the squirt of milk into buckets.

When I woke again it was dark and the hay was tickling my cheek. My joints were stiff, my throat sore, and for just a moment I had no idea of where I was or where Marguerite had gone. Then I remembered. I stirred myself, pushed away the mounds of hay and felt around for my clothes. They were dry, and faintly warm, and smelt of hay and cowdung.

Outside, the weather had changed: a sky scudding with clouds, a bright full moon, stars. How long had I been asleep, I wondered; how much time had passed? A hand strayed down to my belly, round and firm beneath my palm. As I moved across the courtyard, I passed a barrel resting on its side and heard the rattle of a chain as the sleeping dog inside it stirred.

The dairy was pale and cold in the moonlight. I helped myself to a long drink of milk, found two small curd cheeses and dropped them in my pockets. I took apples from the applestore, a piece of bacon from the meatsafe. They didn't have much, certainly didn't have anything to spare, but hunger sends the conscience straight to sleep: it only stirred as day broke on the open road and the last soft crumb of cheese was melting on my tongue. All compulsion gone, I was left with a full belly and the slow aching rise of guilt.

But it was forgotten soon enough. It was two days before I reached the next settlement. Two days in which I found it more and more difficult to stop myself from just curling up beneath the roadside hedge and sleeping. Two days in which my legs became weak, in which I became increasingly aware of my own heart beating, in which all I found to eat were a few frost-softened windfalls lying in the grass of a wayside orchard.

It was mid-afternoon when I first spotted the village across the fields, but it was well into the night before I reached its outskirts. Kitchen gardens lined the road. In the moonlight I saw rows of frost-pinched brussels sprouts, hen-scratched earth and bleached fruit canes. The houses were dark and blindfolded with shutters.

Down back alleys and across gardens, I took a child's

way through the village. I found the gaps in hedges, the loose pales in fences, the hand-and-foot-holds in drystone walls. Here and there I tried a door or window, gently tugging and pushing at the fastenings to see what would shift readily and without much noise. At one house I had barely touched the doorhandle when a dog began to bark, and I ran, scrambled over a wall and dropped down into an alley. I crouched there listening, heart beating fast, until the barking stopped. When doors were left unbolted, I slipped inside and stole whatever I could find. I took the eggs from underneath hens as they slept.

When the sun came up, I was striding out along the road in guilty haste. A child would go without breakfast. A dog would be kicked for sleeping through the theft of that day's dinner. How many chickens' necks would be wrung because it looked like they'd stopped laying? I took an egg from out of my pocket, weighed it in my hand. A clutch of three more still nestled, warm and reassuring, in my pocket. I looked at it a moment, so perfect, smooth and self-contained, then I pierced it top and bottom with a fingernail, and raised it to my lips to suck.

A few days later, in another village, almost big enough to be called a town, there was a bakery: hot and glowing at four o'clock in the morning when, sneaking down an alleyway, I came across its back entrance. I waited outside for almost an hour before I got my chance. I took two loaves, ate the first one so quickly that I'd almost finished it before I'd got beyond the village limits. I gave myself the hiccups.

Long after daybreak and miles further on, I was still wracked with guilt and hiccups. I knew it was wrong, but I couldn't help myself. I was driven by something more pressing, more compulsive than I'd ever known. Something stronger than me was working now, something far more vital. You.

At my feet the rabbit-clipped grass ended abruptly. Below, slabs of turf lay tumbled down on the muddy sand. In front of me stretched a sheet of rippling water, reflecting the grey sky. Gulls rose and fell on the evening air.

The road swung out away to the right, towards the town. The town's walls were grey and high and smooth and the buildings rose up inside them, streets spiralling up a rocky outcrop; on the seaward side, an arm of stone reached out into the grey waves, holding shipping still and close, as if by these displays of solidity the town could assert itself against the ghosts of elsewhere. Port towns are always riddled with thoughts of what might lie beyond, of what has been left behind.

A sharp breeze blew off the sea, pushing back my hatbrim, bringing the blood to my cheeks, making me gasp. It seemed like so long since I'd felt anything like awake, felt anything more than the heavy pulse of blood, the increasing inertia of the flesh. I just stood there a moment, the wind on my face and in my lungs, the blood stirring in my cheeks, the sound of the sea like breath. And then I shrugged off my jacket and shirt, stepped out of my trousers. The cold air brushed my skin into goosepimples. My hand rested on the roundness of my belly. A moment, just standing there, looking out across the silver plane of the water. Then I stepped down the bank, from turf to turf, then on to the sand. Heels sinking deep, toes spreading wide, I walked out towards the sea.

Water sprayed up over my ankles, shins, knees. I waded on until I stood thigh-deep, then dived out and swam. And as I turned and twisted through the water, I felt you move. A flicker, silvery and soft. A minnow in my belly. I stopped, hanging still, and pressed a hand to my cold skin. Perhaps the mermaids crowded close, drawn towards that glimmer, brushing me with a cold hand, a curl of tail, a tendril of saltsoaked hair as they passed by. If they did, I didn't notice them: I was listening for you.

Seventeen

Open-topped, single-masted, she was little more than a
dinghy really, but she seemed canny enough. She was due
to sail on the morning tide. The captain and I established
this between us after much mugging and gesturing on my
part, and a few functional but not unfriendly words on
his. He, like many sailors, port-town publicans, whores
and pawn-brokers, possessed the ability to negotiate in
seemingly any language that was required of him. When I
unknotted my handkerchief and showed him the clutch
of coins Marguerite had given me, he shifted them round
my palm with a fingertip, shook his head sadly.

'Two times,' he said, holding up his fingers to
elucidate, and I closed my palm, rattled the coins a
moment in my fist, then nodded at him.

'I'll be back,' I said.

The glow from the windows was warm and smoky.
Standing outside on the quay, I could hear shouting,

laughter and several voices conspiring to murder a tune. Now and then I'd catch a word or two, a clot of syllables I thought I might have understood if I'd heard more, if I could've just teased them apart in the right places. I ran a hand down the front of Cunningham's old jacket. It hung loose and concealing. Something to be thankful for.

I pushed open the door. The smell of the place — tobacco, spirits and stale beer – made my stomach heave. Eyes peered over the rims of glasses or were narrowed through a stream of smoke. The room had fallen silent. I moved over to the counter, hitched myself up on to a stool. The barman was a big man, pale, with a long rusty moustache. I knew he'd understand me, if he chose to.

'Dandelion and burdock, if you have it,' I said. Everyone in the room seemed to lean in towards me to listen.

He shook his head.

'Ginger beer?' I asked.

'Wine,' he said. 'Beer, brandy.'

'Milk?'

He shook his head again.

'Tea, then.'

He just looked at me.

'It'll have to be a beer then, I suppose,' I said, and watched as he poured it. Then I pushed a coin across the counter. The biggest denomination that I had: Marguerite had pressed it into my palm after a performance in the mountains. I should have left it on a dairy shelf in place of those two cheeses. I should have slipped it on to the baker's floury tabletop, or underneath a hen's warm rump. But I'd known that this moment, or a moment like it, would come eventually. Out of the corner of my eye, I watched as the barman picked up the coin, raised an eyebrow. He began counting out the change.

'Haven't seen you in here before,' he said, setting the glass down in front of me.

'No,' I said, and took a sip; the stuff tasted foul, oily. I placed it back down on the counter.

'In town for long?'

'Not long,' I said, and smiled up at him. 'I just came in on the last boat, it's my first time away from home.' I raised the glass to my lips, let the liquid rest against them a moment without drinking, then wiped away the foam with the back of my hand. 'A year's grace, the old man said, then back home, settle down, take over the family firm.' I glanced at the barman's face. A common enough story: it could, almost, have been my own. But was he falling for it? I didn't have the money to try this again in another bar. I didn't have the time.

'So it's my last chance to live it up,' I said, leaning in, giving him a wink. He picked up a glass, began polishing it with a grimy rag.

'You got money,' he said, 'I can find you a woman.'

'Er, no,' I said, and then cleared my throat. 'No, not that. I was looking for a game of cards, in fact. I heard this is the place for it.'

The barman looked across the counter at me a moment, his pale eyes unreadable. I lifted my glass, tilted it, watched the foam slide and shift inside. Of course I'd heard nothing of the sort, I'd just walked into the first bar I'd come across. But I'd been in enough of these places back in Sailortown to know I couldn't be too wide of the mark. A moment passed. I looked up at him again, gave him my biggest, broadest, most innocent smile.

'Later,' the barman said. 'Midnight. Five card jack.'

I tilted my head. 'I don't think I know that one,' I said.

The wick had burnt down low. Tallow dripped down the candle stump, pooled out into the saucer. Sweat trickled down the side of my nose. I reached up a hand to wipe it away and glanced round the circled faces. I was finding it hard to concentrate.

He had changed, but I would have known him any-where, and in an instant.

He'd come through to the back room after everybody else. He must have arrived at the bar just in time for the game, slipping through the front door as we were moving through to the back. If he'd been in the bar while I was there, I would have seen him. I would have turned to him without thinking, as a compass needle turns towards the north.

He was thinner, and he'd never been heavy. His cheekbones were stark and sharp, his eyes underhung with shadows. He looked faded, worn: his clothes were shiny at the seams and there was grey in his hair. But when he came into the room, scraped back the empty seat and nodded at the other players, I felt a surge of joy. It was all I could do to stop myself standing up and crossing over to him, pulling up a chair and giving him a nudge, a smile. I'd've been back at his side, and happy, before I'd even thought about it.

But I did stop myself. I thought about it. He wasn't the only one who'd changed.

He took his cards, he made his bets, once or twice he scowled down at his hand, but he didn't look up at me. Another change; in the past his face had always been a mask while he was playing. The memory, the intimacy of this private knowledge, gave me goosepimples. I plucked a card out from my hand, replaced it at random between two others. I wouldn't look at him again. I knew, without even taking my eyes off my cards, that he was drunk. He was drunk, he was losing, and he hadn't noticed me.

The barman shunted a final column of coins out towards the heap in the middle of the table. He took his cigarette from his mouth, tapped the ash on to the floor.

'Let's see 'em, then, lad,' he said, a smile twisting up the corner of his mouth. The smell of his tobacco was making me feel sick, was putting me off my game, as if there weren't enough distractions already.

'I think –' I said.

In the corner of my eye, the bowed head, the tremble in the hands that held the cards, the hands that had undone the buttons of my wet shirt one by one, had tugged each fly button loose and grazed the cold skin of my belly.

My mouth was watering. I swallowed. I laid my cards out flat on the table. 'I think that might be what you call a five card jack,' I said.

Someone coughed. Someone's hand, resting on the tabletop, curled into a fist, the knuckles whitening. I tried a smile. No one reciprocated. No one said a word. I reached out to pull my winnings to me.

One of the men was picking up the fans of cards, forming them back into a pack, shuffling them.

Across the table, he looked up for the first time, and I looked straight back at him. I raised an eyebrow. He held my gaze a moment, then he dropped his eyes, pushed back his chair and walked out without saying a word. What had it meant, that glance? What had he wanted to convey? It was too late to ask: he had pulled the door shut behind him, and was gone. I noticed a card land just by my hand, then another. I looked back round at the table.

'Well, that's enough for me,' I said. I dragged handfuls of coin over the tabletop, began scooping it into my pockets. 'I'm done for.'

'You'll stay for another.'

The cards were skimming out across the table, were gathering in front of me.

'No, thank you, I really must be going –'

'One more game.'

'Very decent of you but –' I moved over towards the door, stretched my hand out towards the latch. My pockets were heavy with money, my jacket swinging with its weight. Behind me, I heard the scrape as chairs were pushed back. I pressed down on the thumbplate, began to draw the door back towards me, then a hand was placed on mine: I saw it before I felt it. Blunt-fingered, square-nailed, pale as milk pudding. I turned round, my hand falling away from the latch, his hand falling away with mine, the door standing half-open at my side. I raised my eyes to his face.

The barman said something, and I watched his oddly pink lips move behind the fringe of his moustache, saw the yellowed ridges of his teeth, noticed the patterning of freckles across his nose and down his cheeks, but I didn't hear a word that he was saying, because something was welling up inside me, something blind and ferocious and mad. It wasn't the money, at least, not directly. It was him, standing there, keeping me there when every fibre of my body was crying out to be elsewhere. One more solid fleshy obstacle in my way. I felt my teeth clench, felt my right hand wrap itself up into a knot. I slipped my back foot into the gap between the door and the doorjamb, shifted my weight on to it, and then I punched him in the face.

I was out of the door in an instant. The main bar room was deserted. I ran for the front door, skidded up to it, began to fumble with the bolts. It would have been more satisfying, I found myself thinking, if I could have said something, told him that he was just the last in a long line of offenders, and that when I slammed my knuckles into his nose it was nothing personal. But there wasn't time for regrets or explanations. I heaved the door open, a blast of cold air hit me in the face, and I stumbled out into the quayside.

To the east, the sky was beginning to pale. The harbour was right in front of me. It was nearly high tide. Ships' lanterns scattered light like coins across the water. At the end of the quay, a yellow lamp bobbed and swung, waiting for me. In a little less than half an hour, the sun would be up, the tide would have turned, and my ship would have set sail.

The door fell shut behind me. From inside came raised voices, the sound of movement. I was turning towards the yellow light, about to run for the safety of the boat, when something snagged my eye. Over to the left, in the opposite direction, there'd been a movement, as if the shadows had rippled. I turned back and saw him, just as he went round the corner, just before he slipped out of sight. There was no mistaking it. It was Joe.

I ran after him along the quay, tugging my jacket close, the bulging pockets knocking against my legs. I was out of breath almost instantly, my heart beating fast and heavy, my head tight and spinning from lack of air. But I wouldn't let him get away. Not like that. Not without a word. Not again.

My ankle twisted sideways. I froze, half-crouched, swaying, biting at my lip. I tried my weight on it: a burst of pain, bright and sudden as a firework. I couldn't move.

I glanced over my shoulder. Back at the bar, the door had been pulled open and light spilled out across the cobbles. A dark figure stood there, was joined by another man, then another, until their bodies blocked out the light. They hadn't seen me yet. I wrapped my arms around my belly. One of the men turned his head towards me. The light streamed past him, caught on sandy-red hair, on the dark blood flowing from the barman's nose.

Then something pulled the hem of my jacket and I was tugged, sideways, into darkness.

I lost my footing. As I fell I tore my ankle again. I landed on my right thigh on the cobbles, my hand pressed into something slimy. I hunched forwards, breathing, waiting for the pain to fade. He was there beside me, hunkered down in the darkness: I could feel him rather than see him, but I knew without question who it was.

'C'mon,' he breathed into my ear, and I could smell the drink on his breath as he spoke. But I couldn't move, I had to stay there, curled up, listening inwardly for changes, shifts, for the slightest indication of you.

'They're coming,' he hissed. I could already hear the clatter of footfalls on the cobbles. 'Give me your hand.'

I didn't give him my hand: his fingers wrapped themselves around my wrist. He pulled me to my feet and I hissed against the shock as my foot touched the ground. He jerked at my wrist and was off, dragging me after him in a crouching uneven half-run up the dark alleyway, my feet slipping on the dirty cobbles, my leg and hand stinging from the fall, every step jolting my ankle. I kept one arm wrapped around my belly; half my mind was still wrapped up in the warm darkness inside.

Suddenly we were out of the alleyway and into moonlight. I was hunched, limping and breathless with pain, my wrist still caught tight in his hand. He was striding along beside me, alert and assured, upright as the day he'd stood on the village road and the moonlight had caught his smile. Such a slight thing, a smile. But without it, I would have turned and walked back into the house, and into a different life.

He rounded a corner into a narrower street and I

stumbled after him: we passed through wrought iron gates and were suddenly out in the open, the sky clear above us.

A graveyard. I would have stopped then, would have slumped down on a tomb or kerb, but he dragged me on between the monuments and headstones until we came to a place where the grass grew high between the graves and the stones were crumbling and aslant. He stopped. I put a hand on the lid of a tomb and sat down. I could hear nothing but the blood pounding through my skull. I leant forward, rested my head upon a hand: I was going to be sick, I thought. Any moment now, I would be sick. I made to stand, to turn away, but as I stood a blanket seemed to come down over my senses, lights swimming and clotting, everything scrolling away into the distance, sounds coming to me muffled and distorted. There was pressure on my shoulder, pushing me back down to be seated.

'Whoa, whoa there,' he was saying. 'What's the rush?'

I rested my head upon my hand again, concentrated for a moment on my breathing, on making sure I didn't throw up.

He sat himself down beside me, pushed back his hat. I turned my head and looked at him. The sky was growing paler, the light increasing. It caught the plane of his cheek, the smooth side of his nose. It caught in his eye when he turned to look at me. It picked out the map of lines and wrinkles when he smiled. I closed my eyes, shook my head, leant down more heavily on my hand. I was wrong, I thought. He hasn't changed a bit.

'You're good,' he was saying. 'You're very good.'

I opened my eyes, looked down at the dark fabric of my trouserlegs, and between them the rough cold stone of the tomb.

'With the cards, I mean. The whole shebang, in fact. The innocent abroad; it's not what you'd call original, but it's certainly effective: they had no idea.' He paused a moment, watching me, and I was about to turn to him, to speak. But when it came to it, it no longer seemed to matter how he'd come to lose me in a game of dice, or how remorseful he had felt to find me gone, or what kind of trouble he had been in as a consequence. I found I didn't want to ask him anything at all.

'What's your name?' he said.

I looked up. He was taking a bottle from an inner pocket. He uncorked it, offered it to me. I shook my head. I watched as he drank for a moment, his head thrown back.

'You don't know me,' I said.

He took the bottle from his lips, looked at me.

'Eh?'

'You don't know me,' I said again.

His eyes skimmed my clothes, the bulk of my jacket, my scuffed and patched boots, then turned up again to look at my face.

'No, no,' he said, 'Of course I do. Just give me a minute. You're – erm –'

And he stared at me, blearily, through a fog of drink.

'You're –'

And then his eyes cleared, his mouth fell open. He recognized me.

'Bloody hell.'

He brought a hand to his mouth, leaned in towards me, looked me up and down again. And then he laughed. He laughed, and for a moment I just watched him, watched the shake of his shoulders and the crease of his eyes, smelt the drink on his breath. Then I pulled my jacket tighter round me and stood up.

'No, no,' he said, 'It's just after so long –' He put his hand on my arm, gripped it. And you're still angry with me –' This set him off again. He rested his free hand on his knee, leaning down on it. I pulled away. He shook his head, sobering a little.

To the east, the sky was flushed with golden light, the clouds were pink.

'If you knew half the trouble you got me into back in Sailortown –' he said, and shook his head again. 'And to think I was going to offer you a partnership tonight.'

Looking down at him seated on the tomb, I could feel the heat throbbing in my face. His eyes were wet with laughter.

'I would have said no,' I said.

He wiped an eye. 'Oh really.'

'You're a liability.'

He almost choked. 'I'll have you know that I'm the best –'

I shook my head.

'No,' I said. 'Not any more.'

I tried my damaged foot. It seemed to take my weight.

'You're finished now,' I said. 'You're over.'

And I turned and walked away.

Eighteen

Strange how a road can look so different on the return: you see first the other profile of a hill, come upon a copse from an entirely different angle, notice for the first time a standing stone you must have passed by oblivious on the way out. The same road can look so different, in fact, that it will take something else entirely to make you realize where you are. Something tiny, such as the colour of the stones in the bottom of a stream, or the way the harebells grow in clumps along a bank to catch the sun. Or the smell of gorse.

As I walked those last few miles, a hand to the ache in my back, I could feel you moving all the time. Low down I felt what must have been a fist, and there seemed to be a foot stuck in underneath my ribs. Already struggling against your confines. It made me smile, though for the first time I began to feel afraid of your coming. You seemed so real now, and so ready to come.

It was dusk when I arrived, boots scuffing through the

road dust, the weight of my belly like a mountain cantilevered against my hips. As I came down the hill and out from underneath the trees, the same cottages shambled out towards me from the crossroads, here and there a light glowed in a bedroom window, and in one downstairs room, where the curtains had not yet been drawn, two women leant across a table to talk. I watched as one of them spoke, lifting a hand into the air with a slight dismissive gesture, and then a little later the other nodded. A child came in and was shooed back to bed, then one of the women stood up, lifted a kettle from the stove and made tea. The Clay twins. Grown up into a kind of mild beauty, apparently content.

At the crossroads, the windows of the Anchor were uncurtained, glowing with fire- and oil-light. As I passed I caught sight of Uncle George, leaning on the counter, talking. That same unearned air of authority, the same arrogant tilt of the jaw. It looked like he hadn't changed at all. It didn't seem to matter now.

I carried on across the green, the long grass tangling round my ankles. Birds rose from sleep into the air, their voices swimming up into the sky, dissolving. Yellow eyes blinked at me; goats tethered to graze on the common land. I felt again the chill of bare legs, and remembered the pocked and freckled dockleaf in my hand, the way I'd leaned in, poised to run, tickling the old billy's nose with it. And with the memory came a shiver of apprehension, as if I were a child again. My Da had died and Gran had sent me away.

All I'd ever wanted was someone to love.

In front of me, the schoolhouse stood in darkness. From out of nowhere came the memory of something tiny, the way a plant grew in the gaps between the paving slabs outside the schoolhouse door. It would break out into flowers in the springtime: red, like the open mouths of birds. I realized now, as I set my booted foot on the step, peered down and saw nothing but the dark, that I would never know anywhere so intimately as this. My hand reached out for the latch. The door was unbolted. I stepped inside.

A corner of a table caught me in the thigh: I hissed. A table where no table should have been. I made my way around its edge. On the dresser, the plates were patterned with sprigs and leaves, monochrome in this light. I'd remembered a willow-pattern service. Across the room, the settle sat bolt upright against the wall. And above it hung the map. I crossed the room, climbed up on to the settle, and looked at it. I reached into my pocket, struck a light, held it till the flame scorched my fingers, and looked. I struck another, then another, each one burning down to touch my fingertips, making me flinch and shake the flame away. In the morning, Miss Woodend would find a scattering of charred matches on the floor.

The map was not as I'd remembered it. It wasn't what I'd thought it had been. Obliged to observe without looking all those years ago, my peripheral vision had noted what had seemed to be the map's outlines: a squarish landmass circled by green seas, a scooped out central lake. An island country, washed by waves. I'd imagined the ways away from here, dust rising in a dot dot line across the map. I'd seen myself bobbing around in the margins, sailing right underneath the frame and out across the schoolroom wall. But now, up close, what felt like a lifetime later, I saw two green-tinged coastlines facing each other across a squarish stretch of sea, and in the centre of the sea an island, traced in green.

The cottage was in darkness, the windows shuttered, the doors bolted, but I didn't realize until I'd gone down to the river and found the ferryboat lying aslant on the shilloe, with a tarpaulin lashed over it to keep out the rain, that my grandmother was dead.

I rowed myself across the river, walked the floodplane to the churchyard. I made my way to my father's grave. The turf had been recently lifted and relaid.

It was only then that I realized that when my father had died and she had sent me away, it was because she couldn't look at me any more. She kept looking over my shoulder, expecting to see him.

The next day, I took an awl from amongst my father's tools, rolled a fallen stone from the churchyard wall. I set the stone on the grave, and carved the one word, 'Reed'.

That is all the family I can give you. I hope it is enough.

I gave birth to you two weeks later, in the cottage. As I knelt at the side of the bed, my shirt rucked up about my hips, rocking back and forth and moaning, bleared with fatigue and pain, I knew her at last: my mother on her knees as I was on my knees, eyes squeezed shut on red and mouth open to shout against the pain, and before her other women, grandmothers, great-grandmothers and their mothers before them, all of them swollen and bent, bodies racked with these same waves, this agony, this love. When you slipped, toadfaced and greasy, into the world, and I sank back exhausted. I just looked at you lying there, the cord still trailing from you to me, still pulsing, and I was overwhelmed by the fierce simplicity of what I felt for you.

Then I lifted you to my chest, and touched your bloody cheek, and you opened your eyes. You looked at me.

Martin Sloane

Michael Redhill

Jolene Iolas, a student in upstate New York, encounters Martin Sloane's work while visiting a Toronto gallery. Flush with the confidence of youth, she strikes up a correspondence with the older artist, and eventually they become lovers. She learns Martin's story, and cherishes it as her own.

And then, without warning, without a word, he vanishes. There is no hint of his fate, no chain of cause and effect to be followed. Ten years pass, and Jolene learns to stop trying to make sense of what has happened to her. But before she can fully return to life, the opportunity to confront her ghost arises, when she hears that someone named Sloane has been exhibiting artworks identical to Martin's in galleries in Ireland . . .

Seamlessly crafted and beautifully written, *Martin Sloane* evokes the mysteries of love and art, the weight of history, and what it means to bear memory for the missing and the dead. This is a truly remarkable debut.

'It is rare to read a novel that pulses with such pleasure that you don't want it to end, but this is what Redhill's debut delivers.'
Independent

'Dense with powerful emotional insights . . . Like Martin's art, it inspires a feeling of stillness and calm, of looking down on things from above; while underneath rest layer upon layer of meaning, prompting reflection on the novel's images and understandings long after the last page is reached.'
The Times

'A powerful meditation on the implications of memory and the vacancies opened up by the loss of love.'
Observer

arrow books

ALSO AVAILABLE IN ARROW

A Ship Made Of Paper
Scott Spencer

Daniel has returned from New York to the Hudson River town where he grew up. There, along with Kate and her daughter, Ruby, he settles into the kind of secure and comfortable family life he longed for during his emotionally barren childhood. But then he falls helplessly in love with Iris Davenport, the black woman whose son is Ruby's best friend. During a freak October blizzard, Daniel is stranded at Iris's house, and they spend the night together – the beginning of an affair that eventually imperils all their relationships and their view of themselves as essentially good people . . .

'Superbly captures the giddy roller-coaster emotions of infatuation - the self-deceit, desperation and heights of ecstasy are all beautifully conveyed . . . Compassionate and powerful, *A Ship Made of Paper* is a tempestuous, absorbing journey into the human psyche.'
Time Out

'Irresistible . . . This is a book about love as a torrent, a force of nature that overwhelms families, harrows lives and lays waste to whole towns as it thunders through. Love may be our only hope, but when you put this book down – not an easy thing to do – you may wonder how civilisation survives it.'
Time

'Scott Spencer is a magnificent writer.'
Anne Tyler

arrow books

Say When

Elizabeth Berg

'He felt his stomach tighten, his heart begin to race. The coffeemaker beeped, signalling its readiness, and Ellen got up and poured two mugs. She set one in front of Griffin, one in front of herself. Griffin watched the steam rise up and curl back on itself, then dissipate. He said quietly, "I'm not going anywhere." "Pardon?" "I said, I'm not *going* anywhere. I'm not moving." She nodded. "I see. Well, *I* can't. I have to be here to take care of Zoe." Griffin pictured his daughter, a redheaded beauty who would knock the stuffing out of any man who crossed her. "All right, you can stay, too," he told Ellen. "Griffin. One of us has to go."'

When is a marriage worth saving, and when is it worth letting go?

In *Say When*, Elizabeth Berg negotiates perfectly the fine balance between humour and poignancy as she charts the days and nights of a family whose normal life has been shattered. Told from the point of view of a man who goes overnight from being a husband to becoming his wife's roommate, this is a gripping and heartfelt story.

'Berg oozes warmth, wisdom and generosity of spirit. Her writing is quite brilliant.'
Anna Maxted

'Savvy, wry, and sharply observant . . . Berg's graceful and deceptively simple prose is laced with clear-eyed insights . . . deft and inspiring.'
The Denver Post

'Berg knows her characters intimately . . . she gets under their skin and leaves the reader with an indelible impression of lives challenged and changed'
Seattle Times

arrow books